Duncan's eyes were glued to the destruct button. He saw that the colonel's hand never did get to it. Yet, even as he watched, he saw the red button move downward, apparently of its own volition. The rocket blew into a million pieces, and the button came back up. No one, Duncan would swear, had physically touched the button, yet it had been depressed . . .

RAYMOND BUCKLAND
has written over twenty top-selling non-fiction books on subjects ranging from Ghosts and ESP, to Witchcraft and Voodoo, and is now focusing his attention on fiction. In his early teens, Ray Buckland was loaned a book on spiritualism, which led to experimentation and enquiry into spirit contact and, later, to investigation into the many other fields of parapsychology. As a half-blood Romany, he's an authority on Gypsies; three of his books being about them. Ray has been technical advisor for movies, written screenplays, video, television, and radio scripts, and has taught courses and lectured at universities and colleges across the country. He has been a stage actor in England and played character parts in American movies. He has appeared on numerous radio and television talk shows in the United States, Canada, England, and Italy, and been the subject of many newspaper and magazine articles.

To Write to the Author

If you wish to contact the author or would like more information about this book, please write to the author in care of Llewellyn Worldwide and we will forward your request. Both the author and publisher appreciate hearing from you and learning of your enjoyment of his book and how it has helped you. Llewellyn Worldwide cannot guarantee that every letter written to the author can be answered, but all will be forwarded. Please write to:

Raymond Buckland
c/o Llewellyn Worldwide
P.O. Box 64383-100, St. Paul, MN 55164-0383, USA

Please enclose a self-addressed, stamped envelope for reply, or $1.00 to cover costs. If outside U.S.A., enclose international postal reply coupon.

A Llewellyn Psi-Fi Novel

THE COMMITTEE

Raymond Buckland

1993
Llewellyn Publications
St. Paul, Minnesota, 55164-0383, U.S.A.

The Committee. Copyright © 1993 by Raymond Buckland. All rights reserved. Printed in the United States of America. No part of this book may be used or reproduced in any manner whatsoever without written permission from Llewellyn Publications except in the case of brief quotations embodied in critical articles and reviews.

Cover Painting by Martin Cannon
Design by Christopher Wells

Cataloging-in-Publication Data
Buckland, Raymond.
    The committee / Raymond Buckland
      p. cm. — (Llewellyn's psi-fi series)
    ISBN 1-56718-100-7
    1. Subversive activities—United States—Fiction.
2. Supernatural—Fiction. 3. Occultism—Fiction. I. Title.
II. Series.
PS3552.U3378C66 1993   93-30473
813'.54—dc20   CIP

Llewellyn Publications
A Division of Llewellyn Worldwide, Ltd.
P.O. Box 64383, St. Paul, MN 55164-0383

Announcing Llewellyn's FICTION Line

Llewellyn Publications launches its new line of occult fiction with two titles by best-selling authors of the supernatural: Raymond Buckland and Donald Tyson. Intriguing and entertaining, the books in this series are also highly educational because they are based on authentic and accurate metaphysical practices, written by world-recognized experts in the occult. Look for exciting new additions to the line in the upcoming months.

THE COMMITTEE

The Cold War is back in this psi-techno suspense thriller where international aggressors use psychokinesis, astral projection and other psychic means to circumvent the U.S. intelligence network. When two routine communications satellite launches are inexplicably aborted at Vandenberg Air Force Base in California, one senator suspects paranormal influences. He calls in a writer, two parapsychologists and a psychic housewife—and *The Committee* is formed. Together, they piece together a sinister occult plot against the United States. *The Committee* then embarks on a supernatural adventure of a lifetime as they attempt to beat the enemy at its own game.

Books by Raymond Buckland

NON-FICTION
 Practical Candleburning Rituals
 Witchcraft From the Inside
 Witchcraft . . . the Religion
 A Pocket Guide to the Supernatural
 Witchcraft Ancient and Modern
 Here is the Occult
 The Tree: Complete Book of Saxon Witchcraft
 The Magic of Chant-O-Matics
 Anatomy of the Occult
 Practical Color Magick
 Buckland's Complete Book of Witchcraft
 Buckland's Gypsy Fortunetelling Deck
 Secrets of Gypsy Fortunetelling
 Secrets of Gypsy Love Magick
 Secrets of Gypsy Dream Reading
 Scottish Witchcraft
 Doors to Other Worlds

Under the pseudonym "Tony Earll"
 Mu Revealed

With Hereward Carrington
 Amazing Secrets of the Psychic World

With Kathleen Binger
 The Book of African Divination

FICTION
 The Committee

Acknowledgements

My thanks to Col. Ben W. Hunsaker, USAF (Ret.); Lee E. Klaus, USAF (Ret.); Comdr. Ed. L. Fitzgibbons, USN (Ret.); David Buser; Dan P. Briggs, and many of the members of the Experimental Aircraft Association, Chapter 14, San Diego, California, for their help and constructive criticism.

Author's Note

I call this novel a psi-techno-thriller. That's because the technology of it is that of parapsychology. Although a work of fiction, all of the practices described in this book are factual; the astral projection, ESP, skrying, radiesthesia, etc. Detailed documentation of these and similar practices is to be found at such research societies and institutions as the Duke Parapsychology Laboratory, North Carolina; the Association for Research and Enlightenment, Virginia; the Paraspychology Foundation, New York; the University of Saskatchewan, Canada; the Society for Psychical Research, London; the A. S. Popov Scientific Technical Society, Moscow; and the University of Leningrad, Russia.

Raymond Buckland

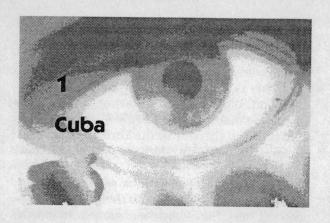

1
Cuba

Fidel Castro did not meet the Iraqi envoy at Havana Airport. Instead, a helicopter whisked the visitor away from the tarmac and the city, over the treetops toward one of the four homes owned by the Cuban leader. This particular one was a farm set in the gentle, rolling hills of the Sierra de los Organos, west of the capital.

The Soviet-made Kamov Ka-18 skimmed the tops of the tall *ceiba* trees, and the many groves of bananas and plantains. Nizar Hammadi cradled his briefcase on his lap. He stared without seeing out of the window of the noisy aircraft, across the silent soldier seated beside him, who was similarly cradling an AK-17 automatic rifle. Nizar's thoughts were on his mission.

Saddam Hussein had personally requested that he come to Cuba. The two had been friends for more than thirty years and, since he hated to leave his wife and family and to journey outside Iraq, Nizar could have refused. But he did not.

"This is important, old friend," his leader had said, big brown eyes staring, unblinking, at his companion. "We have a chance to be a real thorn in the side of the Yankee-Satanists. I can trust this mission only to you." How could he refuse?

The four-man helicopter crossed over open grasslands before rising into the gently rolling, wooded hills. Suddenly there came into view a large clearing in the middle of a section of forest, and the whirring bird dropped down to settle atop a white cross painted on the periphery of a manicured section of lawn. As Hammadi unbuckled his harness and clambered out a figure dressed in green army fatigues came strutting across the grass to meet him.

"Welcome to Cuba!" Castro tightly grasped his arms and bent forward to give a cheek-to-cheek greeting. "Come! Let's talk."

The tall Cuban *Comandante en Jefe* did an about-face and Nizar almost had to break into a run to keep pace with him as he headed for a khaki-colored British Range Rover parked nearby. Behind them the helicopter's twin rotors, which had never stopped turning, picked up speed and the Kamov rose once more into the sky.

Castro waved his driver into the back seat and slid in behind the wheel. Nizar could not help but notice that the Cuban leader's bulk made slipping behind the wheel a tighter task than it probably had been in years gone by. But the Commander-in-Chief slid the jeep into gear and, spinning the rear wheels slightly on the turf, drove off and onto a nearby farm road.

"This is new," he said, patting the dashboard of the vehicle. "Better than those damn Soviet jeeps, but harder to get spare parts."

Nizar glanced at the AK-47 automatic rifle hooked onto the dash and the two communication radios bolted in place. "It's comfortable," he said. He leaned back in the soft seat and remembered Sadam's warning that the Cuban "drove like a pig in a stripped down jeep."

"Where are we going?" he asked.

Castro chuckled. "To *La Habana*," he said.

"Havana? But I just arrived there. You had me flown here."

Castro's chuckle broke into loud laughter. The soldier in the back seat joined in, not knowing what he was laughing at. "We take maybe an hour to drive back," said the bearded figure at the wheel, glancing briefly at his passenger. "But it is an hour with no fear of other ears listening. You understand?"

Nizar nodded. He'd heard of Castro's eccentricities; something which had kept the Cuban leader alive all these years despite the CIA, and who knew who else, endlessly trying to assassinate him. An Iraqi journalist had come to Cuba only a year or so ago to interview Castro. He'd been there for two weeks without success. Then, the day before he was due to leave, Castro had suddenly turned up in the hotel lobby and whisked the journalist away in his jeep, giving him a four-hour interview.

Castro's public appearances were never promoted ahead of time; they were simply reported on after the event. He would appear in the Plaza and give an important speech to whomever happened to be there and then disappear again. The speech would be detailed in *Juventud Rebelde,* the afternoon newspaper, and *Granma,* the official organ of the Communist Party of Cuba; also on the two television channels. Castro seemed to revel in the aura of mystique he generated this way.

"So! Tell me about Hussein. Is he still licking his wounds from the Yankees?"

Nizar ignored the slight and told the Cuban of Sadam Hussein's esteem in the eyes of his people. He spoke of the plans the leader had for his country and of how he was going to revenge himself for the affront that the Devil Bush had rendered him.

"Words!" Castro said. "Empty words!" He obviously had no time for the niceties of diplomacy. Or was it that he knew Nizar was here to ask a favor for Sadam? His next words seemed to bear out that contention. "So! What does Hussein want from the Republic of Cuba?"

Nizar flicked open his briefcase. The soldier in the rear seat immediately leaned forward, his hand on his sidearm. Castro motioned him back. Nizar pulled out a thick, bound document.

"The full details of the proposal Sadam Hussein wishes to make are contained in this document," Nizar said. "You will, of course, want to go through it carefully, but let me give you a brief rundown on the major points."

"Do that."

Nizar cleared his throat. He really wasn't a diplomat and hated having to present a proposal so important to his country and to Saddam. Suppose Castro just laughed in his face? Suppose he was unceremoniously dumped on a plane and sent back to Iraq with his tail between his legs? Suppose . . . but he couldn't sit there like an idiot wondering and worrying. He turned in his seat to concentrate on the Cuban leader.

"Saddam Hussein wishes to position a number of missiles—SCUDs—here in Cuba. Possibly also some Exocets, Mirage jet fighters, MIGs, and Pumas." He paused and mentally braced himself. Castro said nothing. Nizar continued. "He would like to do this as soon as possible, in fact he has included a timetable in the proposal. In return he is, of course, willing to render services to the people of Cuba."

"Services?" Nizar couldn't tell whether it was a sneer or simply Castro's accent.

"In return we are prepared to purchase up to half of your sugar harvest, at a good price on a long term, and to supply you with oil, which we understand you need urgently." Nizar couldn't help adding the last few words. He sat back, mentally breathing a sigh of relief that he had got through it all. He waited.

Castro had been driving at a fast rate, taking blind corners without slowing down, something which unnerved his passenger but seemed not to bother the soldier in the back seat. Suddenly the Cuban leader pulled over to the side of the country road, beside the gate into a field of sugar cane, and stopped the Range Rover. He signalled Nizar to get out and himself slid sideways off the driver's seat. As Nizar came around the vehicle to join Castro he noticed for the first time that they had been followed by two green Soviet-built jeeps containing an escort of armed soldiers. The two vehicles pulled over to the side of the road at a discreet distance and waited patiently.

Castro stood and fiddled with the thick wire fastening the gate. The soldier from the back seat came running up, his automatic pistol in hand, ready to shoot off the offending cable. Castro waved him back to the vehicle and unpicked the wire. He led Nizar into the field, where they walked side by side between the tall rows of sugar cane.

"The Soviets have reneged on their promise to purchase sugar," said Castro. "Also on their promise to supply oil."

Nizar knew this. That was what Saddam had considered his ace card. Iraq didn't really need that much sugar, though it could absorb it. And it could certainly provide the oil.

"Tell me," the Cuban leader continued, "Why does Hussein want to place SCUDs here? Is he planning on attacking the United States?"

"No, no!" He'd been told to expect this question and to assure the man that this was not the Iraqi intention. "It is purely as a gesture. It is—how do the Yankees say it?—to 'thumb our nose at the pigs'."

"Don't you mean to thumb *my* nose at them?"

Nizar caught the gleam of Castro's eyes staring fiercely at him from under his shaggy eyebrows. He swallowed. "Not at all. Satan-Bush and the Devil Clinton will know who is responsible. They will certainly not attack Cuba for it."

"Tell me, does Hussein remember what happened in 1962?" Castro referred, of course, to the missile crisis, when the Soviets were building their silos at San Cristóbal, in western Cuba.

"Of course." Again, Nizar had been forewarned that this would be brought up. "In October of that year the Yankee Kennedy blockaded your island and made you remove all the Soviet military equipment."

Castro snorted. "They made us do nothing! The Soviets eventually weakened and decided to take their toys away!"

There was silence for a moment. Castro stopped and stood still, picking at his teeth

The Committee

with a twig he had snapped off a plant. "There is no way you could bring in your missiles," he said quietly.

"You mean, because of the Yankees watching?"

The bearded man nodded. "In 1962 it was their spy planes that photographed what we had here. Now they don't even need planes." Nizar raised a quizzical eyebrow. "They have 'spy-in-the-sky' satellites. A permanently set-up camera taking pictures continually. If we even attempted to bring in a single SCUD they would know immediately."

Nizar nodded. Now for the more delicate negotiating. Just how badly did Cuba, and Castro, need that oil and need to sell the sugar? "Saddam seemed to think that you would be able to get around that," he said quietly.

It was Castro's turn to raise an eyebrow. "Get around it?"

"Saddam doesn't care how you do it, but he wants to bring in his missiles and other equipment and he doesn't want the Yankees to know about it until they are installed and can be used as a, shall we say, bargaining tool?"

The eyes gleamed again. "You mean he is going to use them to threaten the U.S.?"

"Only to make them leave us—and you, of course—alone and to keep from interfering with our material being here. With it here it will be a permanent thorn in their side and that is really all that Saddam wants, for now."

Cuba

"So how am I supposed to shut off the satellite camera while you move them in?"

Nizar smiled. "Saddam was sure you'd be able to find a way."

Castro suddenly turned and started striding back towards the gate. Nizar broke into a run to catch up. "Hussein is a madman!" snapped the Cuban. "I have always said so. I need no part of this."

"You don't need the oil?" Nizar asked. "Nor do you need to find a new market for that much sugar?"

Castro slowed a pace. "Japan is a good customer for our sugar," he said. "They will take more."

"Not that much. And certainly not at the price we would pay. And what about oil? Japan needs oil herself. She can't help there."

They were back at the gate. Castro stood with one foot on a bar and examined his fingernails.

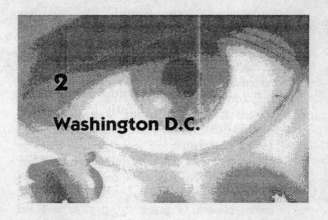

2
Washington D.C.

Senators Bill Highland and Michael O'Cork were opposites in almost every way. Highland was corpulent (frequently described as "jolly"), well-liked, with a clean-shaven, moon face topped by a mop of salt-and-pepper hair. He was in his late forties, of medium height, and always dressed smartly in a three-piece business suit, with shoes brightly shined. He was openhanded and he insisted on his staff calling him Bill. Michael O'Cork, on the other hand, was nearly sixty, tall and thin, with gray hair and moustache, and a lined, gray face. He wore steel-rimmed spectacles which accentuated his grayness. His suits were slightly rumpled two-piece, worn with an ancient woolen cardigan. His shoes were suede Hushpuppies, slightly worn down at the heel. He insisted that every one of his staff call him Senator and had a reputation for being tight with his money.

Washington D.C.

"Senator O'Cork would like a few moments, Bill."

Highland glanced toward the intercom on his desk and nodded. "Okay, Connie," he said. "Send him on in."

With a small sigh, he set down his pen and pushed back his chair slightly from the big mahogany desk. The top of the desk was well covered with papers, though all were in neat piles with yellow squares of paper stuck to the top sheets, bearing brief notes as to what was what. What does "Cranky" O'Cork want, Highland thought? The man usually stays holed up in his office from one week's end to the other. If he ever talks to anyone else it's nearly always by having them brought to his office; he never goes visiting other Senators.

The older Senator came brusquely through the door, a blue file folder clutched under one arm.

"Sorry to interrupt you, Highland," he said. "Won't take but a moment of your time. I know you're busy. Almost as busy as I am, I wouldn't wonder." He looked over the top of his glasses, which sat halfway down his nose. He seemed to be waiting for Highland to rise and greet him. The smiling Senator simply waved him to a chair.

"Take the weight off, Mike. What can I do for you."

O'Cork frowned briefly at the familiarity of the greeting but quickly turned his attention to the matter in hand. He sat on the edge of the chair and pushed the blue folder toward Highland. "What d'you know about this man?"

Highland took the file, glanced at the "TOP SECRET" stamp and tag on the outside, and opened it up. "Lieutenant-General Nathan Beardsmore Wellesley," he read. "United States Air Force; retired 1985—mandatory retirement. Distinguished Flying Cross, two Bronze Stars, three DFCs, DSM, Legion of Merit, Purple Heart. Flew F86s with 51st Fighter Interceptor Wing in Korea. Training Officer in Nam. Wild Weasels out of Thailand. Pentagon duties . . ."

"Yes, yes," O'Cork interrupted. "We know all that. D'you recognize the name?"

"No," Highland said. He thought for a moment. "Though, wait a minute. Yes. Yes, wasn't he the guy who defected to the Ruskies a couple or so years ago?"

"Exactly. August, 1989. He was suspected of passing on classified information. Then, just when we were about to apprehend him, he eluded us. He climbed aboard a Soviet airplane doing a goodwill appearance at some airshow and that was the last we saw of him. Career man, too. Decorated veteran. A real surprise."

Bill Highland tried to think back. "What was his reason for defecting? I'm damned if I can remember."

"We never did establish one," O'Cork said. "It was the surprise of the year, if not the century. Like Harry Truman suddenly turning Republican!"

Washington D.C.

"So what's the scoop? Why are you asking about him?"

O'Cork took back the file and settled into the chair. "With the collapse of the USSR, and the 'retirement', if we can call it that, of Gorbachev, I got to wondering whatever had become, or would become, of the various people who'd defected to the Soviets over the years. They'd gone running off to the other side, slamming the door behind them; now suddenly that door falls off its hinges."

"Hmm. Good point."

"Then, I suddenly remembered General Wellesley. He was one of our bright boys; a special interest of mine."

The younger Senator suddenly sat forward. "Wasn't he involved with satellites, or something?"

"Very much so. Yes. Worked at the Pentagon as civilian staff from the time of his retirement from the Air Force to his defection. He was our number one man when it came to the placement of military hardware in space."

Highland whistled, which brought a frown to O'Cork's face. "No wonder we were sorry to see him go. So, what have you found out? Where is he now and what's he up to?"

"As I said, I got to wondering about these people, and Wellesley in particular." He looked hard at Highland. "I would like to think that it might be possible to repatriate Wellesley, among others. We could still very definitely make use of his expertise when it comes to communications. Now, I didn't say I had discovered anything yet. In fact," his voice dropped a little, "I was wondering if you could help me on this?"

Here's a first, thought Highland. The old fart wants me to help him? Normally he hardly has the time of day for me. He smiled at O'Cork. "Be glad to, Mike. Of course. What exactly can I do for you?"

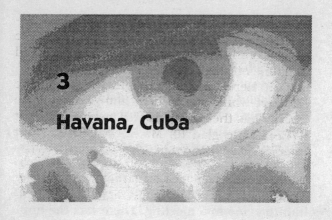

3
Havana, Cuba

Ovideo Carlos de Céspedes Alderaguía had known Fidel Castro for many years. And not just known him; they were like brothers. They were even born in the same month and year: August, 1926. True, they hadn't actually met until thirty years later, but in 1956 Ovideo had been one of the eighty men who joined Fidel and Che Guevera on *Granma*, the yacht from which the revolution had started. He had been in the midst of the battle and lucky enough to be one of the fifteen men to survive. Two short years later they were in charge of the government.

Ovideo went over those events, those memorable days, in his head, as he did many times. He never tired of reliving the excitement of being part of that famous guerrilla force. But like most of those men he was a fighter, not a politician. Fidel had named him Minister

The Committee

of Foreign Affairs yet he hadn't even known where the Ministry building was located. He had to ask his way. The days since then had lost much of their glitter.

Out of habit, Ovideo fingered his thin moustache as he drove, and looked about him with short, sharp movements of his head—movements that some of his associates had unkindly likened to those of a chicken. He swung his Argentinian Ford around the corner and came to a stop at a traffic light. Today he felt a tension in the air. Fidel had asked him to come to a meeting. There was the hint of intrigue; of something big building. He had experienced the same thing just before the abortive *Yanquis'* attack in April of 1961. The Bay of Pigs, they had called it. Good name, he thought. The *Yanquis are* pigs! But what could Fidel have up his sleeve this time? They were both now in their late sixties, though what did that matter? They were in their prime! He revved the engine and, when the light turned green, took off with a little wheel spin. It felt good.

Ovideo drove through Old Havana and headed for Vedado, the newer, twentieth-century section of the city where Fidel had his principle residence. This was another indication of the importance of this meeting, he thought. Anything truly momentous would be dealt with, face to face, in the living room of one of Fidel's homes—never across a table in an office building.

Havana, Cuba

He turned right, then made a quick left, cutting through the narrow Cuarteles Street. He drove past dilapidated buildings with paint peeling from their doorways and walls. That was the least of the decay. Wrought ironwork was corroded. Masonry was cracked and full of holes. Facades had collapsed. He turned onto the Plaza de la Catedral and then to Empedrado. At the bottom of the Paseo de Martí he turned west onto the Malecón and then on into Velado.

Ovideo passed through the once posh Miramar area. The spacious, balconied homes were now depressing government-owned houses and offices. A little further on a blue-uniformed policeman licked an ice-cream cone as he leaned against a large royal palm jutting out from the sidewalk into the roadway. Ovideo pulled around the tree and swung into a driveway next to it. He parked alongside a black, Soviet-made Volga, which resembled a U.S. Oldsmobile of the fifties. Grabbing up his briefcase, Ovideo slid out of the car and headed for the side door of the unprepossessing colonial-era house.

"Ovideo! My friend!" Castro greeted him as though they hadn't met in weeks, yet they had been together only the previous afternoon, inspecting a housing complex in Alamar.

"Come. Sit down." He waved the shorter man to a comfortable chair near the window and signaled for his housekeeper, Alina, to bring them something to drink. She disappeared and as quickly returned with two tall glasses of chilled papaya juice.

Ovideo sipped his drink and looked around the room. He always felt comfortable here. He looked across at Fidel, dressed in his usual green fatigues and lounging in an overstuffed, leather-covered armchair, an occasional table at his elbow. The bearded leader was gazing out of the window into the walled rear of the house, at the well-tended garden resplendent with purple and orange bougainvillea backed by jasmine, gardenias, and jacaranda. Ovideo waited for Fidel to open the conversation.

After a long pull on his eight inch Cohiba *cigaro*, Castro spoke. "Saddam Hussein wants to bring missiles into Cuba."

Ovideo's heart pounded. "Missiles to Cuba? But . . ."

"Yes, I know. October 1962 all over again."

"We could never stand up to another blockade. Not at this time. With the Soviets . . ."

"I know." Ovideo was interrupted a second time. Castro put down his cigar and turned to face his Minister of Foreign Affairs. "I know. But this is to Cuba. Iraq can bring us oil and they'll buy our sugar. We *need* that." He took a sip from his drink. "So the only question is, how can we do it?"

"We can't. It's impossible."

"Impossible? Hah!" Castro threw back his head and laughed. "Nothing is impossible, Ovideo. We proved that thirty years ago."

Ovideo had to agree. He tugged at his moustache. He was always easily affected by Fidel and his enthusiasm for anything. "You're right. Nothing is impossible. But we have the *Yanquis* to contend with. We have them spying on our every move. They would know the very moment we tried to unload a single missile."

"That's right." Castro nodded. "Their 'Eye in the Sky' never sleeps. So what we have to do is get past it. And I want you to tell me how."

So that was it, Ovideo thought. He hadn't the slightest idea how to proceed but was loathe to admit it. He brushed his hand back through his hair, upsetting the perfect setting it had had. "We can do it," he said forcefully, a wan smile on his lips. "We . . ."

"How?"

The smile faded.

"As I thought." Again Castro nodded. "You haven't a clue." Then, suddenly, he again threw back his head and laughed. This time Ovideo joined in, at first uneasily, then, as he realized his friend's good humor, wholeheartedly and with relief. When the laughter subsided Castro got up and began to pace the floor. The room was small and, in addition to the two armchairs, contained a settee, coffee table, sideboard, and a small table with four chairs around it. Castro paced around the furniture in what became an intricate pattern of perambulation. He spoke as he moved, and puffed out cigar smoke till the small room was full of it.

"There is a way, I believe. It may be the only way. As it happens I've been working on this for some time. Not for Hussein, of course. I didn't know he'd come along with his bizarre idea. But we can work into his plans. And get his oil and sell our sugar into the bargain."

"What's the idea?" Ovideo asked.

"You know Humberto?"

"Gavilla? Yes, I know him."

"And did you meet Alexis Militsa?"

"The scientist from Moscow? Yes, I did."

"Well, Humberto Gavilla and Alexis Militsa have been working together on something that I think may bring about what we've been striving for the past twenty-five years—freedom from the *Yanqui* spying."

Ovideo put down his glass and looked hard at his leader.

"Yes," Castro continued. "With a few other people we are bringing in from Moscow, I think we've got a chance to free ourselves, and to cash in on Hussein's deal at the same time."

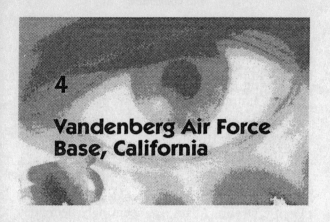

4
Vandenberg Air Force Base, California

Three curving rows of monitor positions faced in toward the huge plotting chart in the main room of the small fort known as the "blockhouse." Seated at each console was a serious-faced technician, eyes glued to a cathode ray screen, fingers alternately poised over and scrambling about the keyboard. More than 150 warning lights flashed intermittently as over a thousand buttons were pushed and pulled, as the technicians went through the check-tests of the internal responses of the rocket.

The blockhouse was two hundred yards from the launch pad. Built of concrete and armored in steel, it had walls eight feet thick and a roof of sand ten feet deep. It could absorb the blast from an explosion of twenty-five tons of TNT at fifty yards.

The Committee

Launch Control personnel scurried backward and forward across the open floor space, some squeezing down the aisles between the monitor rows, delivering and retrieving information pertinent to the polar rocket launch about to take place. For the moment, Space Launch Complex Two of the Vandenberg Flight Control Center was the hub of the universe.

Outside, on the launch pad, a towering Vulcan rocket stood like a giant sentinel poised on Point Arguello, looking out over the Pacific Ocean. At its tip, seemingly delicately balanced, was a Key Hole KH-12b satellite, waiting to be placed seventy-two miles above the Earth, from which altitude it would be able to deliver photographs that could clearly depict a license plate on an automobile parked on a street in Santa Barbara. The satellite's camera possessed two lenses of fixed focal length, together with one telephoto lens. These projected the target's image onto a focal plane of electro-optic sensors. An on-board computer then converted the image to digital information and transmitted it, via a relay satellite, directly to a building on the corner of 1st and M Streets, Washington DC. This building, looking something like a warehouse, was the National Photographic Interpretation Center, better known as NPIC.

Lieutenant Colonel James Settler ran a finger around the collar of his shirt and tried to loosen his tie without it being obvious. It

Vandenberg Air Force Base, California

was warm in the control center and due to get warmer. At T minus nine the heavy armored door of the blockhouse would be closed and locked and the air conditioning would be turned off, to prevent the induction of the gases released by the rocket on the ramp. It was a hot day, reflected the Colonel, and it was going to get even hotter. He didn't realize just how hot.

The Launch Director watched the clock, checked over the projected trajectory, glanced at a half-dozen computer screens, answered a continuous barrage of questions, and listened to the countdown as it continued seemingly inexorably; all with no outward show of emotion. Some Launch Directors grew tense and nervous as the countdown drew closer to the launch, others got angry and started shouting their commands, some even seemed jumpy and indecisive. But Major General "Pug" Schroeder was always cool and calm, reducing tension and assuaging fears.

Colonel Settler glanced at his wristwatch. The uncoupling procedure had taken place and gone smoothly, nearly three-quarters of an hour before. Five minutes ago they had started filling the tanks with liquid oxygen. Contacting the propellant, at -232.6°F, he knew that the pipes would have been giving off alarming creaking noises as they contracted. The first time he had heard it he would have sworn the whole thing was going to explode.

The Committee

"T minus twenty-eight and the count is suspended!"

A knot of people formed quickly around one of the consoles off to the right and Jim Settler strained to see what was going on. "Pug" Schroeder strode across the room and slid in through the press of personnel. Settler heard someone say something about an overheated gyroscope. That could be serious, he knew. But less than five minutes later the count resumed.

This was the tenth such launch that Settler had been a part of. He doubted he would ever get used to it to the point of being blasé. There was too much going on at too rapid a pace for that. But at least he could feel much more relaxed about it all now. For the first two or three launches he had spent the entire time with his eyes glued to a console screen; now he took time to glance around and see more of the overall picture.

There were no more holds, and at T minus two the circuits passed over to the rocket's internal batteries. Settler unlatched the cover over the destruct button. One of his duties was to destroy the rocket should anything go awry immediately after the launch. The last thing the Air Force needed was to have a rogue rocket plunge into a populated area. He scanned the readings on his console and watched as each light, in sequence, flickered to green.

Air Force observers manned the four periscopes in the blockhouse and other personnel crowded about the six television screens

Vandenberg Air Force Base, California

focused on the launch pad. The Director had pressed the master firing button and the automatic sequencing mechanism was in play. At T minus fifteen seconds those watching the television screens saw the nozzles squirting water, hitting the pad at a rate of 30,000 gallons a second, to cool the flame deflector. At T minus ten seconds the umbilical cords detached and the tower moved back from the rocket. At the instance of zero a man at one of the periscopes announced "Main motors!" The combustion chambers emitted their 4,532° F jets. Gradually they built up to maximum thrust, then the steel retaining jaws snapped open and, unbelievably slowly, the massive rocket and its payload began clawing its way into the air.

"We have lift off. The tower is cleared," the Director announced, his voice still calm and natural. A small cheer filled the room and for the first time "Pug" Schroeder allowed a slight smile to touch his face.

"Going through Mach three. On course. Altitude . . ."

When describing his actions later, Jim Settler spoke of watching his own hand as it moved out to the destruct button. It was, he said, as though it belonged to someone or something else. His fingers hovered for just a moment before pressing down. The rocket exploded, destroying itself and its thirty million dollar payload.

"What the . . . ? Shit! What happened?" Schroeder became vocal.

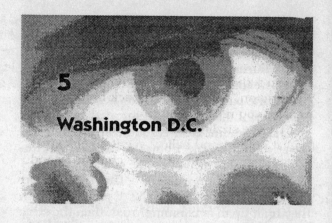

5
Washington D.C.

There was a low hum of conversation throughout the restaurant. Duncan Webster took a moment from perusing the menu to glance about him. Most of the tables were filled, it being well into the dinner hour. He thought he recognized a couple of faces; that was certainly John Cochran, the NBC White House Correspondent, exchanging pleasantries with a presidential aide across a well-laden table. Over on the far side, in an alcove, he thought he could make out the newly appointed supreme court justice, dining alone.

"See anyone you know?"

Duncan looked back to his own dinner companion, his old college professor and now Senator, Bill Highland. "One or two." He smiled. "Not that I *know* them, of course. Just recognize them. You're the one in the know."

Highland chuckled. "Not necessarily, Dunk. You'd be surprised how snooty some of these types can be. Unless, of course, they need a favor."

"Isn't that always the way? Not just in Washington." Duncan went back to the menu. "What d'you recommend, Bill?"

"Try the sizzling scampi. Tastes even better than it smells; and believe me it smells great. Or you're pretty safe with the chateaubriand, if you're really hungry. That's what I'm having, by the way."

Duncan couldn't help glancing at the prices on the menu. He gave silent thanks that the Senator was picking up the tab. He knew it would have blown his budget for the month to pay those prices. "Okay. I'll go for the scampi," he said.

"Good choice." Highland gave their order to the waiter, adding a bottle of red Burgundy to go with his chateaubriand. "Like a Moselle, or a nice dry sauterne or something, to brighten up the scampi?"

"No thanks, Bill." Duncan shook his head and raised his still half-filled glass of rum-and-coke. "I'll stick with this. Some of us have to drive ourselves home, you know. We don't all have chauffeur privileges."

They chatted about old times and their respective careers. Duncan—known affectionately as "Dunk" to his close friends—had been born and raised in southern California, but had opted to go to Columbia University in New York, to "get a taste of the east coast." He had not particularly enjoyed the taste; it was edible but not palatable.

He had started writing as a freshman. Nothing pretentious; mostly poetry. Then, with Professor Bill Highland's encouragement, he had tried a few short stories and non-fiction articles and surprised himself by finding he enjoyed it. To create sentences and string them together into whole paragraphs, then turn those paragraphs into complete stories and articles . . . it could be powerful stuff, though it could also be frightening. He had gone into the Navy for a couple of years, while he decided exactly what he wanted to do with his life. After all, he reasoned, no one could make a living just writing, and his degree in psychology wasn't worth a great deal. How had he known what to major in at that age? Some people seemed to know how to plan their lives right from high school, but he hadn't been one of them. Even after his stint in the Navy he really didn't know what to do with himself. So he started writing again, and actually sending out articles to magazines. No one was more surprised than Duncan Webster when he started getting back checks in return and seeing his byline in little magazines, then bigger magazines, then the national glossies.

He had eventually been approached by a publisher to write a book based on a series of articles he had done for *True* magazine. His first reaction had been panic. To write a book was a big commitment but, as with most things he encountered, he decided to give it a try. He was surprised at how easily the words rolled off his pen (or, more accurately, his computer keyboard). Almost without noticing, the years slipped by and he authored more than a dozen books. None was in the best-seller category, though he liked to think that one day he would hit that. His was what he liked to think of as a more select audience, for nearly all his books were based on his interest in the occult and the supernatural; something that had fascinated him as long as he could remember. He found that there was a perennial readership for such works and that he could make a living at it.

Duncan had reconnected with Bill Highland when he learned that his old mentor had traded in his cap and gown for a senator's desk. The older man had been delighted to find his former pupil again and had applauded, and been not a little proud of, his literary career. From time to time Duncan would get to D.C. to do some research at the Library of Congress and the Smithsonian, as was the case on this present visit, and never failed to get together with Highland at such times.

Thirty years old, with his blond hair, handsome features, and six-foot frame, Duncan Webster was close to being the epitome of the California heart-throb. Certainly he caught the attention of many women, though he remained a bachelor. He was well-built, without being obviously muscular. However, he broke the Southern California image in that he had actually done little surfing as a teen, quickly developing more of an interest in flying and anything to do with aircraft. His income, though adequate, wasn't sufficient to allow him to get a private pilot's license, so he started hang-gliding and then graduated to ultralights. He soon discovered he had more fun with the low-and-slow approach anyway.

"How's your big brother Brian? Is he married yet?" Highland asked, nibbling on a piece of celery.

Duncan shook his head and chuckled, thinking of his taciturn brother who ran a printing business in Long Beach. "Not that wily old bird. Mind you, I think it's just that no one will have him." They both laughed.

"And little sister Martha?"

"Still married to Tony, and still producing young 'uns. She called last week to say she was pregnant with number three."

"Wonderful. Be sure to give her my love next time you speak to her."

"I'll do that."

The polite verbal fencing continued through the meal until they had finished their entrées and sat back to contemplate dessert. The senator viewed the huge tray proffered by the waiter and opted for an extravaganza called "chocolate kamikaze." Duncan settled on a cheesecake.

"Okay, Bill," he said, after the first mouthful. "I know we don't often see one another these days, but to what do I owe this impressive repast? It isn't just for old time's sake, I'm sure."

Washington D.C.

Highland looked at him with feigned offense. "Duncan Webster! How can you suggest such a thing? Of course, I'm glad to see you again."

"Cut it out, Bill. I'm sorry; I know you are. But usually a pizza and a couple of beers covers it, no matter how long the break between visits. And don't forget we did get together just last year, when I was in New York for the A.B.A. convention. No, there's more to it than that. I know you too well."

Bill Highland smiled and picked up a fork to attack his chocolate extravaganza. "You're right, of course, Dunk, though I did feel it was time I really treated you. Mmm! This is good." He savored the dessert for a moment before continuing. "Truth is, Dunk, we've hit a bit of a problem and I know how good you are at solving mysteries."

Duncan wrinkled his brow. "I don't know about that. I do the odd crossword puzzle but . . ."

"No." Highland shook his head. "This is no time for modesty. You've helped me in the past and I've always been grateful. You definitely have a knack for putting your finger on the right button." He suddenly stopped, sat back, and laughed. Duncan looked at him, puzzled.

"What's the joke?"

"Sorry. You'll see. Just a poor choice of phrase, I guess. Or an appropriate one." The senator finished his chocolate kamikaze and looked at the plate as though he wished it would magically refill. Then, with a sigh, he pushed it away and turned his attention to coffee. "Have you ever come across a case where someone has been forced to do something against his will, and has done it without realizing he was doing it?"

He poured cream into the coffee cup, stirred it, and looked at Duncan over the rim as he raised it to drink.

"You mean like through hypnosis?"

"We've considered that. But you've got the right idea. Yes, that kind of thing."

"Why don't you tell me exactly what it is that's been happening," Duncan suggested, sweetening his own coffee. "It's not easy dealing with hypotheticals."

Highland put down his cup and gave his friend his full attention. "You're right, of course. Though I have to tell you this is strictly hush-hush. But, at the same time, it's not *officially* secret—yet—so I feel I can level with you. Anyway, I know you as well as I know myself." He paused for a moment before continuing. "We've had a couple of accidents with launching rockets carrying communications satellites."

Duncan was immediately attentive. "Military?"

"Of course. That's why we're worried."

"What sort of accidents?"

"In two cases recently we've had a good launch—absolutely nothing wrong with it; textbook trajectory—yet within seconds there has been an emergency destruct, even though there was no emergency, and the whole thingamajig was blown to kingdom come."

"You say there was no actual emergency calling for a destruct?"

"None."

"I'm sure you've looked into mechanical faults."

"Immediately." Highland sipped his coffee, then added extra sugar. "Needless to say we've had McDonnell Douglas engineers crawling all over us like ants at a picnic." He looked hard at Duncan. "But I think they're barking up the wrong tree."

Duncan returned the stare. "Why?"

"Because in both cases it was the destruct officer who pushed the button and blew the thing to bits."

The younger man whistled, causing heads to turn at the closer tables. "What was his story?"

"Well first of all, it was a different person each time. Two different launches, both from Vandenberg, but a month apart and each with a different destruct officer. Yet both went the same way. The first was a relay satellite; the latest a Key Hole surveillance satellite. I can tell you, at up to thirty million bucks a time, the powers that be are not very happy."

"So what do these officers have to say for themselves?" Duncan asked.

"Nothing! They had absolutely no explanation. Both the same story. They said it was as though they were watching someone else's hand reach out and push the button."

Duncan thought for a moment. "Background on the men?"

"Career men. Both colonels; one a full colonel, the other a Lieutenant. Exemplary records. You don't get onto the launch team haphazardly, you know."

"And you say you've considered hypnotism?" That would have been his guess, he thought. The situation had all the earmarks of hypnosis.

"That was one of the first things we thought of, yes. In fact we had them both hypnotized and 'regressed', I think they call it. Nothing. Zilch. Now here's the thing." Highland drew his chair a fraction closer to Duncan's. "We've got another launch coming up in a week. This one is a satellite; something to do with making sure Mad-ass Hussein keeps his promises. The top brass, and the Old Man, are very keen that everything goes as it should. They can't afford to keep doing this."

Duncan nodded. "Understandable. So what precautions have you taken?"

"The destruct officer will not be chosen until one hour before lift-off. Then—and this was my suggestion—there will be two Air Force policemen stationed behind him, keeping an eye on him. He won't know they're there, hopefully. They'll be instructed that if they see *any* untoward movement toward the button without getting a nod from the Launch Director, they're to jump in and grab him."

"Sounds dramatic, but necessary." Duncan nodded. "Can't you just have the Launch Direc-

Washington D.C.

tor himself be in charge of the button?"

"He's got far too much on his mind. It's unbelievable the number and variety of things that are going on and have to be watched. And he has to be mobile, so he can move to any location if necessary. The button would tie him down. No." He shook his head. "It has to be in someone else's hands, I'm afraid."

Duncan finished his coffee and thought through the situation. Finally he had to say, "Well, it sounds as though you've got it all covered."

The waiter came and took their order for liqueur. The two men said nothing until it had been served.

"Dunk. This next launch is a week from Wednesday. Would you be available? It's at Vandenberg again. You'll be back in California by then, won't you?"

"You want me to come and watch?" Duncan felt flattered, and very interested. He had never actually seen a rocket launch, especially not from inside the command center itself. And he was always willing to experience anything that would increase his knowledge. You just never knew when it would come in useful when writing. "Sure, Bill. I'd be happy to. Can you arrange it?"

Highland smiled. "One of the joys of being a Senator is that you can arrange just about anything."

"And you'll be there, too?"

"Oh, yes. You can count on it."

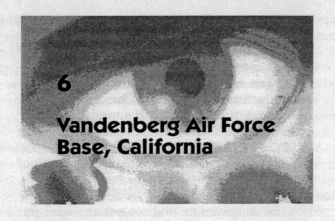

6
Vandenberg Air Force Base, California

Duncan Webster and Bill Highland, both sporting plastic-encased photo-identification passes, followed Major Richard Ward, the short, effusive public relations officer, along the passageway leading to the main control room.

"A mix of liquid hydrogen and liquid oxygen is the most powerful propellant we have at present," the major was saying. "There've been a number of promising experiments with a fluorine-hydrogen mix, but the trouble there is that you get all sorts of corrosion problems. Possibly mixing the fluorine forty to fifty per cent with oxygen could get over it but it's a touchy subject."

"How volatile are these mixtures?" Highland asked.

Vandenberg Air Force Base, California

"They're safe enough, the way we handle them." The major sounded smug.

"So you don't think there's a possibility of the rockets simply exploding of their own volition, just coincidentally with the destruct officer touching, or thinking he touched, the destruct button?" Highland sounded hopeful.

"That would *really* be coincidental," Duncan said. "Especially for it to happen twice."

Highland sighed. "I know. I'm kind of grasping at straws right now."

"This way, gentlemen." With a flourish the major opened a door with his security card and ushered them through into the main control area. It was still nearly two hours before the launch. A tall, sun-tanned, two-star general saw them and crossed the room to greet them.

"Good morning, Senator. I'm Major General Schroeder, Launch Director. Good to have you with us."

"Good morning, General," Highland responded. "I've been instructed by General Berkheiser to call you 'Pug' and stay out of your way—until the launch is successfully completed at any rate."

"God willing that it *is* successfully completed," the Director muttered.

"You were Director for both the aborted launches, weren't you, general?" Duncan asked.

"This is Mr. Duncan Webster." The Senator introduced him. "Dunk is a very good, longtime friend of mine, Pug, and I invited him here to witness this launch."

The Committee

"You know something about rockets, Mr. Webster?"

"Not really," Duncan said. "In fact, no. Nothing. But in the interests of looking at every angle on this problem, the Senator thinks I may be of some help."

"He's a great problem solver," Highland added. "And sometimes it helps to get a completely fresh, outside view."

"Hmm. Well, you must excuse me for now, gentlemen. There's work to be done." The General moved briskly back to the console he had been standing by when they came in.

"Was he agreeing with you, just being noncommital, or expressing disapproval?" Duncan asked, *sotto voce*.

"Doesn't really matter." Highland smiled. "You're here and that's that."

They moved around to the rear of the room, keeping back as much as possible from the engineers at the consoles. Major Ward hovered in the background, within easy reach.

"T minus 140 minutes and the count continues" came over the speakers.

The major drew near. "This is what we call a polar launch," he said. "From Kennedy they are equatorial launches, where we need that extra lift for the heavier loads."

"Extra lift?" Duncan asked. "How's that work?"

"Well," the P.R. officer looked pleased at being able to explain something. "The earth, as you know, rotates from west to east at

Vandenberg Air Force Base, California

about 900 miles per hour. Launching *with* that, traveling east, you get an extra boost; what we call 'rotational boost'. Launching from here we lose that boost because we're going against the rotation. What we call a polar orbit. So your heavy loads, like the manned vehicles, go out of Kennedy, in Florida, but we put up the lighter satellite loads from here."

"I see." Highland nodded thoughtfully.

"Exactly what's happening now?" Duncan asked. "It's, what, just past T minus one-thirty?"

"An aircraft has taken off to check that there's no interference with the frequencies used for telemetry and the missile's remote control. The ocean around Point Arguello has been cleared of all traffic."

"Ever had any problems?"

"Oh, yes." The major chuckled. "We still talk about the time when a Matador began fluttering its control surfaces right after lift-off. Turned out to be a Texas radio-taxi interfering on that wavelength." Highland and Duncan grinned. The major continued, "And then there was the Polaris whose second stage fired prematurely."

"What caused that?"

"We never did find out, though rumor had it that it was a Soviet sub off shore that did it deliberately."

Duncan looked sharply at Highland. "Any chance of that being the cause of our explosions?"

The Committee

The major answered for the Senator. "No, sir. That was one of the first suspicions. But apart from the fact that the Soviets really aren't active any more, there's still the fact that the two officers pressed the destruct buttons."

The count proceeded with no delays. At T minus seventy minutes a siren sounded shrilly over the speakers. Duncan and Highland both looked expectantly to Major Ward. "That's the uncoupling operation starting," he said. "The various stages of the gantry drop their contacts to the rocket. You can see it on the CRT down front there." He pointed and they moved forward. On a television screen they saw the gantry detaching its links; retracting them one after the other. Then the transfer truck pulled the tower away along its rails.

Pug Schroeder was standing right behind them at the T minus sixty count. They both heard him casually say to a nearby lieutenant colonel, "Oh, Colonel Addison. Move back to console seven, would you? Monitor APUs, man the destruct button and verify speed to altitude ratios. Thank you."

Duncan caught Highland's eye as the colonel moved back to take up a position in the last row of consoles. The two of them watched as a pair of Air Force Police sergeants, who had been standing in the shadows at the back of the big room, casually moved forward to stand unobtrusively behind the colonel. Duncan and Highland, in turn, slowly worked their way

Vandenberg Air Force Base, California

back to where they could stand and watch over the Air Force officer.

The rocket's tanks were filled and, on the closed-circuit TV, they saw a white cloud of condensation fill the air around the rocket. The launching ramp was cleared. Calls came in indicating that the Missile Range stations were all ready, that tracking and telemetry equipment was synchronized. Lights flashed and computer screens flickered rapidly as checks were run on flight programmers, gyroscopes and guidance systems. Finally Pug Schroeder fired the master button and the automatic sequencing went into effect.

Duncan strolled along the rear bank of monitors, passing behind the two Air Force policemen and the colonel, timing himself so that he was back behind the colonel at the time of launch. The eyes of most of the personnel in the blockhouse were glued to the television screens as the rocket lifted slowly upward on its tail of flame. It seemed to hover for a moment, as though to get its breath, then moved on upward, accelerating as it went.

Duncan could see the colonel's hands, tightly gripping the sides of the desk on either side of his console. His knuckles were white with the pressure. But, as the rocket climbed, now rapidly, into the sky, one hand pulled free and started to move in toward the destruct button.

One of the AFPs nudged the other. Together they carefully and slowly moved forward. As the colonel suddenly swung his hand across toward the center of the console both men rushed the final two or three feet and grabbed at his hands. They grasped his wrists and pulled him back from the terminal.

Duncan's eyes were glued to the destruct button. He saw that the colonel's hand never did get to it. Yet, even as he watched, he saw the red button move downwards, apparently of its own volition. The rocket blew into a million pieces, and the button came back up. No one, Duncan would swear, had physically touched the button, yet it had been depressed.

7

La Jolla, California

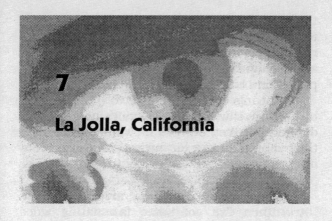

"What do you mean, I'm on the committee?" Earl Stratford looked at his friend with disbelieving eyes. "You know I hate committees. I'm a loner. I hate all groups."

"Aren't you on the faculty of the New School for Social Research, in New York?"

"No. Not really. They let me teach an occasional course when I feel like it, but I refuse to be on the regular faculty. I hate groups. I hate committees!"

"Not this one you won't." Duncan leaned over and topped-up his friend's liqueur glass. "Here, have a little more kahlúa."

Earl accepted it ungraciously, took a sip and sat back scowling. "Tell me about it. Is this your friend Senator Highland's idea?"

"Partly, yes." Duncan sipped from his own glass. "He offered to form a committee to look into what was happening. Of course everyone assumed he meant the usual committee of political know-nothings. But when he got the go-ahead, Bill asked *me* to form my own; with people I thought would know what they were doing . . . people like you, Earl."

"Hrmph!" Earl snorted and took a longer drink. "Flattery, as you well know Dunk, will get you a hell of a lot further than just about anything else. But I'm still not saying yes," he added quickly, as Duncan started to smile.

"Okay. Okay. Just hear me out, though. And then I've got some fascinating video footage to show you." Duncan tapped a VHS cassette lying beside him on the coffee table. He had persuaded Bill Highland it was necessary to have a copy of the tape, though it was now classified top secret. "And, incidentally, the Senator had your service records checked and you're okay for security clearance."

They were in Duncan's condominium overlooking Boomer Beach at La Jolla. The tops of two royal palm trees framed the large picture window, from which there was a striking view of the Pacific Ocean. Off to the right were sandstone cliffs, at the foot of which were the numerous caves of La Jolla Cove. Beyond, the beach curved around to Scripps Institution of Oceanography, with its own pier jutting out into the blue waters, and beyond that lay the infamous Black's Beach with its nude bathers and, above, the cliffs from which Duncan had many times leapt, clinging to a hang-glider and soaring up on the rising currents of air to sweep across the ocean five hundred feet above the waves.

Earl was fifteen years Duncan's senior. With dark hair, moustache and full beard, bespectacled and slightly overweight, Earl's looks strongly contrasted with those of the younger man. He was a parapsychologist and had come into contact with Duncan some years before, when they were both involved in the investigation of a haunted house in Mississippi. Although they lived on opposite coasts—Earl had a small apartment in Greenwich Village, New York—they seemed to keep meeting through one or the other of them traveling to give a lecture or do research. This time Earl was on the west coast to speak at a symposium in San Diego.

Briefly, but not leaving out any important details, Duncan told his friend of the three rocket mishaps, including the one he had recently witnessed. Earl, in spite of himself, became interested.

"What about radio interference? Someone on the same frequency with their own destruct button? You said they had had problems in that area before."

"Yes." Duncan nodded. That had been one of his own earlier thoughts. "But that was quite a few years ago. And the destruct frequency is certainly one they jealously guard and protect. No, it wasn't that."

"You're certain?"

"I've been assured by just about everyone, Earl. I guess that was the most obvious suspicion and one that was really checked-out thoroughly."

"Hmm. And you've considered hypnotism? The destruct officers having been hypnotized by 'person or persons unknown' and made to hit the destruct button whether they wanted to or not?"

"Oh, yes. But it wouldn't cover the last shot—the one I was at—because the destruct officer wasn't even selected till just before lift-off. And it certainly wouldn't cover what happened then, as you'll see in a moment." Again Duncan tapped the video tape box.

"Quite apart from the 'how' we must also consider the 'who' and the 'why'," Earl said, taking off his glasses to polish them. "If we knew either one of those two it would help with the 'how'." He put his glasses back on and turned to Duncan. "Let's have a look at your tape. See if there are any clues you may have overlooked." He peered over the tops of his bifocals before pushing them up to settle on the bridge of his nose. "You know how it is, Dunk? 'Can't see the wood for the trees'?"

"Oh, I agree." He and Earl usually thought along the same lines, Duncan had found. And by the same token they did extremely well sparking one another's thought patterns. They tended to egg one another on; to go just a little further in the thought processes than they might have been content to do otherwise. He

La Jolla, California

got up and slipped the video into his VCR. He closed the venetian blinds to darken the room and took up the remote control. "Okay. There are some shots here of the last rocket blasting off—the one I witnessed—and then, later, exploding. This is official launch footage so you'll see data superimposed on the screen, indicating everything A-okay up to the big bang. Then there are interviews with the destruct officer, one Lieutenant Colonel Eugene Addison. As with the previous officers, he's a top-rated Air Force colonel with an exemplary record."

"Anything else?"

"Uhuh. Most interesting. Interviews with the two Air Force policemen who grabbed Addison to stop him from hitting the button. I think you're going to be intrigued by what they have to say."

"You've no footage of the actual button push, or non-push, as you described it?"

"No, dammit! Wish we'd thought to set up a camera there." Duncan could have kicked himself for not having had the thought earlier. "But, of course, we didn't know exactly what would happen. We thought the two AFPs would simply stop any interference."

They watched the tape, with Duncan operating the remote and giving a commentary on the launch. At the destruction of the rocket Earl leaned forward but said nothing. Then there was the interview with the lieutenant colonel. It was conducted by Pug Schroeder,

The Committee

Bill Highland, and a two-star General named Broderick.

"I have no idea why I tried to push the button, sir."

"Were you aware of the two previous destructs?" Broderick asked.

"Oh yes, sir. It's been the talk of the blockhouse. And that was all the more reason that, when Colonel Schroeder asked me to move to console seven, I was determined not to be the third."

"Just tell us exactly how you were affected," Highland said.

"Yes, Senator. It was strange. One moment I was perfectly relaxed and the next I suddenly felt this pressure on my arm to move to the button."

"You felt pressure?" Pug Schroeder was curious.

"Pressure is the only way I can think to describe it, sir," the colonel replied. "It was almost as though someone had taken a grip of my wrist and was suddenly determined to move it in to the button."

"Did you actually feel fingers?" Broderick asked, incredulous.

"No, sir. I don't think I could say that. It wasn't really as though some*one* had grasped my wrist . . ."

"Isn't that what you just said?" snapped the general.

"Well, yes sir. I guess I did. But what I meant . . ."

"Just take it easy, Colonel," Highland said. "No one is blaming you. You're not on trial here. We're just trying to get to the bottom of this."

"Yes, Senator. Thank you, sir. As I say, it was as though some*thing*, I guess I'd have to say, had hold of my wrist and was pushing it in. I resisted as much as I could but I couldn't stop it. Then, just as I was getting close to the button, I was seized from behind. Next thing I knew, the rocket exploded anyway."

"You did push the button then?" Broderick asked.

"No, sir. I'd swear I didn't. I was pulled away before I could."

"Well someone must have pushed it."

"Not me, sir."

"Did you see the button go down?"

"No, sir. When the AFPs seized me they took me by surprise and my attention was distracted from the button."

Duncan hit the pause control. "That's the meat of what he had to say. They went over it all several times but got nothing more out of him. I'll fast-forward to the next one. The first of the two policemen." He set the tape moving forward to the start of the next interview.

"Were they questioned together?" Earl asked.

"No. Separately. In fact they were separated right away; right after the excitement died down, so there could be no collaboration, conscious or unconscious."

"Good. Okay, let's see what they have to say."

The first man interviewed was a Sergeant Redland. He recited his military background and then moved on to the launch episode. "We had been ordered to grab, er, restrain, the colonel should he move toward the red button without obvious necessity, sir—er, sirs," he stated.

"How were you to determine whether or not there was, as you say, 'obvious necessity'?" General Broderick asked.

"We were told that Colonel Schroeder here, sir, would give a very definite signal if there was to be a destruct, sir. If he didn't give such a signal we were to assume everything was hunkydory and were to act on any untoward movement of Colonel Addison's, sir."

"I see. Go on. What did you see when you did restrain the colonel?"

"Well, sir, I don't know. I mean, what happened was that I, we that is, grabbed him and as we were holding him the rocket exploded. Well, we were all taken by surprise, weren't we sir?" he asked of Pug Schroeder.

"Yes, yes. Of course. Go on."

"Yes, sir. Well, we were all surprised and then I suddenly noticed the red button. It was pressed down."

"What do you mean, it was pressed down?"

"Just that, sir. I didn't see it get pressed, and I'd bet a month's pay we'd stopped Colonel Addison from getting to it. But there it was, down. Then, as I watched, it came back up again. Sirs."

Again Duncan hit the pause. He waited for his friend's reaction.

"Fascinating," Earl said, again taking off his gold-rimmed spectacles and wiping them. He put them back on and sat tugging at his beard. "Let's see the other policeman, unless this first one has anything else to add?"

"No. Just cross-examination." Duncan moved the tape ahead to the next interview. Sergeant Whitehorse Cody, a Native American, was speaking.

"As soon as I saw the colonel starting to move for the button I grabbed him, sir. We'd been told there'd be a proper signal, or something, if a destruct was actually necessary, but there hadn't been anything."

"So you acted on your own initiative?" asked Bill Highland.

"That's what we're trained to do, Senator."

"Of course. Please continue."

"Well, sir, I moved forward and so did Sergeant Redland. We got a good grip on his arms and pulled him, and his chair, back from the board."

"What did you see, at that time?" Broderick asked.

The sergeant paused for a moment, as though to be quite sure of his words before speaking them. "I know what I saw, sir, though I still don't know that I can believe it. My eyes were on the red destruct button as I got hold of the colonel. I wanted to make sure his hand didn't get nowhere near it. We pulled him back but, even as I watched, sir, that button went down and came up again just as though someone *had* pushed it. All by itself, sir, as though some invisible hand had pushed it."

"Hot dog!" cried Earl, and threw himself back in his chair. Duncan smiled and stopped the tape. "I know what you'd told me, Dunk. You said *you'd* seen that button go down. But somehow, just hearing these two other unbiased witnesses say the same thing . . ."

"You think I'm biased?" Duncan demanded. "Thanks a lot!"

"No. No, you know what I mean," Earl said, getting up and moving across to the window. He opened the blinds again and gazed out. "Hot dog! This could be interesting."

Duncan chuckled to himself. He'd known his friend would react this way, that was why he had wanted to have a copy of the tape. "So you don't mind being on the committee?" he asked, innocently.

Earl looked down at the bikini-clad girls on the beach. He watched a couple of suntanned male surfers—blondest of blond hair and deep tans—tossing a frisbee back and forth, trying to impress some of the girls. He saw them but he didn't see them. An unexpected excitement ran through his body. He turned back to Duncan.

La Jolla, California

"You think there's a paranormal explanation for this, don't you, Dunk? I know you. That's why you want me on your damn committee."

Duncan rewound the tape and retrieved it from the VCR, put it back in its box and placed it carefully on a shelf. He must remember to put it away somewhere safe later on, he thought. "The official investigation seems to be getting nowhere," he said. "You saw the tape. Military questions; military thinking. Scientific checking. Radio frequencies, maladjusted hardware, computer whims, sunflare interference . . . you name it, it's all been checked out or damn soon will be. Apparently McDonnell Douglas has started its own investigation, and not only that, but Bill tells me Rockwell and Ryan and everybody else in the industry is pushing for funds to conduct a monster enquiry. But Bill—God bless him—has this hunch, and he's sticking to it. It's why he called me in. He knows the answer's not a mechanical one or electrical or radio or computer or whatever. And we both know the answer's not there. It has to be supranormal. And you and I, and one or two others we both know, are the only ones who stand a chance of finding out that how, who, and why. Thanks to Bill we are the official, if unacknowledged, committee on this. If anyone should get to the root, we should. And, by golly, we will!"

8
Washington, D.C.

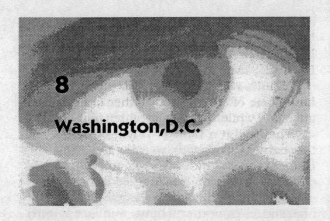

"You've got me running backward and forward across the country like a horizontal yoyo!"

Bill Highland smiled. "Now you know how a politician feels in a campaign year," he said. "But seriously, Dunk, I'm sorry but I honestly think D.C. would be your best base of operations for all this. Sure, we had to be on the west coast for the launch, and it gave you a chance to get things straightened up at home, but here's where you need to be till we get this all figured out. Here's where we've got all the records on everybody and everything, and here's where I can wield the most influence to get you access to those records."

"And it's close enough to my center of ops as well," Earl added. "Only a hop and a skip from the Big Apple."

"I guess you're right. Both of you," Duncan

admitted, thinking wistfully of the La Jolla beach and its bikinied inhabitants. "And let's hope it won't take too long to settle this. I guess I can stay away from the sun for a while."

"Sun!" Highland snorted. "You should have some of our winter weather in California once in a while. That'd straighten you out!"

They sat at a table in "Flying Dutch's," at the corner of Rhode Island and 17th. The place had started out as a semi-private men's club, but had been forced to open up to both sexes and was now a popular restaurant-cum-bar. The walls were still decorated mostly with the original assortment of mounted fish and animal heads, interspersed with autographed caricatures of prominent politicians, past and present. A smattering of prints of Toulouse-Lautrec lithographs and of framed Degas-inspired pastels of ballerinas were the concession to feminism, as was the decor of pink-and-maroon striped tablecloths and lampshades.

Bill Highland was finishing off a large plate of Milanese-style pasta smothered with fresh-grated Parmesan cheese and a side-order of ravioli. He popped half of a garlic breadstick into his mouth and chewed happily, and thoughtfully, for a moment. "So you're a committee of two so far. Who else d'you have in mind, Dunk? Others of Professor Stratford's caliber, I trust."

Earl inclined his head in acknowledgement of the compliment and kept his attention focused on what remained of his veal fricandeau.

"Between us, Earl and I have a number of acquaintances who are experts in various fields of the paranormal," Duncan said. "We've been discussing this and we're pretty sure we'd like to bring in Elizabeth Martin and possibly Fritz Friedermann, if he's available."

"Anyone you say," the senator said. "I have implicit faith in you, Dunk, you know that. Who's Elizabeth Martin?"

Duncan smiled. "Just an Ohio housewife," he said. He thought to himself of the petite redhead's incredible ESP scores, when she was tested and retested at Duke University. Experiments there, originally set up by Dr. J. B. Rhine, had proven beyond a shadow of a doubt that extra sensory perception—the ability to focus in on another's thoughts—was not only a reality but that Beth Martin had that ability in far greater capacity than just about anyone else ever tested.

Highland stopped with his fork halfway to his mouth. "Just an Ohio housewife?" he repeated. Then he nodded and carried on eating. "Okay. And Fritz Whatsisname?"

"An associate of mine," Earl said. "Another parapsychology professor. Very prominent in the field. Only trouble is he's usually very busy. We may not be able to get him."

"Well, as I told you, you choose your own committee," Highland said. "And don't worry about expenses, Dunk. Whatever you need,

I'll see you're covered. Within reason, of course."

"Thanks, Bill. Thanks a lot. I appreciate it," Duncan said, feeling somewhat relieved. The question of expenses was one he had been worrying over. It wasn't a subject he would have felt comfortable bringing up to Highland yet he'd known it would have to be dealt with. He was grateful it was Highland himself who'd broached it. "But, getting back to the problem, the thing is that this obviously isn't just some haphazard happening or occult disturbance. There has to be someone, or some group, directing this; *making* these rockets explode. But who and how?"

"And, as importantly, why?" put in Earl.

"Exactly." Duncan nodded his head and took a quick bite of garlic chicken. "It may just be coincidental that two of these rockets were carrying surveillance satellites. I wonder, would they all have been exploded if they'd been putting up, say, weather satellites, or civilian TV or telephone relay satellites? Somehow I doubt it."

"Mmm." Earl nodded.

"Do you have any ideas at all, at this point?" Highland asked. "I mean, in which direction are you going from here?"

"I called Beth and she's already on her way here. I left a message for Fritz and hope to hear from him within twenty-four hours. As soon as we've got everyone together we're going to have a major brainstorming session.

Until then, to answer your question, no we've really got nothing."

"Dunk and I did kick around the idea of astral projection," Earl said, picking at the last of his veal. "From the point of view of whether or not someone was using it to find out exactly when the rockets were being launched. But despite being a parapsychologist—or perhaps because of it—I'm a bit of a skeptic on some of this stuff, and that includes OOBEs."

"Which is one of the reasons I like him," Duncan said.

The senator sat with the last of his breadsticks in his hand. "And what, might I ask, are OOBEs and astral projection?"

Earl looked at Duncan and grinned. "I said I was the skeptic," he said. "You tell him."

Thanks a lot, Earl, thought Duncan. He looked at the senator. "Do you dream much?" he asked.

"What? What does that have to do . . ."

"Just answer the question, Bill. Do you dream much?"

"Not much, no."

"But you do a bit?" Duncan persisted.

"Sure. Doesn't everybody?"

"No, but never mind. What sort of things do you dream about?"

Highland pushed his plate away and sat thinking. "Nothing, really. By that I mean just crazy, nonsense kind of things. You know, I wake up with just bits and pieces."

"Give me a for instance," Duncan said.

"Well, as a matter of fact I had one just last night. I woke up this morning and remembered dreaming about snowshoeing across the Atlantic Ocean."

Earl's head jerked up. "Say what?"

Highland laughed. "I know. Crazy, isn't it? But I was snowshoeing across the water and I had a golf club in one hand and a file folder full of lecture notes in the other. Now, what d'you make of that?" He looked defiantly at Duncan.

"Interesting." The young man finished off his chicken, took a long drink of water and then sat back. "Let me tell you first about the astral body and then I'll explain your dream," he said.

They each ordered and got a cup of coffee and waited for Duncan to begin.

"The thought is that everyone has what's known as an astral double," he began. "This is an invisible form—invisible to the naked eye—that is an exact duplicate of your physical form. There are extensions of it that you may have heard referred to as the *aura*, but I won't go into that right now. Anyway, your astral body can separate from your physical body when you're asleep, or when you're unconscious for any reason."

"We certainly have lots of documentation on people who have 'slipped out of their bodies', as they put it, while under an anesthetic during a surgical operation," put in Earl. "They also call them OOBEs—Out Of Body

Experiences. These people claim to have been able to hover over the operating table and watch what was going on. Certainly some have been able to accurately describe everything that happened, both in the operating room and in other parts of the hospital, that they could never have known normally."

"I've heard of 'near-death experiences'," Highland said. "Isn't that the same?"

"Very similar." Duncan nodded, relieved that Highland could relate in some way to what he was saying. "Just a step further, if you like. Anyway, the astral body can separate from the physical and, apparently, it does this every night when you sleep."

"Where does it go?"

"It can go anywhere; anywhere your subconscious decides it would like to go. And it can go with the speed of thought."

"So how does this tie-in with my dream?" Highland opened three packets of sugar, poured them into his coffee and stirred.

"Well," Duncan said. "Your dream was fragmented memories of your astral travels. It could be that your unconscious mind decided it would be nice to play a game of golf with a friend. Then, perhaps, you relived a speech that you gave in the past and that went extremely well. After that you might have gone off up to New England and gone snowshoeing, just for the sheer hell of it! And from there, you obviously crossed the Atlantic for some reason—perhaps a quick trip to Britain. When you woke up this morning you just had odd little scraps of memories of these different adventures, but all jumbled together so that you were crossing the Atlantic on snowshoes, with your golf club and speech notes."

They all laughed at the picture. "So how do I get to sort out what's what in these dreams?" the senator asked.

"Just a question of practice," Duncan replied. "As soon as you wake up in the morning, before anything, even before getting out of bed or having a cup of coffee, write down all that you remember of what you dreamed. It'll take a while to remember everything with any accuracy."

"How long a while?"

"Depends on the individual. Could be weeks; could even be months. But eventually you'll remember all of your dreams and, consequently, all your astral journeys."

"There's another step from there, isn't there?" put in Earl.

"Oh, yes." Duncan nodded, this time appreciating the prompt. "Some people have got to the point where they decide where they want to go, on the astral, *before* they go to bed. Then they go to sleep and go there."

"Good God!"

"And again we've got this documented," Duncan continued. "The Society for Psychical Research checked out such a person. They gave this man an address and told him to travel to it on the astral. He'd never been to this place before in his life—I think it was somewhere in Indiana—but he just lay down on a couch and put himself into a light trance. When he woke up, half an hour later, he was able to accurately describe the house at that address, its decorations, furnishings, and occupants."

"Good God!" Highland repeated. "And other people can do this?"

"Anyone can, with practice. The trick is to 'go to sleep' when you're wide awake, thus releasing your astral body. You can do it with just a light trance—similar to the state you put yourself in when you do meditation—or you can go for a good, solid, deep trance through self-hypnosis."

"But the main thing, it seems to me," Earl interjected, "is to remember your experiences when you 'come back', or wake up?"

"Exactly." Duncan nodded. "If you can remember your dreams you are halfway there. You are simply carrying your memory over from one state of consciousness to another."

They continued discussing the astral and out-of-body experiences for a while, then the talk got back to satellites.

"On the subject of who might be destroying these satellites," Duncan said, his face serious, "who would know about the launches ahead of time? I mean, like the dates and times, and all that information?"

"A relatively short list," Highland replied. "And, as you might guess, we've already gone down it and checked everyone on it very carefully."

"You're sure you covered everyone?" Earl asked.

"Yes. But there is something interesting. About a month ago Senator O'Cork was asking me about a man who defected to the Soviets a couple of years ago. Asked me if I knew what had happened to him. Interestingly enough this man was a satellite expert."

"Military?"

Highland nodded. "Yes. You may recall him. A General Nathan Wellesley."

"The name sounds vaguely familiar," Earl said, taking off his glasses and cleaning them on his napkin.

"Doesn't mean anything to me," Duncan said, running the name through his head. "So what about him, Bill?"

"Well, at O'Cork's request I started an investigation and found that, with the break-up of the U.S.S.R., our old friend Wellesley recently moved from Moscow to Havana."

Earl stopped polishing his glasses and looked at Duncan. They both then turned to the senator.

"Havana? Cuba?"

"That's the only Havana I know," Highland said.

"No, actually there's one in Illinois," Earl said. "Though I doubt he went there."

"Why do you think he's gone to Cuba?" Duncan asked.

Highland shrugged. "Who knows. As it happens he didn't go alone. For whatever reason quite a little party of Ruskies went. It just so happened that General Wellesley went along with them."

Again Duncan and Earl exchanged glances. "You don't happen to know who they all were, do you?"

"Not off the top of my head, no. But I can find out and let you know. You think this could be important?"

"I honestly don't know at this point," Duncan said. "But I've got a gut feeling that there's some connection here. Yes, Bill. Let me know the names as soon as you can, will you?"

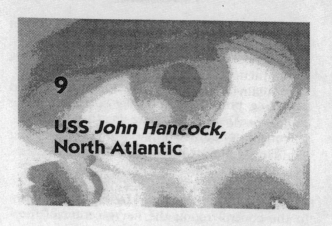

9

USS *John Hancock*, North Atlantic

"Diving officer, make your depth four hundred feet."

"Four hundred feet, aye. Ten degrees down-angle on the planes."

"Ten degrees down, aye."

The USS *John Hancock*, a Los Angeles class SSN 6,080 ton nuclear attack submarine, moved down through the dark green waters of the Atlantic Ocean, slowly increasing speed as she went. Three hundred sixty feet long, she carried twelve torpedo-tube-launched Tomahawk cruise missiles (SLCMs). One pressurized water S6G (GE) reactor supplied her single shaft with 35,000 shp of power through two geared turbines, giving her a top speed of over 30 knots. She carried a full crew of twelve officers and 115 enlisted men. Her skipper was Commander Julian Page.

The Helmsman eased back on the control column. The submarine slowed its descent and started to level out. The ballast tanks no longer let in water and the creaking and groaning of the hull, as it adjusted to the changing pressure, gradually subsided. The huge vessel leveled to where its attitude would be constantly adjusted by computer.

"Steady at four hundred feet."

"All ahead full."

"All ahead full, aye."

Commander Page stood by the chart table in the control room; the nerve center of the craft, situated directly below the fin, or conning tower. "Set a course two-two-zero, west-south-west," he said.

"Two-two-zero, west-south-west, aye."

The *John Hancock* had been absorbed in the NATO exercise USEFUL PORPOISE for the previous six weeks, and had been at sea for another week before that. After the prolonged intensity of the exercise all the men were happy to see it come to an end and to be able to relax a little. They now looked forward to the end of the voyage and to twenty-five days in harbor.

Lieutenant Jim Harrison bent over the chart table. "Are we going home, sir? I'm sure ready for that."

"Not directly, I'm afraid," Page said. "We have to make a courtesy call at Bermuda first. Some little political pomp-and-ceremony, I believe. We have to show the flag."

USS John Hancock, *North Atlantic*

The navigation officer groaned. "Not a service dress appearance?"

"'Fraid so. But don't worry, it's only a brief stop and then straight on back up to Norfolk from there."

The submarine was cruising at 20 knots and life settled into its routine. However, with no indication of daytime or nighttime possible below the surface, time was divided into six-hour one-in-three rotating watch cycles. With this device it didn't take long to lose track of what was when, in terms of normal daylight. Conventional submarines have to make frequent trips up to the surface for air. Nuclear submarines don't. They can remain deeply submerged for weeks at a time. Two distillers make 5,000 gallons of fresh water a day, by distilling seawater. Fresh air is made by electrolysis; passing electricity through fresh water. Just one pint of water can produce enough air for the crew for one hour. CO^2 "scrubbers" absorb the stale gasses from the air.

SSN nuclear attack submarines are larger than the older diesel-electrics, and there is a little more elbow room for the crew. The captain and officers have separate cabins; the enlisted men share cubicles with bunks and lockers. There is a dining hall, lounge and even a library. Each evening a different movie or video is shown, these frequently being newly released films.

Commander Page was resting in his cabin when there came a tap on the door. Wearily he swung his legs off the bed, where he'd been stretched out, and moved across to answer it.

"Skipper, I think we have a problem. A big problem. You'd better come to conn." Lieutenant Commander Ed Carroll was known for his cheery disposition and his constant grin. This time his face was grave and the Skipper sensed something was seriously wrong.

The commander's cabin was just off the control center, so that he was never far from the action, consequently the two were soon peering over the shoulders of the chief of the watch and the helmsman. Lieutenant Harrison was already there, moving backward and forward between his charts and the SINS display.

Navigation is accomplished through the SINS system—the Ship's Inertial Navigational System. This is amazingly accurate, allowing a submarine to circle the globe and end up back at exactly the same spot from which it started. The system uses gyroscopes to keep frames of the unit pointing exactly north-south, east-west, and perpendicularly up-and-down. When the submarine alters course the gyroscopes stop the frames from moving with it. Accelerometers then measure the strength of the forces needed to keep those frames from turning. A computer calculates how far, and in which direction, the ship has turned, based on those measurements.

"Who gave the order to alter course?" The Commander's voice was quiet but those who knew him could immediately tell that he was not pleased.

"No one, sir," responded the officer of the watch.

"But we were on a heading of two-two-zero, I believe?"

"Right, Skipper." The Lieutenant Commander nodded his head. "And, as Smitty says, no one's countermanded that. No one would dream of doing so," he couldn't help adding.

"I don't understand." The captain's voice remained quiet but icy cold. "I read a heading of two-one-six."

Even as he spoke the submarine turned a fraction more to port and the heading changed to two-one-five. "What the . . . ! Helmsman!"

"I—I'm sorry, sir. I'm not doing it! I swear I'm not. In fact I'm trying to turn back to starboard."

After taking the helm himself, and failing to bring the submarine back on course, Page's next step was to question the instruments. For two hours officers and men ran to and fro exhaustively testing, checking and rechecking all the navigational instruments. Everything seemed to check out, yet despite all efforts the ship seemed to have a mind of its own and continued to swing to port, finally settling on a heading several degrees south of Page's original one.

"Take her up to periscope depth," the commander snapped.

Within five minutes the upward angles of

the diving planes, coupled with using compressed air to expel water from the ballast tanks, had brought the great ship to within a few feet of the ocean's surface. It was not uncommon to occasionally double-check the SINS by the use of some of the more conventional methods of navigation. These were the satellite navigational systems (SATNAV), such as the Global Position System known as NAVSTAR, also radio aids such as LORAN C and OMEGA and there was even celestial navigation, that could be done by looking through the periscope and measuring the positions of the stars or the sun. Many of these were tried now. All they did was confirm that what the SINS said was correct; the submarine was apparently turning of her own volition.

"Bring her back to ten knots."

"Ten knots, aye."

The *John Hancock* slowed.

Word spread quickly through the ship. For all the sophistication of nuclear propulsion, sailors remain a superstitious lot. It didn't take long for there to be mention of the Bermuda Triangle.

"Remember the *Scorpion* went down in the Triangle," said one older Warrant Officer, knowingly.

"*Scorpion*?" a younger ensign asked.

"Yeah," someone else chimed in. "I had a mate on that. Real weird that was, if you ask me."

"What the hell are you talking about?"

USS John Hancock, North Atlantic

A small circle quickly formed about the three men.

"May, 1968," the W.O. said. "The U.S.S. *Scorpion* went into the Bermuda Triangle and just never came out."

"What d'you mean, she never came out?"

"Just that. She disappeared, with all hands. Was six months later they finally located her. Sitting on the bottom under two miles of water, 400 miles southwest of the Azores. Miles away from where she was supposed to be."

"That's the Triangle all right."

"Aye!"

Commander Page was stumped. He called a meeting of his top officers, in the ward room.

"Ideas?" he asked.

There was an uneasy silence, then Lieutenant Harrison tentatively broke it.

"We've checked and double-checked all instruments, Skipper. You saw us do that yourself. Which means there's no mistake; we've changed course without trying to."

"Anyway," put in Ed Carroll, "even without checking instruments we can see that no matter how hard we try to change course, she's not responding to any input on the helm."

"Yes. That's the spooky thing."

"Belay the 'spooky' talk," Page snapped. "The last thing we want is to start a chain of ghost stories or Bermuda Triangle nonsense."

"'Fraid that's too late," Carroll said. "I've already heard the men muttering something to that effect."

"Jesus Christ!" Page raised his hands above his head and brought them down hard on the table. "We're at the end of the twentieth century in a nuclear powered submarine, for god's sake!" He looked around the table, his face grim. "Let's pinch out that sort of thing before it gets any further." Heads nodded.

"Would it help to talk to COMSUBLANT, Skipper? Ask if they've had any similar problems on other boats?" It was a Lieutenant (jg) who asked.

Page shook his head. "No. Leastwise, not yet. Let's see if we can deal with this ourselves before we go running to daddy."

The conference broke up with nothing accomplished, other than a decision to keep checking instruments and to try various maneuvers to change course.

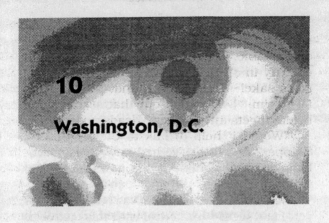

10
Washington, D.C.

Duncan picked up Elizabeth Martin at Washington National Airport and, on the drive to the hotel, filled her in on all that had been happening.

"Is Professor Friedermann coming?" she asked. "You mentioned him on the phone."

"No." Duncan shook his head. "Apparently he's tied-up doing some television series. So Earl had an idea and called Rudolf Küstermeyer. He's flying in from Frankfurt . . . on the Concorde."

"The Concorde!"

Duncan smiled. "Well, time is all important and Bill Highland did say he'd cover expenses. So, why not?" He glanced at his passenger. He had always loved her red hair. She had let it grow since the last time he'd seen her, and now it reached to just below her shoulders.

"I guess you're right." She gazed out of the window, her hair blowing in the wind that sneaked in at the lowered top. "Didn't Küstermeyer write that book on astral projection?"

"He sure did. That was one of the things that made Earl think of him. We'd been trying to explain projection to Bill."

"You think we may need to use it? I guess this could be more complicated than I thought." She caught at her hair and snagged it back behind a barrette, giving Duncan a clearer view of her lightly-freckled face.

"Oh, it could get complicated all right," he said, turning and crossing Pennsylvania Avenue, heading north up 16th to M Street. "We just don't know how much, at this point. And don't forget, Beth, all this is very important to the security of this country. This evening, when we all get together, you'll probably get a better idea of what's what. By the way, how's John?" He'd almost forgotten to ask after her husband.

There was a short silence. "Didn't I tell you, Dunk? We've separated. We're going to get a divorce."

"No. I—why, no." He didn't know what to say. He had never really cared for John, who was a workaholic insurance salesman with no interest whatever in his wife's ESP abilities. They drove on in silence.

*

Washington D.C.

They met in Duncan's room at the Jefferson Hotel, on 16th Street NW just four blocks from the White House. Bill Highland had booked him into a suite so there would be plenty of room for such meetings, and to set up an office of sorts. Duncan was amazed at the opulence of the hotel; one of the best in the world, Highland had declaimed. Each of the 104 rooms was uniquely decorated; Duncan's had an antique four-poster bed with a plump, eyelet-trimmed comforter and pillow shams. There was a Napoleonic cherrywood bibliothèque filled with rare books against one wall and a French Empire Louis XVI bureau at another. Beautifully framed original oil paintings decorated the walls and Persian rugs covered the floors. An Italian crystal chandelier hung from a carved-plaster rosette-motif Adams ceiling.

Room service brought up a huge tray of coffee and assorted scones, pastries, and finger sandwiches. Rudolf Küstermeyer was in his seventies, thin almost to the point of emaciation, with a bald pate poking through his thinning grey hair and with penetrating, black eyes staring out from under bushy, gray eyebrows. He sat on the edge of an elegant straight-backed chair balancing a cup and saucer on his knees. He was in deep conversation with Elizabeth, who sat back in a comfortable armchair. Duncan and Earl were at either end of the rose-and-gold silk-covered Chippendale sofa, sorting through a small pile

The Committee

of papers that lay between them.

"You must call me Rudy," Rudolf was saying. "Everybody does."

"I don't," said Earl, without looking up from the pile of papers.

"You do not count, *mein lieb Freund*," the German responded, with a chuckle.

Duncan straightened up and looked around at each of them. "Okay, let's get going," he said. "I'm sure Rudy has got jet lag, in spite of the swiftness of the Concorde, so I don't want this to run too late." The German graciously inclined his head. "Let me bring you all up to date. I've got here a list, from Bill, of the Russians who have opted for Cuba and, presumably, are there in some way connected with Nathan Wellesley."

"Just what do we know about this Nathan Wellesley, before you get into the other people, Dunk?" Elizabeth asked, her green eyes searching his face.

"Well, as I told you on the way here from the airport, he was a top Air Force general with a very impressive background. He's an expert on satellites and telecommunications. He worked at the Pentagon for several years and was in on the planning of military satellite placement."

"Satellites for what?"

"Mainly for surveillance. We have one biggy, generally referred to as our 'eye-in-the-sky', that keeps tabs on Castro and the

Cubans, then there are others strategically placed around and above the globe watching potential trouble spots."

"There are also a whole bunch of relay satellites," Earl added. "They do just that, they relay the information from one satellite to another and from satellites to good old *terra firma.*"

"And General Wellesley knows where all these military satellites are placed?" Rudolf asked, his bushy eyebrows meeting over his beak of a nose.

"Yes," Duncan responded. "He was the original mastermind behind them. Then, for whatever reason, he started giving information to the Ruskies."

"For money?" Elizabeth asked.

"I'm sure he did get paid, and handsomely, for the info. But whether or not that was the reason, or the only reason, we don't know." Duncan paused to pour himself another cup of coffee. "Anyway, it didn't take too long for military intelligence to cotton on to him and try to grab him."

"*Try?*" Earl's brow wrinkled.

"Bill's got a feeling there was some sort of internal leak, giving him warning," Duncan continued. "Just when they were about to grab him he did a bunk."

"How?"

"He was at Oshkosh, for the big E.A.A. convention. He climbed aboard the huge Soviet An-124 that was there and asked asy-

The Committee

lum of the captain. He flew back to Russia with them."

"Okay. So now who's gone with him to Cuba?" Elizabeth asked.

Duncan looked at a sheet of paper. "Here's the list Bill gave me just this afternoon. See if any of you recognize any of these names." He did what he could with the unfamiliar Russian pronunciations. "Petrov Aksakov, Anna Blavatsky, Boris Vyrubova, Praskovia Yussoupov . . ."

"Praskovia Yussoupov?" Rudolf cried. "You don't mean . . ?"

"Hold on a second." Duncan held up his hand. "Let me read the rest of the names—or try to." His eyes caught Beth's and they both smiled. "See if you recognize any others. Nicephore Pecherkin, Catherine Nikolaevna, Josef Romanov . . ."

"I've heard of him," Elizabeth said. "Oops! Sorry. Go on, Dunk."

"Natalia Purishkeyevitch, Vasilly Godunov, and Helene Petchukocov."

"*Ja*," Rudolf burst out. "*Und* Helene too. I know of Yussoupov and Helene Petchukocov."

"And I know of Josef Romanov," Elizabeth said.

"Well, they're all Greek to me," Earl said. "Though I have to admit, like Rudolf, Praskovia Yusso-whatever sounds vaguely familiar."

"All right," Duncan said, now enjoying himself. "What's the common denominator with these you've heard of? What do you know about them?"

"PK, of course," Rudy said. "At least for Yussoupov and Petchukocov." He turned to Elizabeth. "What about Romanov?"

"Exactly," she said. "Yes. PK."

"That's it all right," Duncan agreed. "They were involved in those early PK experiments in Leningrad, Kiev, and Moscow, back in the early sixties. I'm sure we all remember that dumpy Moscow housewife—what was her name?"

"*Frau* Nelya Mikhailova," Rudy said.

"Right. She was able to move objects with the power of her mind." The others nodded.

"I'll never forget that film that was taken, showing her doing just that," Rudy said.

"She just concentrated on a magnetic compass and caused its needle to spin 'round and 'round at an incredible rate," put in Elizabeth, sitting forward on the edge of her chair. "And I remember they put a big glass or clear plastic cover over a bunch of stuff on a table top and she still made things move. She had cigarettes rolling across the table, matchbooks sliding around, she stopped the pendulum of a grandfather clock. Wow! Yes, I remember that film. And none of it was trickery, right?"

"Oh, *nein*," Rudy said. "They put the plastic dome over the table so she could not blow things, or move them with threads, or make any physical connection. It was very well controlled, *Ja*." He put down his empty coffee cup, took an old, curved briar pipe out of his pocket and started filling it with tobacco.

"But this Moscow housewife isn't one of those who's gone to Cuba, is she?" Earl asked, perplexed.

"No, no," Duncan said, turning to his friend. "But she was the star, if you like, of this PK research thirty years ago. I guess most of these other people are newcomers. They've certainly come on the scene since her time."

"Yussoupov is from the mid-seventies," Rudolf said, puffing smoke from his pipe as he lit it. "By that time he was far more advanced than *Frau* Mikhailova. He was moving furniture, and some other quite heavy stuff."

"Wait a minute! Wait a minute!" Earl got up and started to pace the floor. He had his glasses off and was polishing them furiously. "Now, just what have we got here? You're all talking glibly about people moving things by just thinking about it? And now moving heavy furniture? You've got to be kidding!"

Duncan glanced at the others and then joined them in friendly laughter. "No, Earl. It's absolutely true. Believe me. Back in the early sixties—and continuing on, I guess, though it seems they kept quiet about later developments—but back then the Russians were doing a lot of experiments with PK. That's Psycho-Kinesis. Moving objects by the power of the mind. It's been well researched and well documented and it does exist. Certain people really are able to make things move just by thinking about it."

"The Czechs were into it, too," Rudolf said. "There were reports, I remember, in *Evening Moscow*, in the late sixties about it and there were papers—I have copies of them at home—issued by the Popov Scientific Technical Society in Moscow."

"I believe *Pravda* ran several articles," Duncan added.

"*Psychic Discoveries Behind the Iron Curtain*. That was the first book I read on the subject," Elizabeth said. "That came out in 1970, when I was doing my thing at Duke."

"Yes!" Earl stopped pacing and replaced his glasses. He peered around at them. "Yes. Now that you mention it, Beth, I do remember that book coming out. I guess I glanced through it at the time but I didn't really get into it."

"Did not the United States do similar experiments?" Rudolf asked.

Duncan nodded. "Yes. A few, for a while. But they didn't persevere."

"Probably a matter of budgeting," Elizabeth murmured.

Duncan caught her eye and smiled. "I'm sure you're right. Anyway, for whatever reason we didn't keep up with the potential of PK. Certainly not on the scale the Russians did. My god!" He thought for a moment. "That was all of thirty years ago. Just think what tremendous strides they must have made if they've been keeping up on it ever since then!"

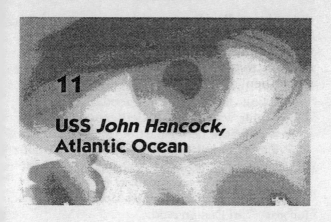

11
USS *John Hancock,* Atlantic Ocean

"Reduce speed to eight knots."

"Aye, skipper. Reduce speed to eight knots."

"Eight knots, aye."

In the reactor control room, toward the rear of the submarine, the five men on duty studied the multitude of dials, gauges, and monitoring instruments, and adjusted the amount of steam going to the turbines. Control rods passing down into the core of the nuclear reactor control the amount of heat produced by the neutron particle bombardment of Uranium 235 atoms. The heat from the reactor is used to heat water, which flows in a sealed, primary circuit around it. This primary circuit in turn heats water in the steam generator. It is this secondary water that produces the steam to drive the turbines. As the temperature is reduced it, in turn, reduces the steam and the turbines start slowing. Throughout the ship officers and men could feel the change as the great vessel slackened its rush through the ocean waters.

A half-dozen officers stood around the chart table watching the Lieutenant plot their course. For the better part of thirty-six hours the *John Hancock* had stuck to its new, unofficial heading, straight across the Atlantic Ocean toward the east coast of Florida.

"Well, we're going to miss Bermuda, that's for sure," an Ensign said.

"Looks like we're going to end up in West Palm Beach," Lieutenant (jg) "Woody" Williams added. "Haven't been there in years. Wonder if it's changed much?"

One or two officers standing close to him sniggered but most were mindful of Commander Page's grim countenance.

"Estimated time to the mainland at eight knots?" the skipper asked.

"Twenty hours forty-five minutes, sir."

"Conn, reactor." It was the voice of Lieutenant Tepps. Page took it.

"Conn, aye. What is it, Tepps?"

"Sir . . ." the Lieutenant was hesitant. "We can't get the speed down."

"You what?"

"We—we can't slow down, sir."

Page's eyes swept the instruments in the conn. The speed gauge was registering fifteen knots. "You've got a problem with turbines . . .

or the reactors?" A thousand thoughts went shooting through the Commander's head.

"No, sir. It's not that. The throttle responded as normal but the vessel isn't slowing. We can't bring her down below eighteen knots."

"Kill the engines! All stop!"

"All stop, aye."

Everyone heard the turbines slow and stop. There was quiet throughout the ship. Quiet but for the dull roar on the hull as the submarine continued moving forward through the water. The speed gauge remained set on eighteen knots.

Julian Page was used to being in command, of himself and of his ship. Now he seemed to have lost that command. He couldn't turn the sub and he couldn't stop it. He was worried. This was unlike anything he had ever encountered in his whole naval career. He straightened up and addressed Lieutenant Commander Carroll who had the conn, with a junior officer of the deck and seven enlisted men. "Take us up, Ed. I guess we're going to have to call into Norfolk, whether we like it or not."

And Page didn't like it. Not one bit.

The engines were restarted and kept turning over at what would normally be the equivalent of ten knots. The submarine climbed up to periscope depth and Ed Carroll raised the periscope and ESM masts. This was standard procedure to check for surface traffic. With everything clear, and no sign of any ships or

The Committee

aircraft within at least five miles, a laser transmitter and a UHF receiving mast were raised.

"All ready, sir," the duty radioman reported to Page.

He bit his lip. While the submarine had been rising to the surface, the Commander had been composing and encoding his message. He hated to send it; it was tantamount to admitting defeat. But he had no alternative. He couldn't control his craft so his men's lives were at risk. He gave his message to the radioman. "Transmit." The radioman sent it to COMSUBLANT, the Commander of the submarine force in the Atlantic.

When decyphered, the message read:

Z140321ZAPR
TOP SECRET
FM: USS JOHN HANCOCK
TO: COMSUBLANT
INFO: CINCLANTFLT

1. REPORT COURSE DEVIATION EFF 0245Z 19APR TO 212WSW. UNABLE TO CORRECT. ALL INSTRUMENTS NORMAL OPERATION. CONSTANT ATTEMPTS TO CORRECT COURSE INEFFECTIVE.

2. SPEED DEVIATION FOLLOWED EFF 1154Z 21APR. DESPITE SHUTDOWN OF ENGINES JOHN HANCOCK MAINTAINS CONSTANT 18 KNOTS. UNABLE TO STOP.

3. REQUEST ASSISTANCE. SUGGEST RENDEZVOUS 200 MILES EAST OF FLORIDA.

Page imagined the confusion that would be taking place in the Vice Admiral's office. A runaway submarine? Unheard of! Yet something would have to be done. Probably they'd send out helicopters by the score, half a convoy, and a tug to act as a buffer. After the sub surfaced the tug could get in front of the *John Hancock,* match speed and make physical contact, then gradually slow both itself and the sub till both were at rest. It sounded simple enough. But they'd sure need one hell of a big, powerful tugboat. A 6,080 ton submarine moving along at 18 knots would not be easy to stop!

The response from COMSUBLANT was not long in coming. Page could read the sarcasm between the lines, as he decoded it and learned that, as he had expected, a Navy tug and attendant ships would rendezvous with them 150 miles out from West Palm Beach.

But a few hours later the Commander was once again summoned from his cabin by Ed Carroll.

"We're changing course again, sir."

"Damn! What now?"

They both hurried to the conn.

"Looks like we're making a great sweep around to come down among the islands," Harrison said. "At the moment we're bound for Great Abaco, in the Bahamas. Of course, that may change."

"Take her up, Ed. We'll have to let COMSUBLANT know. We won't be able to meet up with the tug now, unless they've got something else tucked away down in the islands." He scratched his head. It was completely beyond him. How could the submarine develop a mind of its own? It was like the old science-fiction movies he had loved as a kid, where a spaceship's computer takes over and decides it knows better than its programmer. Only this wasn't a movie, it wasn't a spaceship and it sure as hell wasn't being run by a computer. But what was it being run by? He kept thinking himself around in circles. There was nothing wrong with any of the instruments; or any of the submarine's equipment, either directional or propulsional. Yet someone or something was in command and was taking them he didn't know where. How could that be?

They stayed near the surface for the next several hours, relaying their new headings to the mainland as they changed.

"It's no good, Ed," Page said, scanning the horizon with the Barr & Stroud CK34 search periscope. "We'll be getting into shipping lanes soon. Wouldn't do to ram the Love Boat! Better surface, though we'll still have to watch out when we get in among the islands. We may even end up running aground."

"Well, at least that would stop us," smiled the Lieutenant Commander.

Page chuckled in spite of himself. "True. Perhaps that's the best we can hope for."

"Too bad we're not an old SSK deisel-electric, then we might at least run out of fuel."

*

"It's some sort of remote control, obviously."

Page and Carroll were standing side by

side on the bridge at the top of the submarine's sail. The ship had just crossed the Tropic of Cancer and was on the surface approaching Samana Cay. They had come too far south for the tourist ships and had seen nothing but fishing boats for the past hour, though they had picked up some company. A huge Army six-bladed MH-53J "Pave Low III" helicopter and a smaller Marine VH-3 helicopter now hovered uselessly overhead, while a US Navy frigate and a 140-foot US Coast Guard cutter steamed along on a parallel course, as they had done since meeting the USS *John Hancock* off Eleuthera.

As though guided by an unseen but knowledgeable navigator, the submarine moved around shallow areas and skirted small islands till it began traveling east again, running parallel with the north coast of Mayaguana, the Bahamas island closest to Caicos.

"We've slowed to ten knots," Ed Carroll observed.

"Yes. With no input on our part."

"Think we're bound for Cuba?"

"Who knows?" Page said. "Could be we're going down toward Jamaica. Let's go below and look at those charts."

Page called down for a Petty Officer to come up and act as lookout, then he and Carroll descended the twenty feet to the pressure hull, then on down to the control room. For the next hour they plotted their movements.

"Son of a gun, I was wrong." Page looked at the chart and watched as the projections showed them swinging south again then, eventually, west to run along the south coast of Great Inagua, the southernmost island of the Bahamas. "Too bad. I was hoping we might be guineapigs for some sort of top secret remote navigational aid that was going to take us into Guantánamo Bay and our naval station there."

"That would have been nice."

The submarine slid smoothly along the coast of Inagua, then slowed to five knots and turned north into an inlet. Page was back up on the bridge at the top of the sail.

"All stop!" he ordered. It was one thing to have the submarine moving of its own volition when the turbines were still, but it might be something else again for the turbines to be running when they were supposed to be stationary in the bay. "Supposed to be?" By whose orders, he asked himself? If only he knew. He picked up the microphone for the PA system.

"This is your captain speaking. As you know, we have been the object of some as yet unknown force which has directed us across half the Atlantic Ocean. It has now seen fit to bring us into some remote bay in the Bahamian island of Great Inagua. Just who is responsible I do not know. But hear this. This is an unknown situation. Stand by condition yellow till further notice."

He put down the microphone and studied the landscape.

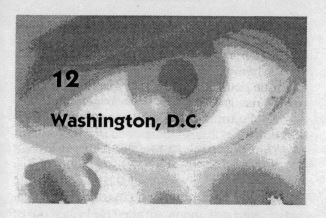

12
Washington, D.C.

The four of them climbed into the limousine that Bill Highland had sent to the hotel. Duncan assisted Elizabeth in and then sat beside her, in the back seat, with Rudy on the far side of her. Earl sat on the fold-down seat, facing them. There was a window separating the rear seats from the driver, so they were able to speak openly.

"I don't suppose we'll see anything exciting," Earl said, apologetically. "Marshall was very loathe to let us come along at such short notice, but," his eyes glinted behind his gold-rimmed spectacles, "he owes me one."

"I've heard of the Arlington Parapsychologists," Duncan said. "I know how this guy Marshall must feel. I certainly wouldn't want a whole load of people suddenly dropping in on me when I was in the middle of an experiment."

The Committee

"Well, we're not just *any* 'load of people'," Earl responded. "And as a matter of fact—I wasn't going to tell you this—Marshall admitted he'd be pleased at getting to meet you. Though don't ask me why! I guess he's read a lot of your books."

"Oh!" Duncan was always slightly surprised, and a little embarrassed, at his own not-insignificant fame. When people approached him at book-signings, clutching a pile of his books and being obviously elated to get his autograph, he had difficulty accepting that he was indeed a "famous author." He looked out of the window of the moving car and unconsciously changed the subject. "Oh, look! We're going to pass the White House." He turned to Elizabeth. "Have you seen the White House before, Beth?"

She shook her head. "Only on T.V." She leaned across him to get a better view as they went by. "Looks smaller than I expected."

"That's what they all say," Earl chuckled. "What d'you think, Rudolf? Look big enough for you?"

Duncan sat back as much as he could, to give the German a good view. He was conscious of Beth's head pressed against his shoulder and had to resist the impulse to reach up and caress her beautiful hair.

"I have seen it before," Rudy said, looking out, his unlit pipe clenched between his teeth. "Though it was some time ago. Hmm. It does not appear to have changed much in ten years."

Washington D.C.

They drove on, past the Ellipse and the Washington Monument, then turned along Constitution Avenue and took the Arlington Memorial Bridge across to Arlington. Within twenty minutes they pulled up in front of a large red brick building just off Glebe Road. A small brass plaque on the massive oak door said "Arlington Parapsychology Research Institute."

"Professor Stratford . . . Earl! How great to see you. Come on in." Marshall Perchard, a short portly man in an overlarge white lab coat, introduced himself to them and then led the way through the dark walnut-paneled foyer and into the library.

Duncan looked around at the floor to ceiling books that covered all four walls. "Boy! I envy you your library, Marshall."

Perchard smiled. "Thanks. Coming from an author, I appreciate that. I might say that more than one of your books is included here. You've done some fine work."

"Thanks." Duncan felt his face redden.

"We're dying to hear—and hopefully see—what you're doing here in the way of PK," put in Elizabeth.

Duncan nodded vigorously. "Yes. Have you been into PK for long?"

"About five years. We're at about the same stage the Russians were at back in the midsixties. Though in one area in particular we're ahead of them, I think. As you'll see."

"We were just recently talking about the Russians and their PK," Earl said.

The Committee

"Remembering Nelya Mikhailova," Rudolf added, puffing on his pipe.

"Ah, yes. The Moscow marvel." Marshall opened a second door out of the library and led them through. "Come on. I can see you're all anxious to get to our experiments."

They found themselves in a large room set up as a laboratory. Closest to them was what Duncan recognized as a mechanical dice tumbler, of the sort first used at the Duke Parapsychology Laboratory in North Carolina. A young girl, in her late teens, sat in front of it, concentrating on the two dice resting on the bottom platform. Behind the machine was a lab-coated assistant, clipboard in hand, recording the teen's successes and failures as she tried to influence the fall of the two dice.

"Exactly how does this work?" Earl asked.

"The tumbler shakes up the dice and then throws them," Marshall explained. "Our Jennifer Prentice, here, tries to influence which faces of the dice land upwards. In other words, she's not just trying to guess what faces will come up, she decides before the machine throws the dice and then *makes* those faces land uppermost."

"She'd be useful in Atlantic City, or Vegas." Earl smiled.

"Oh, we've tested some consistently good rollers from both those places."

"Tell me, why dice?" Rudolf asked.

"The advantage of using dice in a PK experiment is much like using zener cards in

ESP testing, the results you get can be statistically analyzed."

"You mean you can calculate the odds against it just being chance?" Earl asked.

"Exactly."

"What sort of scores are you getting?"

"On average Jenny is getting results that wouldn't come up more than once in a billion times if it were chance alone that was at work."

"Wow!" Elizabeth looked at the teenager with admiration. "That's even better than my ESP scores."

In another corner of the room Duncan noticed a second dice experiment, this one using a large number of dice all mechanically thrown at the same time. Other experiments utilized varying numbers of dice or small wooden cubes with their faces painted in different colors.

"Oh, look at the kitty!"

Duncan turned to see what Beth was talking about. In a far corner of the lab he saw a section of floor painted something like a child's hopscotch board, but with three columns of eight rows, the squares randomly numbered. Sitting in the middle of the "board" was a young kitten. A skinny, nervous-looking young man, dressed in corduroy pants and jacket, stood at one end, staring at the cat. As they all watched, the kitten got up and moved across to sit down again on the number seven. "A hit!" another lab assistant murmured,

The Committee

recording it on a clipboard.

"Is that psi or ESP?" Duncan asked of Marshall.

"What d'you mean?"

"Well, it could be that the kitten is being moved by the young man's psi powers . . ."

"Yes, that's what we're presuming."

"But," Duncan studied the man and the cat, "it could just as well be, I suppose, that the cat is picking up telepathically where he is wanted to go and then going there of his own accord."

There was silence for a moment.

"Damn!" Marshall Perchard said. "Where were you when we were setting up these experiments?"

"Sorry." Duncan thought that perhaps he should keep his comments to himself.

"No, no, I appreciate any input." Marshall seemed to get over his surprise and be pleased. "Thanks very much. That's a new wrinkle we'll have to check out."

They wandered around the large lab and saw many examples of mind over matter being demonstrated. Then Duncan thought that Marshall seemed to show extrasensory perception himself, by picking up on the thoughts of all of them. "Why don't we take a look at some more impressive stuff," he said, with a smile. "All this is important, believe me, in proving the existence of PK, but I know people of your caliber want something more. Come on."

Perchard took them out to the corridor and then up a wide, winding, balustraded staircase and into another large room on the second floor. Banks of dials, meters, and oscilloscopes covered one of the walls. Computers were very much in evidence. Around the rest of the room small areas had been sectioned off as separate cubicles.

"Here we use just about every sort of measuring device you can imagine," said their guide. "Oscilloscopes, thermisters, magnetometers, electroencephalographs, electrocardiographs, EKGs and EGGs—you name it and we've probably got it. Er, if you don't mind, Professor Küstermeyer, I must ask you not to smoke."

"Of course. Of course." The German took his pipe out of his mouth and, after checking the bowl, stuck it in his pocket.

"And what are you doing with them?" Earl asked.

"We're amassing an incredible amount of data proving the existence of psychokinesis; PK."

"Proving it?" Rudolf was interested.

"Oh, yes." Marshall nodded. "We've proven beyond a shadow of a doubt that it does exist. We've—many of us of course—known of it for years but there's a need, for the scientific community, to produce repeatable experiments. We've certainly been able to do that."

"What sort of things have you accomplished?" Duncan asked.

The Committee

"See for yourself."

They strolled around the lab as they talked, peering into various sectioned-off areas where experiments were underway. They saw a young boy no more than ten years old, connected up to an EKG machine, who caused an apparently solid metal ruler contained inside a glass bell-jar to twist and turn until it looked like a pretzel.

"I thought key-bending and the like had been shown to be all bunk?" Earl asked.

"Not at all. Just because a stage magician can do something by sleight of hand and substitution doesn't disprove that that same thing can also be done by what we might term paranormal means; by concentration of the mind."

"I guess not."

"More than one way to skin a cat," Elizabeth muttered.

They saw a middle-aged woman sitting back from a large flat table, again with her vital signs being monitored, making a toy car run backwards and forwards at varying rates of speed on the table's surface. The little car followed along a twisting track drawn on the tabletop and then did the same thing in reverse. They saw two elderly men sitting one at either end of a table-tennis table, with the surface marked out like a miniature football field. They were mentally controlling half a dozen small rubber balls which they moved around, trying to get past each other to score a goal. They saw a teenage boy throwing a

Washington D.C.

large styrofoam model glider and mentally directing it to land inside a marked circle.

"Come with me," Marshall said, one last time. He took them through to another small room which, for a moment, seemed to Duncan to be bare. But one wall was the back of a two-way mirror. They crowded together to peer through at what was going on in the adjoining room. "The reason for the two-way mirror is so that we'll in no way distract the attention of the subjects inside," he explained. "You'll see that that is very important."

Duncan saw eight people sitting around a large, circular, wooden table. Suspended about two feet above the center of the table was a metal safe.

"What's this?" Earl asked.

"Just look at the safe," Marshall said.

Duncan studied the object. It looked like a normal office safe. Not new; its paintwork slightly marred and its handle worn. Then he gave a start. The safe was not held up in the air by anything visible. It was suspended in space!

Marshall smiled when he saw the reaction of Duncan and the others. "Yes. Those people sitting around the table have raised that heavy safe off the table by the power of their minds alone."

Earl and Rudolf paced up and down, occasionally stooping down to try to see the safe from different angles.

"I assure you its a genuine phenomenon,"

Marshall chuckled. Duncan thought he looked deservedly smug.

"I believe you," the German said. "Though I would not have done so, should I not have seen it for myself."

"How long have they held it up there?" Duncan asked.

"Well, here's another interesting thing. We've been working in teams. It takes a lot of concentration, as you can imagine, on everybody's part. Therefore we don't let anyone go for more than ten minutes. Then another person slips into a seat to relieve them and they go to rest. With forty-eight people of good psi capability, we've been keeping that safe in the air for twenty-four hours now."

"Wow!" It was Elizabeth's favorite expression. Duncan smiled and mentally added his own "Wow!"

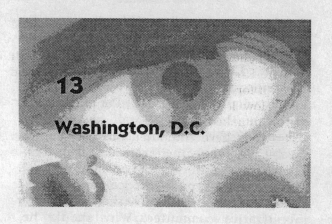

13

Washington, D.C.

"I have absolutely no idea whether or not there's a connection between the rocket explosions and our submarine being taken over by some phantom helmsman," Highland said. "All I do know is that I have a group of extra special people working on finding out if there *is* any connection."

O'Cork snorted and felt annoyed, though he didn't really know why. "Extra special people? Your idea of what constitutes specialness and mine are hundreds of miles apart, Senator Highland. This was not what I expected when I asked your cooperation." He felt extremely angry with the younger man.

"You merely asked for my help in locating Lieutenant-General Wellesley. I'm doing that, Mike. In fact I've done it. He's in Cuba."

"Please do not call me 'Mike', Senator." The nerve of the man, he thought.

"Sure! As you wish, Mi--. Senator!"

"You have created a comittee of gross amateurs; strange people who are into who knows what gobbledygook. I'm sure this is not what the Chiefs-of-Staff had in mind when they gave you the go-ahead. It's certainly not what the President expected." There. It was out. He had been annoyed—all right, perhaps even a little jealous—that the younger senator had been asked to form the investigative committee. Why should he, Senator Michael O'Cork, have been passed over? He was always being passed over, it seemed.

"How do you know?"

"What?"

"How do you know it's not what the President expected?"

"W-well . . . well, I'm *sure* it's not what he would have expected." O'Cork's mouth set in a straight line. The younger man seemed to have seen a tiny crack in his armor and leaped for it.

"You can't say, with any degree of certainty, Senator O'Cork, that the President has no knowledge of the people comprising my commitee. You don't know whether he's approved of them or not."

Suddenly O'Cork was on unsure ground. Highland was right; he really knew nothing at all about this whole committee business. He had overheard Highland confiding in another senator in the washroom, while he'd been busy in one of the stalls. He now felt it his duty to straighten out the man. "Er—and has he? Has the President approved?"

"I'm afraid I'm not at liberty to say." Bill Highland's face was straight. "And I would also point out that, *in their field,* these people are very well-known, very well respected and far from being amateurs."

"Their field being?"

"Parapsychology. Metaphysics."

"Hmmm." O'Cork had little idea of what fell under those headings. He thought it was something to do with ghost chasing and the movie *The Exorcist,* but wasn't absolutely sure.

"So, if you have no further business, *Senator,* I have important things to do." Highland was glaring defiantly at the older man.

O'Cork stood for a moment, bristling. He had to save face. "Do you have my folder on Colonel Wellesley?" he asked, imperiously.

"What? No, I don't. You took it with you when you left, the first time you came and asked me about the man. I haven't seen it since."

"Oh! Well then, never mind." O'Cork swung on his heel and, as dignified as he could, walked to the door. He turned. "And don't think you've heard the last of this. I have the President's ear, you know." He stalked out of Highland's office, leaving the door open.

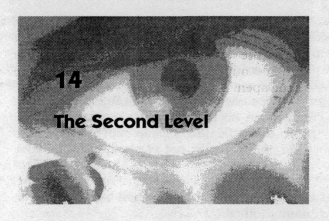

14
The Second Level

Duncan was slower than Rudolf in leaving his body. Of course Rudy was much more the expert at astral projection, Duncan acknowledged. While Rudy had studied it and practiced it for years, writing a number of respected books on the subject, Duncan had done it infrequently and more often involuntarily than purposefully. He had needed a lot of coaching that evening before they left.

Duncan looked about him. Below he could see his physical body lying silently in the four-poster bed at the Jefferson Hotel, while his astral double floated on a level with the ceiling. It always seemed strange to look down on yourself, he thought. He could make out the gentle rising and falling of his chest, reassuring him that he was indeed still alive. But he couldn't help noticing the odd twist of his body as he sprawled across the big bed. He really must try to lie straighter, he thought, or he'd need a chiropractor on a regular basis.

"Are you coming, or are you just going to float there admiring yourself?"

The words came into his head. It was as though someone had spoken to him yet there had been no sound. He looked around and saw Rudy floating beside him. "Sorry," he said/thought. "I'm not as used to this as you are, you know."

"I know. Come on, *mein Freund*. You are doing all right. Oh! You might want to put on some clothes."

Looking down at his astral body, Duncan saw that he was naked; the way he always slept. Remembering Rudy's earlier instructions, he concentrated on having himself dressed in a simple track suit, as Rudy was. Even as he thought of it, he found his astral body dressed that way.

Together they moved up through the ceiling, through the rooms above with their sleeping occupants, until they came out in the night sky above the old hotel. Duncan was dimly aware of the faint, thin, slightly fluorescent thread that stretched back down all the way to his body. Known as the "silver cord," it was infinitely elastic and was a living connection between the two bodies. Wherever he went in his wanderings he knew he would always be able to get back by way of that cord.

"Which way?" he asked.

"The way of thought," Rudy's reply came to him. "We think of where we want to go and immediately we go. *Kommen sie!* To the launch site."

Side by side they streaked across the sky, under the low-lying clouds that blanketed the city, across the Potomac River, into Virginia and onward to the west. They were quickly out in clear sky with a million stars glimmering above. The moon was in its first quarter and seemed to shine with a brilliance Duncan had never previously known. Before he knew it they were over the Rocky Mountains and then swooping down the west coast, past Big Sur and San Simeon, toward Point Arguello. Duncan caught the German's thought: "*Gut!* That was even faster than the Concorde!"

Bill Highland had advised them of a night launch that was to take place. He knew—or thought he knew—that Duncan couldn't get to it, but wanted to tell him anyway. The Committee had decided that it would be a good idea to monitor the launch, from the astral. If the "enemy," whomever that happened to be, was indeed responsible for the previous launch failures it seemed highly probable that they were getting their information by astral means. Rudy and Duncan were elected as the two to go and check it out.

On arrival at the site they immediately passed into the blockhouse, passing through the eight-foot thick walls as though they weren't there. With the launch only minutes away, the center was a hive of activity and reminded Duncan of the launch for which he had been present.

"We can stay in here or be out on the ramp itself," Rudolf said.

"Out on the ramp?" Duncan thought of the 4,532° F temperature as the rockets blasted off. Then he remembered that, of course, his astral body would be completely unaware of that great heat. They certainly could stand right up against the rocket and be totally unaffected. "No," he said. "This is where they'll be, if anywhere."

"Then we'd better be inconspicuous," Rudy said. As he spoke he suddenly became dressed in the uniform of an Air Force Lieutenant Colonel. "No one here physically would even know we are present," he explained, "but if the people we seek are here they would immediately spot us. This will make it harder for them."

Duncan thought himself into a similar uniform and looked around carefully. There didn't seem to be anyone there who should not have been, though a couple of times translucent figures wearing night attire passed completely through the blockhouse as if intent on errands. Rudy explained that they were the astral forms of personnel asleep in other parts of the Air Force base; figures off on their own dream journeys.

After a while Duncan's attention was drawn to a Major who seemed to be keeping

The Second Level

close to the Launch Director. At first he thought the man was simply an Aide, but then the Director turned suddenly to move off on a change of direction and Duncan could have sworn he actually passed through the left shoulder of the Major. He tipped off Rudy. After a quick look Rudy indicated they should get closer.

As he studied the man, Duncan saw that in fact he could catch the glint of computer screens right through his body. The "Major" was almost solid but not quite. Obviously he had done the same thing that Duncan and Rudy had done and put himself in a uniform, just in case anyone else was there on the astral.

As it came time for the launch they saw the Major lean forward and study the screen in front of the Director. He seemed to be memorizing information. Then, suddenly, he turned and moved rapidly up toward the ceiling, becoming more and more transparent as he went.

"Go back to the hotel!" Rudy's voice rang inside Duncan's head. "I'll meet you back there."

As Duncan turned to question his friend he saw the German shoot up after the departing spy and disappear through the ceiling. It took a moment for it to sink in that Rudy was going to follow the intruder. By the time Duncan got back up into the night sky himself there was no sign of either of them. Annoyed that he had been too slow, Duncan headed back to the east coast.

*

"Didn't he see you following him?" Elizabeth asked.

"*Nein* . . . no," Rudy answered. "He was too intent on getting where he was going as quickly as he could think. And he did not seem to suspect that anyone knew what he was up to, so he did not trouble to look behind him. Besides," he allowed himself a smile, "I changed my appearance two or three times, just in case."

The four of them were once again in Duncan's suite, having early morning coffee together before going down to breakfast. They had agreed to meet there at first light, to review what had happened to Duncan and Rudy on their astral journeys.

"Changed your appearance?" Earl was having trouble with the whole concept of astral bodies and traveling on what Rudy termed "the Second Level".

"*Ja*. At one time I would have looked to him like an old man with a long white beard. At another time I would have looked like a young teenage girl. There are many, many people traveling about the astral at night, of course. He was being cautious at the Air Force base but after that he would have no way of knowing if someone was following him or if there just happened to be others traveling along similar paths."

"Hmm. I'm going to have to study one of your books." Earl still looked slightly bewildered.

"But let's get the details of what you found," Duncan said, eagerly. "Where did you both go?"

"Of course. I am sorry I digressed. He went on southward and then to the east. We went across a great area of water—I guess the Gulf, is it? The Gulf of Mexico?—and then on to an island; a long, thin island it seemed, as seen from up high. There we rushed down to the near end of it, where there was a low range of hills, and entered a house overlooking the ocean."

"Sounds like you crossed to the Caribbean," Earl said.

"Go on," Duncan urged. "What did you find at the house?"

"The man I followed was possibly Spanish/Mexican? He was dark of complexion, with a full, drooping moustache and a mop of black hair. His name was Humberto Gavilla. I know this because one man at the house called him by his first name and another by his family name."

"Good. Go on."

"Hold on a minute." Earl interrupted them. He had pulled his diary out of his pocket and turned rapidly to the pages at the back that included a miniature atlas of the world. Holding the small book up close to his glasses, he had been studying it while Rudy spoke. "A long, narrow island you said? How about

Cuba? That's as long and narrow as they come, and right across on this side of the Gulf of Mexico."

"Cuba. Of course! That makes a lot of sense, Earl." Duncan felt a thrill of excitement. He had long been wondering who could possibly be working against the United States, in whatever way and for whatever purpose. Cuba seemed to make sense. At least it would do as a working hypothesis. "Okay. Let's consider it as Cuba for the moment and see if everything else fits in with that, or if there's anything that conflicts."

The others nodded in agreement.

"There are pine trees on Cuba?" Rudy asked.

"Plenty." Earl nodded. "Especially in the west, which would have been the end where you were."

"And palm trees also?"

"Oh, yes."

"Good. For there were lots of pines over the hills, but there were also palm trees around the house."

"The man you followed, Rudy?" Duncan tried to be patient.

"Of course. *Ja.* He went back to the large main room of this house where his physical body was lying out on a daybed. Others were sitting beside it waiting for his return."

"How many others?"

"Two men who seemed to be on more or less equal terms with our friend the traveler, plus there were about ten or twelve others—men and women—who sat around in a circle of chairs outside on the patio, overlooking the ocean."

"Really?" Duncan leaned forward in his chair. Suddenly the telephone rang. With a silent curse for the interruption he got up, walked over, and picked it up.

"Hope I'm not calling too early, Dunk." It was Bill Highland.

"Not at all. We've all been up for ages. What is it, Bill?"

"Two bits of news. First, that launch I told you about yesterday. It went off okay . . . up to a point."

"What d'you mean, up to a point?"

"Well, at least it didn't self-destruct. But what it did do is deviate from its designed trajectory."

The others had started talking quietly amongst themselves. Duncan waved them to silence. "Come again," he said.

"The rocket went up as planned, and followed along on its intended course for about twenty minutes. Then, suddenly, it veered off."

"What?"

"Nothing drastic; just slightly off, but enough to cause a minor panic in control and to get the boys running around in small circles getting it back on course again."

"Did it then stay on course?"

"Oh, yes. And there's no reason that anyone can see for its having gone off in the first place."

Duncan looked around at the others as he spoke. "Well, we may just have something on that for you later this morning, after we've thrashed out some details. What was the other piece of news, Bill?" He heard the senator shuffling papers at the far end of the line.

"Remember that submarine I told you about yesterday? The one that was so mysteriously diverted?"

"How could I forget? What about her?"

"Well, she's just as suddenly been released, if that's the right word, and now she's on her way back to Norfolk. She'd ended up in the bay of an island called Great Inagua, down the bottom of the Bahamas."

"Great Inagua?" Duncan leaned across and picked up Earl's diary which still lay on the table, open at the maps. "Isn't that right opposite Cuba, Bill?" Everyone strained to listen when they caught the name Cuba, as though they might hear the other end of the phone conversation.

"Yes," said Highland. "Yes, you're right, Dunk. It's just across the road, as it were."

Duncan thanked the senator and again told him he'd get back to him later in the morning, then he hung up the phone. He turned back to the others.

"Well! That could certainly confirm the Cuba tie-in. The sub that was hijacked, or whatever you'd call it, ended up in a bay close to Cuba."

"Is it all right?" Beth asked. "Everyone okay?"

"Oh, yes." Duncan came back to his chair. "In fact Bill was saying that it has now been released from whatever was holding it and directing it and is on its way back to Norfolk."

"But it was close to Cuba?" Rudolf persisted.

"Definitely." Duncan took a deep breath and looked around at the others, looking hard into the eyes of each one of them. "I don't know about you guys, but this makes quite a bit of difference to me. I have to admit that I've been sort of playing along with all of this. Taking it seriously, of course, but really, I guess, treating it as some sort of a jaunt just to placate my old friend Bill Highland."

Earl nodded.

"But now it seems it's rather more than that," Duncan continued. "It seems there's something very real going on here and, since Cuba is involved . . ."

"And, implicitly, Fidel Castro," Earl put in.

"Right. Since they're involved, well, I feel it's much more a *duty*, if you like. This might well be something that's threatening our country."

"What sort of thing, do you think, Dunk?" Elizabeth sounded worried.

He gave her a small smile. "I don't know any more than you yet, Beth. But what I'm trying to say is that I'm going to be in this all the way. I haven't the slightest idea what it might grow into, but I very definitely want to be a part of it."

Earl looked around at the others. "I think you're speaking for all of us, Dunk." They all nodded.

"You do realize, *mein lieb Gefährtes*, that this could well evolve into a much greater conflict than just between the United States and the Republic of Cuba?"

"You mean, like a world war?" Elizabeth asked.

"*Nein.*" Rudy shook his head impatiently. "I mean like a war between Good and Evil."

"Oh, come on!" Earl broke the emotionally charged atmosphere by laughing and getting up to get himself another coffee. "I agree with Dunk, here, that we need to take this very seriously and that it's probably something that's on a higher scale than we'd previously realized. But Good versus Evil? Come on, Rudy! That's late night movie stuff."

"Do not you be so sure." The German's bright eyes stared out at Earl from under his bushy, gray eyebrows. "It may not be 'hip', do you still say? It may not be fashionable to speak of such things, but that does not mean that they have disappeared. *Nein!* The eternal battle still rages."

There was an uncomfortable silence. Duncan surprised himself by finding that he was inclined to agree with Rudolf. He had never thought much about it before but, on brief reflection, he did feel that there was far more

The Second Level

to the metaphysical aspects of life than most people would acknowledge. He cleared his throat and spoke.

"We're all into metaphysics to an extent. Some of us more knowledgeable than others, for sure. So I don't think we should disregard Rudy's thoughts and feelings on this. Let's keep an open mind for now and see what we find. The main thing is, we're all committed. Right?"

"Right!"

"Okay." Duncan's eyes locked briefly with Beth's and he gave her what he hoped was a reassuring smile. He felt a warm glow when she smiled back. "Okay. Then let's get back to last night's astral detective work. Rudy? Fill us in on the rest of it."

"*Ja.*" The German sat forward in his chair. In short sentences he told them of the return of Humberto Gavilla to his associates in Cuba. The two men who sat awaiting his return were apparently military, or ex-military. One was a Russian colonel named Alexis Militsa and the other apparently an American lieutenant-general, whose first name was Nathan.

"Nathan Beardsmore Wellesley," said Duncan. "That's the guy Bill Highland was tracking for that other senator. What's his name? O'Cork."

"Well," Rudolf said, "he is in Cuba."

"What about the others there?" Earl asked. "The group out on the patio?"

The Committee

"Ah, yes." the German nodded and tugged at his ear. "They, I believe, are much like the good people we saw at the research institute yesterday. The ones holding up the safe. Our astral-flying friend, Humberto, gave them some figures—coordinates I would now guess. They all took hands for a few moments and then seemed to do a sort of group meditation."

"PK?" asked Beth.

"You can bet on it!" Duncan could see the pieces falling into place. "To change the course of that rocket! They're the guys from Moscow . . . probably they've also got some local talent, brought in to swell the energy. I wouldn't mind betting they're the ones who moved the various colonels' hands to the destruct buttons, who dragged the submarine into harbor and now they've changed the course of the rocket."

"You think they're that strong?" Beth asked, astounded.

"I'm sure they are," Rudolf said. "It's been thirty years since they were doing the relatively simple things we saw being done at the good Doctor Perchard's establishment. Thirty years! Imagine what they must be capable of today!"

"Damn! Then what on earth can their final goal be?" Earl demanded.

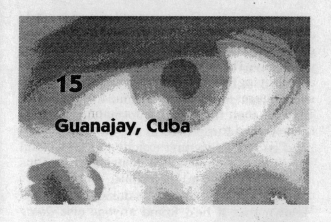

15

Guanajay, Cuba

Nathan Wellesley leaned on the old stone balustrade and stared out through the royal palm trees at the ocean. He sighed. He was tired. It wasn't just from having little sleep the previous night; his whole being was tired. He was seventy-three years old but he knew there were plenty of men of his age, and older, who were spry and energetic. He could think back to his days in the Pentagon and name at least a dozen such people. No, he thought to himself, he was more than just physically fatigued, he was dangerously close to being mentally, totally, burned out.

He was tired of running. He'd just run from the crumbling U.S.S.R., where he'd gone after running from his homeland; from the United States of America. Damn! He'd been so stupid. He'd got caught up in the nightmare sickness of compulsive gambling and then thought he'd found an easy way out. That Russian from the embassy—he couldn't even remember the man's name now . . . Grigori something-or-other; nice young man he'd seemed. It had looked like such an easy way out of his financial problems to let Grigori have those little bits of information. Nothing much, it had appeared at the time. Just odds and ends that weren't exactly top secret and that brought him enough money to pay off his gambling debts and then some.

Oh, he'd known he was doing wrong. He'd known that if he'd found anyone else doing what he was doing he'd have been down on them like a ton of bricks. Treason, that's what he'd have called it in anyone else and, let's face it he thought, that's exactly what it was. But somehow he hadn't seen it as that, in himself, at the time. He'd found excuses. And then he found himself getting in deeper and deeper, with no way of getting out.

And how had he got caught up with this present set of weirdos, he asked himself? Playing mental games and flying off on the astral, for God's sake? He supposed they knew what they were doing. Certainly they had excellent credentials. Back in the U.S.S.R. the group had been under the personal aegis of Dimitri Tupolev, righthand man to none less than Mikhail Sergeyevich Gorbachev and, after him, to Boris Yeltsin. As he understood it they had been set up in a huge building just off Red Square, with luxurious living quarters and with attendants to cater to their every whim. Alexis had hinted that they had been instrumental in obtaining a wealth of American secrets through what he termed "astral spying" and had said that even the Germans had dabbled in that back in the last days of World War II.

Nathan now found himself teamed up with this group due to his background in U.S. military satellite placement. This Cuban jaunt was something important, apparently, that needed both his expertise and theirs. Tupolev felt that something was owed to Castro—or perhaps it was just that there was no more need for any of them in Moscow. Who knew?

He heard a footstep behind him and turned to see Alexis Militsa emerging from the villa.

"Good morning, comrade."

"Morning, Alexis," Nathan replied. "Have you caught up on your sleep?"

"Oh, I do not need so much sleep. I am fit." The younger man stood, hands on his hips and feet apart, taking deep breaths. His fair hair was cropped short and his feet were bare. He was dressed in black cotton pants and a sleeveless tank top. Wellesley, by contrast, was in cut-off denim shorts, an old USAF tee-shirt and white Nikes.

"Is Humberto up and about?" Nathan asked.

"*Da*. He is stuffing his body with too much breakfast. He grunted to me as I passed him by. He should join us soon."

When the three of them finally sat down together on the patio Nathan was feeling better. Perhaps it had just been the lack of sleep that had been getting to him, he thought. He looked around. A tall *ceiba*, or silk-cotton tree, stood off to one side of the garden that sloped down to the beach below. The tree was over a hundred feet tall, standing out above the palms, plantains and frangipani, the brilliant bougainvillea, and the multitude of flowering trees and shrubs that made up the property around the villa. Yes, he reflected, this was decidedly better than being cooped up in a windowless office in one of the inner rings of the Pentagon.

"So!" Alexis said. "Let us recapitulate. After your very fine journeying, Humberto, to get us the necessary figures, Comrade General Wellesley was able to calculate where the Alpha group should focus to do their work. They did exactly that and, so far as we know, completely disrupted the flight of the American rocket. We shall be getting confirmation of our success shortly."

"It seemed to me the group took a long time to get focused," Humberto said, taking out a packet of Popular, the Cuban cigarettes, extracting one and lighting it. "I thought they were better than that? Are they getting lazy?"

"I don't know about lazy but they're sure powerful, to my way of thinking," put in Wellesley. He had been astounded to find that the group was able to influence something as big and powerful as a nuclear submarine.

Sure, it had taken the combined groups to do it, but that was all right. It was still damned impressive to him.

"No! They are not getting lazy," snapped the Russian. "I would never allow that, as you should well know, Comrade Gavilla. But do remember that such power as we are using dissipates quickly as you aim it away from the earth's surface, into the atmosphere and beyond. It does take longer to focus and it takes more energy. We cannot do everything by simply flitting about in our astral bodies!"

Armando, one of the servants, appeared in the doorway.

"What is it?" demanded Alexis.

"Teléfono."

The Russian got up, grumbling, and Wellesley watched him follow Armando into the building. He was only gone a few minutes before he reappeared, a sour look on his face, to stand looking at the other two men.

"What is it?" Humberto asked.

"We did not have the impact I expected last night."

"What d'you mean?" Wellesley asked.

Alexis said nothing for a moment. He turned and walked over to look out at the ocean. Finally he spoke back to them over his shoulder.

"I am told that we had little effect on the American rocket. Oh, we turned it slightly off course, yes. But we did not move it anywhere near as much as I had hoped."

He paused. Wellesley glanced at Umberto but the Cuban seemed not to be listening to Alexis and was leaning back in his chair puffing on his cigarette.

Wellesley shrugged. "Well, you just said yourself that the energy dissipates when sent up like that. Obviously what can be done to something as big as a sub down here can't be done as effectively out of the earth's atmosphere. And what we've got to do is work on something miles above the earth's surface!"

Humberto sat forward and tossed his cigarette butt off in the general direction of the ocean. "I said they were getting lazy! *Jesucristo!*"

Alexis swung around, his fists clenched. "Comrade Gavilla! . . ." His hands slowly relaxed and opened. "Laziness is not a factor. It must not be and it is not. *Nyet!* The groups simply need more practice."

"More practice?" Humberto spat on the floor. Wellesley saw Alexis's eyes narrow. "We practiced making men push buttons. We practiced moving a nuclear submarine. We've just practiced changing the course of a rocket. How much practice do they want?"

"Enough to do what is to be done," Alexis said quietly.

"How long do we have?" Wellesley asked.

"Fidel says two weeks. Ovideo tells me only one." Alexis replied. "One week or two . . . it will suffice."

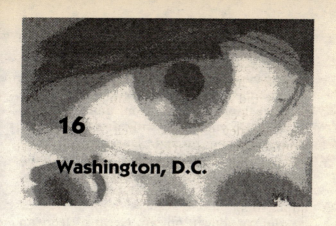

16
Washington, D.C.

Elizabeth led the way into her room at the Jefferson Hotel. She placed her bag on top of the red-lacquer Chinoiserie case, which was tastefully filled with objets d'art, and crossed to open the French doors onto the balcony. As she turned back to Duncan her eyes caught sight of a beautiful bouquet of red roses that had been placed in a vase on the eighteenth century occasional table near the canopy bed.

"I just love staying at this hotel," she sighed. "It's like living in another world."

"I know what you mean," Duncan replied. "A far cry from my little condo on the beach and its California-modern decor!"

"I could very easily get used to this sort of thing."

"I don't know about that," Duncan laughed. "I feel a whole lot more relaxed when I can just be me. You know, walk around in

I can just be me. You know, walk around in my skivvies and not have to think twice about which knife to use at the dinner table?"

Beth looked at him from under lowered lashes. "Do you really walk around in your skivvies?" she purred. Duncan reddened and she was immediately sorry for having embarrassed him. "I was just kidding," she said. "So, Dunk, where do we go from here on all this?"

He sat down on an elegant Georgian loveseat and stretched out his long legs in front of him. "I'm not too sure," he said. "Not yet, anyway. I let Bill know what we discovered last night." He chuckled. "Poor man was a little bewildered at how we could have been both here and in California at the same time. And especially how we were able to know what was happening in Cuba. But, give him credit, he didn't laugh in my face and he did seem to take it all seriously."

Elizabeth crossed the room and sat down beside him. She had always been attracted to Dunk. They had known each other for nearly ten years, having met when she was at Dr. Rhine's Foundation For Research On the Nature Of Man, in Durham, North Carolina. Dunk had been there doing research for a book and she had been there as one of Professor Rhine's best subjects. She had quickly learned that she had exceptional ESP faculties. She had been attracted to Dunk even in those days, though still married to John;

albeit she and John had been on separating paths for almost as long as they had been married.

She studied Dunk's tanned face and the worried frown that marred his brow. How handsome he was, she thought. His blue eyes always seemed so brilliant, as though lit from within. And she was fascinated by his frequently unruly blond hair, which would occasionally fall across his face so that he had to flick it back with a quick twist of his head.

"What was it like, astrally projecting?" she asked.

He was surprised by her question. "You've never done it?"

"No, never. Not so far as I know, anyway."

He twisted around and looked her full in the face. She shivered. "It's incredible," he said. "I'd done it once in a while before, but mostly without trying to. It was just something that sometimes happened and sometimes didn't. I really had no control over it."

"But last night you did?"

"Yes, thanks to Rudy's coaching. And, Beth, it was exciting. Really exciting."

She stretched out her arm along the back of the loveseat and gripped his shoulder. "Could you teach me?"

"I don't know. I guess so. Rudy is really the expert."

"I know, but I'd like you to teach me, not Rudy." Their eyes remained locked for a long moment.

"Sure. Sure. I'd love to. In fact it would probably be a good idea if we all learned to do it, as soon as possible. Even Earl." They laughed.

"Poor Earl," she said, dropping her hand again to her lap. "He has a hard time accepting the reality of a lot of this and yet he'll go off, merrily checking-out haunted houses in various parts of the country, and totally believe in ghosts."

"I know."

"So what's the next step, Dunk? I know you just said you weren't sure, but you must have some inkling as to what we might do."

He reached out and took both her hands in his. Her heart beat a little faster. "We'll have to discuss it this afternoon. We must all be in agreement. But I do think it may be necessary for us—or at least one or two of us—to go down to the Caribbean."

She squeezed his hands. "To Cuba?"

"I doubt we can do that. Not in today's political climate. At least . . ." He trailed off.

"At least what?"

"Well, . . . I was going to say, I doubt we could do that legally."

"You're suggesting we get in there illegally?"

He shrugged. "It depends on how important it becomes, I suppose. Are you afraid?"

She moved closer to him. "No," she said. "Not with you, Dunk." She leaned forward and they kissed.

Washington D.C.

*

Immediately after lunch they all met once again in Duncan's suite.

"Okay, Dunk," Earl said, tugging at his beard. "What's the next step?"

"I've already been asked that." Duncan smiled and looked around at them all. "Here's what I suggest. See what you think. We know the 'enemy'—and I think we can refer to them as that, at least for now—we know they're based in Cuba and that they are employing occult means to work against the United States' government."

"Possibly against the positive forces of the whole world," Rudolf suggested darkly, puffing on his pipe.

"Well, we don't know that for sure, as yet," Earl said.

"Anyway," Duncan continued. "They have been interfering in U.S. actions, destroying rockets and satellites and diverting subs. Enough, I think, to merit some sort of countermeasures."

"Agreed," Beth murmured.

"So, I've spoken with Bill and I suggest that we shift our base of operations down to the Caribbean itself, since that's where they are."

Earl's eyebrows went up. "Sneak into Cuba, you mean, Dunk?"

"No. At least not yet. Who knows if it will come to that. No, I suggest we set up our HQ in the Bahamas."

"The Bahamas! Sounds delightful," Beth said. The others nodded.

"A paid vacation in the sun," Earl murmured. He took off his spectacles and held them up to the light to examine the cleanliness of the lenses. Apparently satisfied, he put them back on his face.

"Well, it remains to be seen how much of a vacation it might be," Rudolf said. "What do we take with us, Duncan? How do we prepare ourselves?"

"There are a few things I've asked Bill to lay on for me," Duncan replied. "Other than that I'd suggest taking as little as possible. But one important thing: we're all familiar with psychic cleansing—I think we need to start a strict regimen immediately. No more pizzas . . ." Earl groaned. "No more junk food of any type. No sugar. Cut out refined flour. Complete sexual abstinence." He darted a quick glance at Elizabeth, who looked back at him from under lowered eyelashes and giggled. "No smoking; not even a pipe, Rudy." The German nodded and reluctantly tapped out the one he had been enjoying.

Duncan continued. "I'd suggest meditation periods first thing in the morning and just before going to bed, to strengthen your auras and build up your kundalini. Any personal psychic protection methods you've developed, please employ—and feel free to share anything you've found to be really effective. One more thing—I plan to get in touch with Guillemette

Flaubert. She's down in Nassau and can help us with accommodations and other things. In fact, if you're all agreeable, I'd even like to ask her to join the Committee. I think she could be very useful to us."

"Who is she?" Beth asked.

"Did she not write those books on Santería?" Rudolf asked.

"And Voudoun," Earl said. "Yes, Dunk. I think she'd be an asset. We really don't know what we might run up against and she is very knowledgeable on the sort of occult problems that might come up in that part of the world."

"Have you ever met her?" Beth turned and looked at Duncan.

"Briefly," he said. "We were once both guests on a TV talk show out of New York. It was a couple of years ago and I only got a chance to talk with her briefly off-camera. She seemed a very nice person," he added.

"I was impressed with her last two books," Rudolf stated.

"Okay, then. Let's have her join us." Earl looked around at his friends. They all nodded.

"Good." Duncan looked pleased. "I think it'll really help to have someone familiar with the geography of that area, never mind her metaphysical expertise. I'll give her a call later."

"When will we leave?" Beth asked.

"Bill's going to get us on a flight out at the weekend. He can't get us out before, all the flights are full. We'll fly down to Miami and then across from there on one of those little airlines, to Nassau. We've got two days between now and then."

"During which we do what?" Rudolf asked.

"I'd suggest we monitor the enemy," Earl said. "If only Beth and I could both project we could all take turns in watching them and what they're up to. Certainly Dunk and you could do some of that, Rudolf?"

"Agreed." The German nodded. "And perhaps I can give some pointers to you others as to how you might learn the process. It is not difficult. *Nein.*"

"That's what I told Beth," Duncan agreed. "I've already volunteered to help her."

"You both project already, in your dreams," the German said. "It is simply that you do not remember where you go. Nor are you able to determine where you will go before you go there. Ach! We can soon alter all that!"

He looked at his now-empty pipe as though longing for a puff, Duncan thought. "You just have to remember that we have a different set of laws, or 'rules of the road' if you like, when we're operating in the astral realms," the younger man said.

"*Ja.* Well put, my young friend." Rudolf's head nodded up and down. "To help you grasp the concept, think of yourself as some sort of amphibious creature. Or better yet, perhaps, just as yourself but underwater, with a breathing tube extending back from your face mask to an air source on the surface. Up on the beach you can walk and breathe quite naturally, but once you enter the water you are in a *different element*. You can swim; you can move easily in all directions. And you can breathe quite easily through the infinitely flexible air tube. This is comparable to traveling on the astral though there, of course, you are able to 'swim', or move from one place to another, with the speed of thought if you so desire."

He looked around at the others, his dark, bright eyes staring out from the shadow of his bushy eyebrows. "Just as being in the water changes things, changes the element for the swimmer, so being on the astral changes things for the astral traveler." He smiled. "Yet, you will easily adjust, I know."

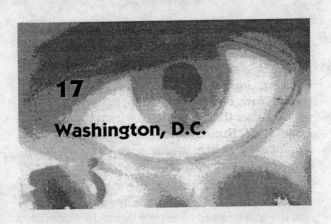

17
Washington, D.C.

Earl went first, with Rudolf. He had trouble getting free of his body; a number of times he found himself halfway out but then, excited at the prospect of accomplishing the act, he lost his concentration and slipped right back in again. Eventually Rudolf talked him through it. As Earl lay there he heard Rudy's voice inside his head, or so it seemed.

"Just relax, Earl. Relax. Slow, even breaths."

The German's voice was soothing and reassuring. Earl found himself calming and relaxing in spite of his excitement.

"Now just let it happen, *mein Freund*. Breath in deeply and, as you breath out, see yourself slipping out through the top of your head . . . that is it . . . excellent!"

Suddenly Earl was standing—if "standing" was the right word; he was six feet off the

Flaubert. She's down in Nassau and can help us with accommodations and other things. In fact, if you're all agreeable, I'd even like to ask her to join the Committee. I think she could be very useful to us."

"Who is she?" Beth asked.

"Did she not write those books on Santeria?" Rudolf asked.

"And Voudoun," Earl said. "Yes, Dunk. I think she'd be an asset. We really don't know what we might run up against and she is very knowledgeable on the sort of occult problems that might come up in that part of the world."

"Have you ever met her?" Beth turned and looked at Duncan.

"Briefly," he said. "We were once both guests on a TV talk show out of New York. It was a couple of years ago and I only got a chance to talk with her briefly off-camera. She seemed a very nice person," he added.

"I was impressed with her last two books," Rudolf stated.

"Okay, then. Let's have her join us." Earl looked around at his friends. They all nodded.

"Good." Duncan looked pleased. "I think it'll really help to have someone familiar with the geography of that area, never mind her metaphysical expertise. I'll give her a call later."

"When will we leave?" Beth asked.

"Bill's going to get us on a flight out at the weekend. He can't get us out before, all the flights are full. We'll fly down to Miami and then across from there on one of those little airlines, to Nassau. We've got two days between now and then."

"During which we do what?" Rudolf asked.

"I'd suggest we monitor the enemy," Earl said. "If only Beth and I could both project we could all take turns in watching them and what they're up to. Certainly Dunk and you could do some of that, Rudolf?"

"Agreed." The German nodded. "And perhaps I can give some pointers to you others as to how you might learn the process. It is not difficult. *Nein*."

"That's what I told Beth," Duncan agreed. "I've already volunteered to help her."

"You both project already, in your dreams," the German said. "It is simply that you do not remember where you go. Nor are you able to determine where you will go before you go there. Ach! We can soon alter all that!"

He looked at his now-empty pipe as though longing for a puff, Duncan thought. "You just have to remember that we have a different set of laws, or 'rules of the road' if you like, when we're operating in the astral realms," the younger man said.

"*Ja*. Well put, my young friend." Rudolf's head nodded up and down. "To help you grasp the concept, think of yourself as some sort of amphibious creature. Or better yet, perhaps, just as yourself but underwater, with a breathing tube extending back from your face mask to an air source on the surface. Up on floor—and looking down on his sleeping body. He turned to Rudolf.

"I did it!"

"Easy, *mein Freund.* You could still slip back in. *Ja.* You did it, just as I told you you could. Now, come with me."

Together they turned away from the sleeping form and, Rudolf taking Earl's hand, they passed up through the hotel and into the night sky. The German gave his friend a few moments to adjust to the beauty of the heavens.

"Very well, Earl. We must be on with our task. *Kommen sie.* Just stay close beside me."

The two astral figures moved off rapidly across the darkened city, heading south. In the blink of an eye they were passing over the night lights of Florida's east coast cities and then were moving across water.

"How do we find them?" Earl's thought flashed to Rudolf.

"I simply think of where I was last time, when I followed our Cuban friend Humberto," came the reply. "See? We are here."

Earl found himself sitting on a stone balustrade at the end of a patio, outside a villa on the seashore. Off to one side was an unusually tall tree, towering above a group of smaller palm trees. Plants and shrubs grew profusely about the property. The garden sloped down to the beach below, where the surf rolled in and broke gently, in a curving white line, along the sand. In front of him the house was in darkness.

"Come! Let us see where the fiends are."

Earl followed the German as he moved forward and passed through the walls of the villa. There was a small oil lamp, its wick turned low, burning in the dining room in which they found themselves. There was no sign of anyone. Rudolf moved down a long passageway to their left and then passed through the first door he came to. Earl followed.

They were in a bedroom. Earl was momentarily alarmed at the first sound they had heard—a sudden, sharp gasp followed by a moan. He looked in the direction of the bed and saw the shapes of two people moving under the sheet. A smile spread slowly across Earl's face.

"Kommen sie!"

Rudolf disappeared through the wall to the left and Earl hurried after him, not to be left behind. They found themselves in another bedroom. In this one there were two beds, each occupied by a sleeping woman. The German studied them for a moment before nodding to Earl and moving off again.

In a short space of time they had covered the entire building, finding a total of twenty-six people asleep in the main house and in two outbuildings. Those outside were probably servants, Rudolf explained.

"So what now?" Earl asked.

They had returned to one of the larger bedrooms, where the figure of the man they had come to know as Humberto lay silently under the covers. Rudolf studied the man intently.

"His astral body is away somewhere. We do not know where. Perhaps he is up to more of his nefarious schemes. We should have got here earlier!" He sounded angry.

"I'm sorry," Earl said. "It was my fault . . . that trouble getting out of my body. It's just that I'd never done it before, Rudolf."

"I know. I know." the German's voice softened. "Do not fret, *mein lieb Freund*. It was no fault of yours. We should simply have started preparing much earlier. It is no matter. We cannot watch over them every single minute."

"So what now?"

"We wait." Rudolf floated up near the ceiling.

Earl, down on the ground from habit, found it somewhat disconcerting to see his friend drifting in space. But eventually he, too, let himself move up beside the German.

Somewhere in the house a clock struck the hours. Time passed quickly, it seemed to Earl, considering that they were doing nothing but sitting on air. Eventually, after hearing the clock several more times, Rudolf stirred.

"*Kommen sie*. We must return and let our friends take up this watch."

It seemed to Earl he had hardly turned to go than he was back in the Jefferson Hotel, in Washington, D.C. Before he knew it he was sitting up in bed and seeing Duncan's and Elizabeth's anxious faces. Across the room Rudolf was getting up from the settee where he had slept for the sake of their astral journeying.

"So what's happening, Earl?" Duncan asked.

"Oh, wait a minute, Dunk," Beth admonished. "Give the poor boy a minute to get back fully."

"Sorry."

"That's okay," Earl smiled. "Wow! That was something. I can see how it could become addictive."

The tall German came over and sat on the edge of Earl's bed. He looked at Duncan.

"Now you two must go out. There is nothing to report. All there were asleep."

"Well, they were all in bed, at least," Earl interrupted. "There were two, at least, who weren't exactly asleep." He chuckled. Duncan and Beth looked at one another. Rudolf continued unabashed.

"The Cuban was already away from his body so we were not able to follow him. The most you can do is to be there when he returns in case he has need to report his travels to one of the others. I would urge you to go immediately."

"Of course."

Duncan took Beth's hand and together they went to her room. They lay together on top of the queen-size canopied bed and, taking a series of deep breaths, started the relaxation techniques that Rudolf had taught them. As they relaxed their bodies and gradually sank down into somnambulism, their astral bodies separated from their physical counterparts and the two of them, in perfect unison, lifted up and out.

"Incredible!" Elizabeth exclaimed.

"You did that in textbook fashion," Duncan said, admiringly. "You must have done this a lot before, whether you'd realized it or not."

Hand-in-hand they rose up and out of the building and were quickly on the patio of the Cuban villa. A light was on in one of the rooms.

"I hope we're not too late," Elizabeth murmured.

They passed through a wall and, gliding silently across one room, moved through an arched opening into the room with the light. A stern-faced young man with close-cropped hair sat at a desk, studying some papers. He was wearing a loose robe and had a mug of steaming coffee beside him.

"Probably couldn't sleep," Duncan said.

"Sssh!" Elizabeth put her finger to her lips.

Duncan chuckled. "Don't worry. He can't hear us." He moved across and peered over the man's shoulder to look at the papers he studied. It seemed to be some sort of timetable and Duncan guessed it was written in Russian. "I can see how this astral projection business could come in very handy in the spy trade," he said. "Hmm. I've no idea what this is all about. Guess we'd better go find our boy Humberto."

The Committee

They moved off down the main passageway. It didn't take them long to find the right room. They recognized the figure in the bed, from Rudy's description.

"Well, I suppose we just camp here till he comes back," Duncan said. "Then, when he gets back into his body and wakes up, we can go with him to whoever he reports to."

"But won't he see us here when he comes back?" Beth asked.

"He might," Duncan said. "But there are all sorts of people wandering around on the astral at this time of night, because everyone's sleeping. Unless he's suspicious he'll just think we're a couple passing through. We could be the astral bodies of a couple of tourists or anyone; he wouldn't know. He's got no reason to suspect that anyone is on to his astral spying so there's really no reason for him to be suspicious. But, to be on the safe side, we need to keep a low profile and, if he does see us, we need to look as though we have no interest in him whatsoever."

Duncan and Elizabeth took up position near the window and waited. They didn't have long to wait. Within a matter of minutes a dim figure materialized and stood beside the bed. Though it was semi-transparent, they both recognized the duplicate of the sleeping man. It was Humberto Gavilla.

"That's him!" cried Elizabeth.

The shadowy figure looked up sharply. Duncan felt a sudden ice-cold sensation pass through his astral body as the dark eyes of the Cuban bored into him. He grabbed hold of Beth's hand. "Let's go!" he cried.

They turned and zoomed up and away. In less than a heart's beat they were back in the hotel, sitting up on the bed, their hearts racing and their physical bodies drenched in sweat.

"What happened?" Earl asked. He was sitting on a chair drawn up beside the bed.

Rudolf jumped up from another chair and ran towards them with something in his hand. The next moment Duncan reacted to water being sprinkled on him.

"What the . . .?"

"Rudy! What are you doing?" Beth asked.

"I'll explain in a moment," said the stoic German. "First, you tell me your story."

Duncan found his heart was calming down. He turned and held Beth to him for a moment.

"Are you all right?" he asked. She nodded. He returned his attention to the others and briefly described what had happened.

"He saw you?" asked Earl. "I mean, I thought it was pretty safe . . ."

"He heard them," said Rudolf. "He heard Beth say 'It is him', or whatever her exact words were. Enough to tie them to him."

Elizabeth turned to Duncan. "But I thought you'd just told me that they couldn't hear us?" she said.

"Ah!" he said, realization coming to him. "No. That was when I was talking about the man in the other room. He was in his physical body so he couldn't hear us. But Humberto was on the astral, just as we were. Of course he could hear us."

"Oh, no!"

"Don't worry, Beth." He pulled her to him. "We got back all right. That's the main thing."

"I think not."

They all turned to look at Rudolf. His face was grim.

"What d'you mean?"

"You got back, *Ja*. I guessed something like this just might happen, so I was prepared." He held up a small glass flask of what looked like water. "I sprinkled you with a mixture of sea-salt and water; a potent spiritual cleansing agent. Baptismal water, as I am sure you all know, is simply water with salt in it. Call it 'Holy Water' if you will. It is an excellent protection in case of attack by any evil entities."

"But how could anyone hurt us once we've got back?" Earl asked.

"Oh, believe me, they could!" Rudolf nodded his head wisely. "But I don't think our friend Humberto was intent on doing that this time. He must have followed you . . . he'd be a fool not to, and I am sure he is no fool. No, he followed you to see where we are located. He can now return here at any time, at his leisure."

"You're saying he can attack us from the astral, Rudy?" Beth was worried.

"If he is as powerful as I believe him to be, yes, he could."

"Oh, no! And it's all my fault."

"We must move fast." Rudolf continued.

"And do what?"

"Humberto has been out on the astral all night. We know that. Then, when he came back to return to his body, he was surprised by you and had to come chasing after you, here. He will now almost certainly have returned to Cuba, believing that he can come back to attend to us later. Certainly after he has reported to his superiors or partners or whatever."

"So I still don't see where that leaves us," Earl said.

"We must move quickly." The German suited his actions to his words and moved off towards the door. Looking back he said: "We must move out of here immediately. Get away to somewhere while he is back in Cuba and before he sleeps again to come after us. Pack your things as quickly as possible. We should all meet in the lobby, downstairs, in ten minutes." He was gone.

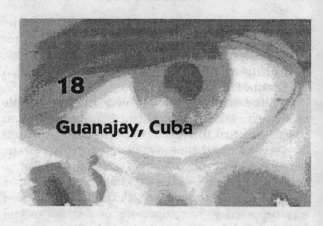

18
Guanajay, Cuba

Humberto Gavilla passed through the wall of his room and moved forward toward his inert body lying on the bed, lightly draped with a single sheet. He felt good. He had had a good journey; one he had been promising himself for some time. Enough of this spying! Enough of memorizing facts and figures from *Yanquis'* computers. That was all very well—and necessary, he recognized that—but once in a while a man needed to get away and just do what his nature directed. Too much enforced direction and you woke up in the morning as tired as when you went to bed. No, a man needed carefree excursions, just as much in sleep time as in waking time. Smiling slightly, he moved forward to enter his body.

"That's him!"

For a micro-second Humberto froze. Then he spun around and looked in the direction from which the voice had come. Two astral figures—one a man and the other a woman—hovered in front of the window, staring at him. He focused on the man. A *Yanqui*-Devil!

The man said something and the couple turned and were gone. But Humberto was an old hand at this game. He was right on their heels. Yet he hung back enough to pursue them rather than catch them. Even caught so off-guard, he had the sense to realize that he needed to know where they came from and why. Better to follow them now; he could destroy them later.

"The Jefferson."

He made a mental note of the hotel name as he entered the building on the heels of the fleeing couple. They led him to a room where two men sat waiting. In the flick of an eyelid the duo were back in their bodies and waking up, near hysteria.

"Good!" he thought. They were obviously amateurs. But were they *harmless* amateurs? Somehow he doubted it. No, they had recognized him, or the woman had. Obviously, then, they knew who or what he was and had been waiting for him.

He moved closer. One of the two other men in the room passed around and Humberto felt a sudden burning fire hit his body. He leapt backwards, finding himself out in the clear night sky again.

"Shit! What the hell was that?"

The Committee

He didn't hurry to return to the room. No, he knew where they were, he could come back any time, he decided. He returned to his own body.

*

"Let's get this straight, Comrade. You say there was someone here waiting for you last night?"

"This morning. Yes. A man and a woman."

"They weren't just a couple of passing OOBEs?" Alexis asked.

"Random astral journeyers? Out-of-Body travelers who 'just happened to be in the area'? No! I tell you they were waiting for me. And then when I saw them, they turned and ran."

"And you say they 'ran' to Washington District of Columbia?" Alexis's gaze was intent.

"Right! Look, I've been over this three times so far."

"And you will go over it twenty-three times if I feel you need to." Alexis fixed Humberto with his ice-cold eyes.

"Fuck you!" Humberto was not to be browbeaten. "The astral is my turf, *Comrade* Militsa. I'm the one who goes out on it and takes the risks."

"Risks? Hah!" The young Russian threw back his head and laughed. "If you ask me this was one of those young girls you go out spying on, coming after you with her boyfriend. Oh, yes!" He nodded emphatically as Humberto's head snapped around to glare at him. "Don't think I don't know how you go out of your body so you can look in on women in showers and couples making love in their beds."

"Fuck you! I'm too advanced for that shit."

"Too advanced? Too advanced? My old aunt in Kuntsevo is a more advanced spirit than you will ever be!"

"I was a personal student of Wolf Grigorevich Messing. I spent years studying with him."

"So? That and a couple of rubles . . ."

"What the hell's going on in here?" Nathan Wellesley's worried face came around the doorway. "You two are yelling so loud the whole villa can hear you. What the hell's happening?" He came in and sat down.

"It's Humberto," said Alexis, waving his hand in disgust. "He thinks he's being chased on the astral."

"I don't think I'm being chased!"

General Wellesley flapped his arms at them. "Calm down! Calm down! Let's take it easy. Gavilla? What happened?"

Once again Humberto went through his story. He was gratified to see that the American seemed to take it more seriously than did the Russian.

"This could be serious, Alexis," said the older man.

"You really think so? How so?"

"It could be a damn good indication that they've tumbled to what we're up to. To the astral spying at any rate."

The young Russian got to his feet and walked over to look out of the window. He was silent for a moment. "You are right, of course, Comrade General. It does bear looking into." He turned to face them. "Humberto, what would you suggest we do—you being the 'astral expert'!"

Humberto ignored the obvious sarcasm of the last sentence. "As you know, we all have a meeting with Ovideo this morning," the Cuban reminded them. "It was because of this that I did not stay and get all the details that I might have done, from these *Yanquis*. However, I do plan to return to them tonight."

"And if they should no longer be there? If they should have run?" Alexis asked quietly.

"I have already thought of that. As you know, Alicia Ordóñez is one of the local women who is part of our team. But you may not know that in addition to PK she has good abilities with astral projection. She should be reporting here within the next few minutes. I will send her to Washington District of Columbia, to the Hotel Jefferson, to watch these people. If they move from there, she will report so to me."

"If they have not already moved," Alexis muttered drily.

*

Ovideo did not care for the Russian, Alexis Militsa. Truth to tell he didn't care for any Russians. He found them arrogant; acting as though the Cuban people were beneath them.

This young one seemed especially imperious. Ovideo was pleased that it was a Cuban who was the expert in this astral business, though he did not understand that at all. He smiled at Humberto.

"Fidel is well pleased with what you have achieved so far," he said.

"What we have done so far is as nothing compared to what we are going to do!" Alexis interjected.

Ovideo kept his eyes on his fellow countryman and ignored the Russian's remark. "You have come a long way in a short time, I understand. That is good."

"Our side of it is well in hand, Minister," Humberto said, ingratiatingly. He glanced at Alexis. "I wish I could say the same for the other side."

"You fool!" Alexis burst out. "Don't you see that we are both on the *same* side? It's not Russians against Cubans, it's both of us against these despotic Americans."

"Er, even that is something of a generalization, I feel." Nathan Wellesley looked uncomfortable.

Ovideo sighed and raised his hand for silence. The last thing they needed was infighting. There was a strict timetable that had to be adhered to and petty squabbling was not going to keep them to it. He straightened up in his chair and tried to be more of a Minister of Foreign Affairs. "Yes. For this exercise at least we are all in this together. All equal." He looked hard at the Russian. "Fidel is *insistent* that we do not fall behind in this. The final objective must be achieved within seven days. Next Friday at the very latest. Is that understood?"

The three men nodded dutifully. Ovideo could feel the unrest and resentment but he couldn't bother with that. They had to sort it out between themselves. His job was to keep them on target and on time. That was what Fidel had entrusted to him and he would do it.

"If these people know where we are, I think it might be good to move to another place." Ovideo spoke his thoughts aloud. "It's a nuisance but we must preserve our secrecy."

"Excellent!" Humberto said. "We do need absolute quiet for the team to concentrate. We certainly don't need thoughts of possible astral prowlers."

"How do we know they aren't here right now, Minister?" Wellesley asked. "Listening to you telling us we need to move somewhere else?" He looked around uneasily, as though he might spot some astral being lurking in the shadows.

"Yes. Well, we could get quite paranoid about this if we wanted to, I suppose," Alexis said, sourly. "Somehow I always associate astral projection with the night hours. Because you usually do it when you sleep, I suppose. Anyway you're right, Comrade General. We obviously can't guarantee that they're *not* here now, so what do we do?" He looked expectantly to Ovideo.

The Minister looked back at him, silently, for a moment. Was the Russian challenging him, he wondered. He decided to accept the remarks at face value. "All right. We will move and we will accept the fact that they may know we're going to . . . they could assume as much anyway. I will write down the new address and you will each look at it in turn, taking care that no unauthorized person can see it."

Covering the paper he wrote on with his left hand, and feeling a little like a child scribbling notes behind the teacher's back in school, he wrote down the address and directions to get to another villa. It was one he had almost decided upon originally, before settling on the present house. "This is not such a large building as this one," he said, folding the paper and passing it to Humberto. "So some of your people are going to have to double-up in their sleeping arrangements. Also, it has been empty for some time and there are no servants at this house—and I want it to stay that way, for security reasons—so you will have to fend for yourselves."

Humberto groaned at this but both Alexis and Wellesley nodded, their faces grim. Then Humberto had an idea. "We will need to keep the *Yanquis* busy while we relocate," he said. "So they do not simply follow us."

"You can take care of that," said Ovideo. "And you might also give some thought to

The Committee

keeping them busy—very busy—closer to the date, so that your team can perform with no fears of interruption."

"Agreed," Wellesley grunted.

"Now!" Ovideo rose. "I will get back and assure Fidel that everything is under control." As he spoke he looked hard into each of their faces in turn. "I will tell him everybody is happy and that there is going to be no problem with reaching the deadline. Am I right?"

"That same deadline even though we have to uproot and move everybody and everything?" Alexis glared.

"That same deadline! No later."

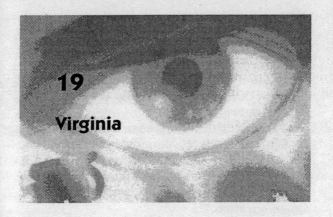

19
Virginia

"Do you think we shook him off?" Earl asked.

"That's something we'll find out, I'm sure," Duncan responded. He peered over the shoulder of the taxi-driver. "With any luck the Cuban had other more important things to take care of before he came back looking for us."

Although it was now past sunrise there was a light rain falling and the day was starting out overcast and murky. There were not many vehicles on the streets and, as they turned from Glebe Road onto Highway 50 and passed through Arlington, the four of them began to relax. In the cold light of the new day the idea of Cuban astral attackers chasing after them began to seem absurd.

"Are you sure we're doing the right thing?" Elizabeth asked, thinking of the comforts and delights of the Jefferson Hotel, now many miles behind them.

"There is no question," Rudolf said firmly.

"I have to agree." Earl nodded. "I don't know too much about astral projection but I do know of psychic attack, and I've seen some ugly examples of it."

Duncan grunted agreement. "Thank God for Bill," he said. "He's incredible. I woke him out of a sound sleep, told him we needed a safe house right away, and he puts his own place in Virginia at our disposal . . . without a single question."

"I thought he lived in D.C." Beth said.

"He might as well, according to him," Duncan chuckled. "He says he hardly ever gets out to the house any more. Just occasional weekends. Well, that's the life of a Senator, I guess. Couldn't pay me enough to do it."

Twenty minutes later they turned off the main highway onto a secondary road and, shortly after that, onto a private road.

"Did that sign back there say 'Sleepy Hollow'?" Earl asked.

"I think it did."

"Hmm. Somehow that seems rather appropriate."

"Yes." Duncan nodded. "Bill said his house is somewhere between Sleepy Hollow and Ravenwood, off on a private road."

The house itself turned out to be large and was built in the popular style of an English Elizabethan manor house. Rudolf referred to it as "Stockbroker's Tudor." The taxi dropped them off outside the iron-studded, double oak doors and disappeared back towards the big city. A frail, white-haired old man answered the doorbell and let them in.

"My name is Webster," he said. "My wife and I are Senator Highland's caretakers. He called to say you were on your way here."

Webster insisted on carrying one of Elizabeth's bags, in spite of her claim to be well able to carry them both herself. The others followed along as the old man led them down the main hall and then up the winding staircase.

"Mrs. Webster is airing out the guest rooms right now," puffed the white-haired figure, as he reached the top landing and paused to catch his breath. "Rather more than we are accustomed to, I must say, but we'll manage. Oh, yes. We'll manage." He started off again down the long hallway, the four of them following.

Mrs. Webster appeared even older and frailer than her husband, but she had already prepared three of the rooms and was hard at work on the fourth.

"This is actually Mr. Highland's own room," she said. "But he said I was to let the young lady have it." She looked at Elizabeth as though uncertain whether or not the Senator had made a wise decision.

"That is so sweet of him," Elizabeth gushed. "But please, don't go to any trouble."

"No trouble," said the old lady, shaking her head and tut-tutting to herself as though it were actually more trouble than she had ever had to bear before in her whole life.

"We'll manage," added her husband, watching every move from the doorway. He had set down Beth's bag in the middle of the floor and backed away from it as though reluctant to finally break contact.

Suddenly both the caretakers were gone and the four friends stood alone in Bill Highland's room. Beth started to giggle and soon all four of them were laughing out loud, their strained nerves finally starting to relax.

"Sssh!" Elizabeth hushed them. "They'll hear you."

"Oh, I'm sure they're two dear, sweet people," Duncan said, tossing his head to shake back a lock of blond hair. "It's just that they're obviously not used to having a bunch of guests suddenly dropped on them, at a moment's notice. Especially in the early hours of the morning."

An hour later they were all seated at the dining table, enjoying a breakfast of eggs, Virginia ham, sausage and scrapple, with fruit juice, coffee, and homemade croissants. Mrs. Webster was still shaking her head and her husband was still assuring them that "We'll manage." Indeed, thought Duncan, the excellent breakfast proved that they would.

"So what's our plan?" Earl asked, finally pushing back from the table and contemplating the empty dishes.

"If I may suggest . . . ?" Rudolf offered, looking at Duncan.

"Go ahead, Rudy."

"I think we should sleep through the day, taking it in turns for one person to watch over the others."

"Sleep through the day? Why's that?" Earl asked.

"I think I know," Duncan said. "The enemy were sleeping all night. They would eventually have to wake up; you can't sleep forever any more than you can stay awake forever. They'll probably be taking care of business through the day and will be back on the astral again tonight. It's when they're on the astral that they'll be the most threat to us if we're also there. Am I right, Rudy?"

The German nodded. "*Ja.* If we are on the astral with them, they could attack us most easily there."

"How?" Beth asked.

"You know about the silver cord, that connects our astral and physical bodies?" Duncan asked. Beth nodded. "Well, at death that separates, because we are not going back to our physical shells. On the astral, under normal circumstances, the cord is always there, incredibly elastic, and serving as a connecting link—an umbilical cord, if you like—between the two. But the bad guys can attack on the astral and break that cord. If they do that, there's no way back to your body."

"You're dead!" Earl said.

Elizabeth shivered. "I don't know that I like this astral projection after all."

"*Nein, nein!*" Rudolf said. "Normally there is no way the cord can get broken. It certainly cannot happen 'accidentally', as some people might have you believe. It would be most unusual circumstances for you to be attacked by people so evil that they would try to cut it."

"But these Cubans and Russians might be that evil? Right?" Earl asked.

Rudolf paused a moment, then nodded.

"So what you're saying is, if we sleep all day we can be awake tonight, which is when they're most likely to be out on the prowl, looking for us?" Earl summed up.

"Exactly."

Despite Mrs. Webster's work setting up the guest bedrooms, it was decided to all stay together in Bill Highland's room, which was the largest of those upstairs. Duncan and Earl pulled the mattresses off two of the other beds and set them down on the floor beside Bill's bed.

"Mrs. Webster's going to kill us when she sees this," Beth fretted.

"Can't be helped," Duncan responded. "Which would you rather face, the mean guy on the astral or Mrs. Webster?"

"At this point I'm not quite sure," Beth laughed.

The Websters were obviously wondering what three men and a woman were doing up

Virginia

in the bedrooms all day long, but they were too well trained to ask. Duncan arranged for himself and Earl to go downstairs and get a couple of lunch trays for them, at noon, and then to return the trays later. The Websters went along with that.

"Remember, it's only for a couple of days," Duncan urged. "Then we're off to the Caribbean. I'm sure these Russians and Cubans will have forgotten about us by then." He sounded more positive than he felt.

"It would be nice to so think," Rudolf said.

The sleep periods passed uneventfully. No one tried to journey to Cuba to check on the enemy; it was deemed best to just lay low. That night they sat up reading, listening to the stereo, and playing cards. The night seemed to drag by. Finally Elizabeth pulled back the heavy drapes and the early morning sun broke through the window. They all gave a tired cheer.

"One down, one to go," Beth murmured.

"I guess the bad guys didn't follow us after all. We get through today and tonight, then tomorrow we're off to the sunny islands." Earl sounded very pleased.

"Off to the sunny islands *and* to crossing swords with the enemy, don't forget," Duncan said.

"Spoil-sport!" Earl pouted.

Again the day seemed to go well. By early afternoon they had all had some rest. During his turn at watch, Duncan had talked to Bill

Highland and brought him up-to-date. Now he climbed back under the covers, on one of the mattresses on the floor, as Earl settled down to take his second turn at watch.

Earl sat by the window, where the shades had been pulled down to dim the light in the room. There was still sufficient light for him to read a magazine and he flicked through the pages of a recent parapsychology journal, glancing up occasionally to look at the sleeping forms.

Half an hour later Earl stretched and got up to close the window, but was surprised to find that it was already closed. He shivered. The room seemed to have become very cold. Careful not to disturb his friends, he quietly crossed to his suitcase, which lay open on top of a small table, and extracted a sweater. He put it on and settled down in the chair again.

"I'm freezing!" It was Elizabeth. She sat up in the big bed and reached down to pull the comforter up over the other bedclothes. "Would you mind closing the window, Earl?" she asked.

"I'm for that!" It was Duncan, sitting up and rubbing his arms. Rudolf similarly sat up.

"Hate to tell you guys," Earl said. "The window's closed already."

"Quickly!" It was Rudolf. He jumped up from his mattress and pushed it off to one side. "Here!" He motioned for all of them to come to where he now knelt in the middle of the room. They swiftly moved to his side and knelt also.

"All take hands," he said. They did.

"What is it, Rudy?" Duncan asked.

"I've got it!" Earl cried. "That's a psychic coldness. You know, Dunk, how temperatures really plummet when there's some kind of psychic disturbance, like a poltergeist or some such?"

"Right!"

"Exactly, *mein Freunds*." Rudolf nodded. "Only this is no *poltergeist*. *Nein!* I think it is a visit from our friends of the Cuban island."

"You mean they *did* follow us?" Elizabeth asked.

"Apparently so." The German looked grave. "Though why they have waited till now I do not know. Now, let us concentrate our energies. Take hands; right hands over left hands. *Gut!* If any of you are especially religious then to say a favorite prayer will not hurt. Then let us all concentrate on the ball of blue light, *Ja?*"

Duncan worked on seeing a stream of white light and positive energy coming up from the earth and ground below and filling his body, driving out all negativity. As his body filled with it, so the white gradually changed to a light blue and then to a slightly deeper shade of blue. From there he could see it, in his mind's eye, slowly expanding beyond his body, out to meet similar light coming from each of his three friends. The agglomeration made a large ball of light totally enclosing them all. He then concentrated on giving the ball a finite outer edge, like the shell of an egg. This, he knew, strengthened the psychic barrier they had erected and also gave a means of concentrating, and thereby increasing, the light force protecting them. It was, in effect, a powerful group aura of protection they had constructed. As it came into being they each became aware of a rising of the temperature till, once again, they felt warm and comfortable.

"*Gut!*" Rudolf muttered. "*Das ist gut.* Keep that light there, my friends. No negativity can penetrate it. Nothing can harm us."

For how long they remained there none of them knew. It seemed like hours. But eventually they were able to relax a little, though still seeing the protective light about them.

"Do you think they've gone?" Beth asked, in a whisper.

"I would doubt it," Duncan said. "I think we can adjust ourselves a little to be more comfortable, but I'm afraid we're probably stuck like this till the sun comes up in the morning."

"What?" Earl wailed. "I'll never make it! My knees will give out long before then."

"Courage!" Rudolf said. "We have beaten the initial attack. That must have taken quite a lot out of the fiends and they may well have fallen back to regroup. We can, perhaps, do the same. Now, we may break hands but keep the blue light around you at all times, *Ja?*"

"You bet!" Earl murmured. He let go off the others and sat back on the edge of the nearby mattress, stretching his legs and rubbing his knees.

The tall German went to his suitcase and returned with the phial of water they had seen him use back at the hotel. He passed from one to another of them, dipping his finger into the water and then marking a cross on their foreheads.

"Thank you, father," Earl said in mock piety.

"This is no time for joking!" Rudolf said sternly.

"I'm sorry." Earl sounded contrite.

"And apart from that, this is not a religious thing that I am doing."

"But didn't you mark the cross on us?" Elizabeth asked.

"*A* cross, as opposed to *the* cross, or the Christian cross." Rudolf explained. "*Ja.* You are all familiar, I am sure, with the cross being used to ward off vampires and werewolves and the like?"

They nodded.

"In late-night movies on TV, at any rate," Earl chuckled.

"But the cross, to keep away these creatures of the night, is not used because it happens to be a religious symbol," Rudolf continued. "Long before the start of Chris-

The Committee

tianity it was a symbol for the sun; for light. Some early depictions show it as an equal-armed cross within a circle; others without the circle. So, it is the sign of Light; of Good over Evil."

"Which ties-in with the vampire's fear of the sunlight," Duncan said.

"Exactly."

"Well, I feel better for that," Earl said. "Because I have to admit I am no great church-goer, so I wouldn't have too much faith in a cross from that point of view. But an ancient symbol for light I can accept."

"Now to make ourselves comfortable, for it will be a long night." Rudolf, helped by Duncan, stripped the covers off one of the mattresses and pushed it into the middle of the room. They all sat on it and Rudolf used the last of the water to trace a circle on the floor all around them.

"I don't really understand," Elizabeth said, when they were all settled. "I didn't think that someone on the astral could physically touch someone on this plane."

"That's what I thought," Earl agreed.

"Generally true, but there are exceptions," Duncan said. "Earl, you'd mentioned that you'd seen evidence of psychic attack. Which, incidentally, brings up the point that this might be just that."

"True. It may not be coming from the astral at all but from someone sitting quietly in his own home."

"Right," Duncan continued. "But, as to whether they could get at us from the astral. From your investigation of poltergeists, Earl, you've seen the psychic energies at work there. Objects are thrown through the air and there've been cases of people actually being hit by them and injured."

Earl nodded, then took off his glasses and looked around for something to clean them on. Finding nothing he pulled out his shirttail and used that.

"It's unusual for someone to be harmed that way," Duncan went on, "yet it has happened. But poltergeist energy is not the same thing as someone on the astral. Is it?" He looked at Rudolf.

The German felt for his pipe, remembered he must not smoke and abandoned the search. "Poltergeist power is just that; power. Or energy, if you like. Raw and uncontrolled. As you know it usually occurs when there is a child of the age of puberty in the house. But psychic energy is psychic energy. From a poltergeist it is uncontrolled. But from someone who knows what they are doing, *Ja*, it can be very much controlled. And it can be directed through from that second plane to this one."

"You say 'someone who knows what they're doing'," Duncan said. "So our Cuban friends are not simply adept at astral projection?"

"Oh, no." Rudolf shook his head. "I think we have very formidable opponents here. One or more of them must be very accomplished not only in projection but also in forms of psychic energy manipulation . . . what some people might term *Magic*."

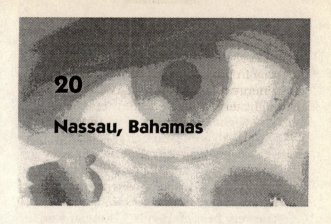

20

Nassau, Bahamas

Temporary barriers around construction areas caused the passengers of American Eagle Flight 5773 to meander in a long, straggling line, from the newly arrived airplane out on the ramp to the customs hall of Nassau International Airport. Dark-skinned workers, seemingly in no hurry to complete their tasks, took time to look over the new arrivals and wonder about their points of origin. Heads turned and eyes followed the bright red hair of Elizabeth Martin as she and her three companions ran the gauntlet of the construction workers and entered the concrete-block building.

"There's Guillemette!" said Duncan, waving to an attractive black woman dressed in an eye-catching red dress, who stood on the far side of the entry officials. She saw them and waved back, her face breaking out in a full smile accentuated by gleaming white teeth.

She was about forty years old, Duncan guessed, yet still retained a trim and athletic figure. Her hair was long and brushed to a glistening ebony. Her cheekbones were high and prominent. But most striking were her eyes. Of deepest brown, they twinkled with mirth, yet echoed lifetimes of wisdom.

"Duncan! You haven't changed a bit," she cried, throwing her arms around him and giving him a kiss on the cheek. "And these are your wonderful friends?" She turned and similarly greeted each of the others.

"The very best of friends," Duncan said.

They piled their luggage into the midnight-blue Chevy Blazer that Guillemette drove, and were soon on their way into Nassau town. Along the way they gazed out to their left, at the brilliant blue ocean water and listened to Guillemette as she talked of how wonderful life was in the Bahamas.

"Are you a Bahamian native?" Elizabeth asked.

"No, child, I am not. I was born and raised in Haiti, just a short hop southeast of here. Born in a *hounfor* up in the hills above Petionville. I came to Bahamas only a few short years ago, when the politics on my own island drove so many native children away."

"Will you ever go back there?" Duncan asked.

"Lord, Duncan, I hope so! That is a land I dearly love with all my heart. I am only half a person away from it."

Nassau, Bahamas

They drove past the American Embassy which was tucked behind a modern MacDonald's restaurant, contrasting with the big old British Colonial Hotel opposite, then turned right up the hill and past Government House.

"Tomorrow, child—or whenever we have some quality time for ourselves—I take you to the Straw Market," Guillemette said, her eyes sparkling as she looked at Elizabeth.

"As you say," Rudolf said, "'whenever we have some time for ourselves'. But who knows when that may be?"

The black woman's face was instantly serious. "You must tell me more about this business. Duncan, dear man, told me only the bare bones on the telephone. Here! We are home. You are staying at my humble house. You shall take time to freshen yourselves and then we shall sit and eat and you can bring me fully up to date."

The Blazer turned into the courtyard of a house that appeared small as it lay tucked behind seemingly overgrown grass and short scrubby trees. But as the vehicle pulled around the side of the building the four friends saw that in fact it was a house of some size, stretching back from the dusty road and surrounded by a large garden of native flora.

Guillemette had put the three men together in one large bedroom with a big, brass-framed, double-bed, a single bed and a camping cot, and placed Elizabeth in an adjoining room with its own brass-framed, single bed. Guillemette's own room was across the hallway from Beth's.

By the time all were settled it was lunchtime and they finally sat down around a solid wooden table in the dining room. Guillemette had prepared a magnificent seafood salad which she served with oven-warm bread and homemade lemonade, and they all tucked in as though they hadn't eaten in days. As they ate Duncan told Guillemette how he had been approached by Bill Highland, how he had formed the Committee, and what had happened to bring them down to the islands.

"You say these people psychically attacked you in the house in Virginia?" Her eyes searched Duncan's face.

"Yes. At least they attempted it. None of us—so far as I know—has ever experienced a psychic attack before, though of course we've heard of them and even met with people who've survived them. As you know, Earl and I do a lot of research in many occult areas, and Rudolf's no stranger to fields other than astral projection."

"I'm the odd one out, I guess," Elizabeth said, with a smile. "My thing is ESP. I've been told I'm extremely good at it, but outside of that I don't have much of a clue."

"I think you're being too hard on yourself." Duncan smiled at her, looking deep into her green eyes. "You've picked up a lot of knowledge along the way, and you've certainly been very useful to the Committee."

"The Committee." Guillemette mouthed the words. "I like the sound of that. A committee dedicated to fighting evil in the world. We need that, my man."

"Well," Duncan said, "it's actually just formed to work through this present crisis. Though, who knows, perhaps there will be other needs for us afterwards?"

They sat and talked about what the people in Cuba might be doing; how the Russians and the defected American were all tied-in together.

"It's like having half the pieces of a jigsaw puzzle," Elizabeth said.

"Yes, and no picture on the box to go by," Earl added, with a grim chuckle.

"Ah, but these pieces, they are beginning to fall into place I think," Rudolf said. "We just need a little more information."

"Then let's see if we can get it."

They all looked at Guillemette, whose eyes seemed to burn with a new intensity.

"You have an idea?" Duncan asked.

"Just a beginning," she said. "I thought we might all have a skrying session this evening. It would give us much the same sort of information you can get on the astral but without the danger of actually going there."

"Skrying?" Puzzled, Elizabeth looked to Duncan.

"Basically it's a form of crystal-gazing, though it doesn't have to be an actual crystal," he said. "You can use any good reflective surface: a glass full of water, a blot of ink, a polished copper bowl. It's a very ancient form of divination found going way back into prehistory."

"How exciting!"

*

The room was lit only by a low-flamed oil lamp, which sent large flickering shadows out to the walls. Aromatic incense wafted across the table where the five friends sat in quiet contemplation. Elizabeth sniffed and thought she'd have to find out from Guillemette, afterward, exactly what incense it was. She thought it was wonderful.

"Remember, build first the blue light around you, to give you full protection," Rudolf cautioned.

They breathed deeply and sat quietly developing their defenses. After a few moments Guillemette, looking resplendent, even in the dim light, in a deep-purple robe trimmed with gold embroidery, intoned what Duncan assumed to be a short prayer. At first he thought it was in French, but then realized it must be in the patois of the Haitian peoples. He recognized reference to the names *Legba*, *Damballah*, and *Gédé*; gods, or *loa*, of Voudoun. Then again all was silent.

Elizabeth did as she had been coached, after their filling midday repast. She tried to clear her mind and then gazed down into the glass bowl on the table in front of her. The crystal had been filled to its rim with clear, fresh, spring water. It stood on a piece of black velvet so that, as she looked down into it, there was nothing around to distract her. She had been told to look into the center of the water and let anything come into her head that may. She breathed deeply and tried hard to relax, though the very act of doing the experiment itself caused tension. Suddenly she gasped. It looked for all the world as though the bowl of water was filling with white, misty clouds. She blinked. Yes, there were definitely clouds of what looked for all the world like white smoke. What was happening?

Her hands gripped the edge of the table but she didn't let her eyes leave the bowl. Then, as she looked, the smoke started to dissipate. Gradually it thinned and faded away. As it did so it left behind a clear picture. It was like looking at a tiny television set, she thought briefly. There, in front of her, was a run-down, dingy house sitting in an overgrown garden. The house's shutters were all closed, though one or two had long since fallen off to reveal grimy, cracked glass in the windows.

"Why am I seeing this?" she asked herself. "What does this have to do with anything?" She remembered Guillemette's instructions and tried to pick up all the details of the scene before her. The house looked as though it had once been a fine villa. There were red tiles on the roof, though many of them broken or missing. A stone balustrade ran around a patio, though, again, sections had crumbled away. The garden was wild and overgrown, trees growing right up against the walls of the house. She wondered what sort of a setting the place was in. No sooner had the thought entered her head than the scene changed as though a movie camera had zoomed back and up to a high wide-angle shot. She saw that the house was buried in the woods about a half mile from a deserted beach. Waves broke gently on the shore but there was no sign of life anywhere near.

As Elizabeth shifted slightly in her chair, the image in the crystal bowl started to fade. Soon there was nothing left; she gazed once more into the clear water. As she had been instructed, Beth closed her eyes, took three or four deep breaths, then sat back and looked up and away from the bowl. She could see, in the semi-darkness, that the others were doing what she had just done. Both Guillemette and Duncan had actual balls; Dunk's being a fine quartz crystal and the Haitian woman's a very large obsidian one resting on an ornately carved wooden stand. Earl was looking into a bowl of water, similar to hers. Rudolf was sitting with his eyes closed, presumably having just finished his skrying. In front of him was a highly polished brass plate, slightly concave.

It was another ten minutes before all of them had finished their tasks. Finally Guillemette, the last to finish, sat back and let out a sigh.

"Wonderful!" she murmured.

"You got good stuff?" Earl asked. "'Cause I'm damned if I did! I thought my eyes were going to bug out, I stared so damned hard."

"That may have been your trouble," Rudolf said, his eyes glinting from under his bushy eyebrows. "You were told not to stare but to simply relax and look. Did you blink your eyes?"

"Was I supposed to?"

"If you needed to, yes," smiled Guillemette. "You should have just looked naturally, blinking as you needed to. Didn't I tell you not to get into a set stare?"

Earl looked abashed. "I guess so," he said.

"Anyone else have problems?" Duncan asked, glancing in Beth's direction.

She shook her head. "Far from it," she said. "I couldn't believe it! I actually saw something."

"*Gut!*" The German produced a notebook and pencil. "Then let us put together all of our sightings."

Elizabeth told them of her rundown villa by the ocean. "I guess it's got nothing to do with what we're doing," she said. "But I was just excited to get anything at all."

"I said you were useful," Duncan said, reaching across and squeezing her hand. "I'm pretty sure that has everything to do with what we're after. What d'you think, Guillemette?"

"I agree," she said. "Well done, Beth. You see, I saw that house too."

"You did?" Beth was incredulous.

"Oh, yes. And I wouldn't mind betting we weren't the only ones." She looked at Duncan and Rudolf, her eyes bright.

The German shook his head but Duncan nodded enthusiastically. "Right on! I saw it from a different angle, I guess, but there's no doubt it was the same house. I saw it briefly from the outside, then I was inside."

"Inside?"

He nodded. "I started going through rooms that looked as dilapidated as the outside, but then, suddenly, I was in a large room that was brightly lit and clean—or relatively so. It had a group of people sitting around a table . . . the Russian group, I'd guess!"

"Well done!" Guillemette murmured.

"What was the group doing?" Earl asked.

"I don't know. They seemed to be just sitting there. I didn't see the Cuban or the Russian, or General Wellesley. By the way, Rudy, I assume the young guy with the close-cropped hair, that Beth and I saw on our astral trip, is the Russian Colonel you saw on your first journey?"

The German nodded. "*Ja.* Alexis Militsa they said his name was. You say he was not in your vision just now?"

"I didn't see him if he was."

Rudolf seemed to consider Duncan's reply for a moment, then he spoke. "I had an interesting view from my skrying. I saw not the house you all saw. But I did see our young Russian. *Ja*, he was in my own sighting. He was sitting in a small room by himself. Where that room was I do not know—perhaps it was in the house, perhaps not—but he did not appear happy. He was writing something. I could not see what; a letter I think. And he was muttering to himself as he wrote. I could hear nothing, of course, but he seemed very angry. He even stopped writing at one point and hit the table with his fist."

"D'you think it's us he's mad at?" Earl asked.

"Who knows?" Duncan shrugged. "That's where astral projection scores over skrying— you can be right there and hear things and then not leave until you want to leave . . . or *have* to leave." He grinned at Beth .

"What about you, Guillemette?" Elizabeth asked. "You haven't said what you saw."

Guillemette rose from the table and turned up the oil lamp so that Rudolf had more light by which to write his notes. He nodded his thanks.

"I saw your house," she said. "But only at the end of my sighting. I started with another villa. It was similar to the old one but in good repair. It, too, was by the ocean. There were trees—with one tall *ceiba* poking out above the palms . . ."

"Ah! That was the previous house—the one we visited in our astral traveling," Duncan said.

"I thought it probably was. Well, from there I must have followed their movements. I finally arrived at the dirty, overgrown villa and moved around the outside of that. But first, I found myself traveling along many roads at high speeds. It was almost dizzying. There is a fairly good road, quite wide though not much traffic, only a short distance from the decrepit place. Then an overgrown, deeply rutted driveway, that winds a lot, leading in."

"See anything interesting around the house?"

She shook her head. "No. Though, wait a minute . . . yes! Yes, there was a small hut, like a gardener's hut or toolhouse, back from the main building. And from that there seemed to be a path that had been freshly cut, running through the underbrush and then down toward the shore."

"Good," Duncan said. "Make a note of that, Rudy."

"So what's next?" Earl asked. "I guess we can gather from all this that they've moved their HQ. We must have scared 'em."

"Do they know where we are now?" Elizabeth asked.

Duncan caught the slight tremor in her voice. He moved his chair a little closer to hers. "Since we were able to find them this way, it's possible they've done the same to see where we are," he said quietly. "But that's presuming that they think we're important enough to trouble with. The thing is, they're up to something—something big. And right now they may not have the time and spare energy to devote to chasing us."

"Especially if they decide we're small potatoes," added Guillemette. "No, child. Don't worry. We are in good shape. And my little house here is not entirely unprotected from the likes of them, you know."

"Oh?" Earl sounded interested.

"Yes. What exactly do you mean, Guillemette?" Duncan asked.

She shook her long hair and chuckled. "I told you I was born in a hounfor in Haiti," she said. "A *hounfor* is a Voudoun 'church', as it were. That is where the *Houngan* and *Mambo*—the Priest and Priestess live. Growing up there I learned many things . . . My mama was the *Mambo*. She taught me how to protect myself, and my home."

There was a moment of silence. Rudolf broke it.

"Does the Senator Highland know where we are?" He looked at Duncan, who nodded.

"Not this exact location, no. But he does know we're in Nassau. Don't forget he got the tickets for us. But thanks for reminding me, Rudy. I must give him a call and bring him up to date."

21

Nassau, Bahamas

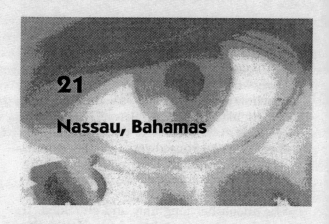

"Do you know where this villa is?"

"No, Bill. Not exactly," Duncan said. "We know what it looks like and we know it's quite some way from the other villa they were in. But no, we don't know exactly whereabouts on Cuba it's located."

"Can you find out? I mean, I don't pretend to understand your methods, Dunk; all I know is you're getting results and that's what counts. But do you have a way of finding out where they are?" The Senator sounded anxious.

"I'm sure we can. It's just a question of astrally projecting. By focusing in on them we should be able to flash straight there. Then, I guess, we'll just slowly pull back and see where 'there' is."

"Gobbledygook, yes! No offense, Dunk. I just don't understand it and I don't even want to. If it does the job that's all that matters."

"The only problem . . ." Duncan hesitated. "It's no longer exactly safe on the astral, now that they know we're after them."

"So how much damage can they do to a ghost?" Highland laughed. "Sorry!" He got serious. "Danger is the name of the game, Dunk. I'm sorry to have dragged you in to this extent. But it seems these guys are up to something major, and you and your Committee are the only ones who have any kind of an inkling as to what's going on."

"What is going on, Bill?"

There was a pause.

"This line is not secure. However, I guess I can tell you, there's been a sudden movement of our surveillance satellite . . . the one that keeps an eye on Cuba."

"What d'you mean, 'a sudden movement'?"

"Just that. A satellite is in an orbit that gives us excellent pictures of all that's going on in Cuba. No more surprise build-up of arms like we had in the early sixties. Anyway, for no reason that any of the lab boys can determine, the satellite has suddenly started drifting off course. If it continues to do that, we could lose sight of our target."

"You mean, no longer keep an eye on Cuba?"

"Exactly. At least, not without starting a whole other complex program of spy planes again, and they're nowhere near as accurate and sophisticated as the satellite."

"But don't you have a way of correcting for movement of that sort?" Duncan asked.

"To an extent, yes," the Senator said. "But only up to a point. As I say, this movement is something that they can't explain. In other words, it doesn't seem to be a natural drift caused by gravitational pull from the Moon, or whatever. And it hasn't been hit by a meteorite, throwing it off course. No. Something—or someone—is influencing it in some way we don't know how. I strongly suspect your bunch down in the Caribbean."

Duncan whistled. "Wow! Now the pieces of the jigsaw puzzle are filling in fast."

"What?"

"Sorry, Bill. Something Earl said last night. Now I can see how this all fits together. The rocket launch manipulations and then the psychic take-over of the submarine. That was one hell of a bit of PK."

"What the hell are you talking about, Dunk?"

"Never mind, Bill. As I say, it's falling into place. Yes, we've got to stop them, whether on the astral or on this plane. We'll do everything we can, believe me."

"I know you will, Dunk. And don't forget, if there's anything you need, just let me know and I'll see what I can do."

"Good. I'll remember that. Thanks, Bill."

*

Nassau, Bahamas

Earl put down his breakfast orange juice and gave out a long whistle. "So that's it! They've brought the PK team from Russia to move the satellite and stop Uncle Sam from watching over them."

"Which means they have something else in mind," said Rudolf.

Earl looked at him. "What d'you mean?"

"Well, surely they are not going to all this trouble and effort to move the satellite just so they can sit there and be happy they are not being watched!" The German busied himself buttering some toast.

"You're right, Rudy," Duncan said. "They must have something planned that they don't want us to see. They're up to something big all right."

"What can we do?" Elizabeth asked.

"We can destroy their concentration, if nothing else."

They looked at Guillemette. She was gathering up their breakfast dishes but stopped to join in the discussion. "We all know how much concentration it takes to achieve anything psychokinetically. And to work on moving an object up in space, well that must take the most concentration you could ask for. I would bet they couldn't do diddly if that focus was broken."

A smile spread across Duncan face. "You're right, Guillemette." He turned to the others. "Remember at Marshall Perchard's place, back in Arlington? Remember how we had to be behind a two-way mirror so as not to distract his team?"

"That's right!"

"So," Duncan looked at Guillemette again and smiled. "If I read you right, you're saying we should put all our efforts into distracting them."

"Which might be easier said than done," Earl said.

"Oh, I'm sure it's not going to be easy," Duncan agreed. "Okay. Ideas?"

"It would be so much easier if we were physically close to them," Elizabeth said, hesitantly. "Don't you think? I mean, we could throw rocks through their windows, or something."

They all laughed.

"There's something in that," Duncan said. "But first things first. We need to establish exactly where they are. Bill was asking me about that and we sure need to know. I told him we could probably find out by projecting, but the enemy's on their guard against that now."

"Even so," Rudolf said. "You are correct. I will volunteer to clarify their position." He turned to Guillemette. "My dear lady, do you happen to have a good map of the islands; of Cuba in particular?"

"Wouldn't be without one," she smiled. "Let's clear off this table, then we can spread the map and form our battle plan."

Quickly the Committee turned the big table from a breakfast smorgasbord into a conference table. Guillemette produced a large-scale map of the Caribbean islands, from the tip of Florida down to Trinidad. Unfolded, the map covered most of the table. They all pored over it.

"Did we ever establish where their last villa was?" Elizabeth asked.

"Only roughly," Duncan replied. "It was west of Havana, probably in this Pinar Del Rio section, from what Rudy said that first time he followed Humberto Gavilla there from the rocket launch."

"*Ja.*" Rudolf studied the map and nodded. "*Ja*, I remember how the coastline looked as we approached it. That is where it must have been."

"But where have they gone now, that's the question?" Earl asked.

"Maybe I can help." Guillemette studied the map. "When I was skrying, as I told you, I seemed to fly along the roads, probably taking the same path they had taken in their Jeeps when they switched bases. Let me see . . ."

Her finger picked up the main Cuban highway that tracked along the spine of the island, from Cardenas down to Holguín, Bayamo and Santiago de Cuba. As she picked it out Duncan noticed that she half-closed her eyes, as though actually traveling the route. Her finger tracked along for quite some time then paused and wavered over the town of Camagüey. It then left the main highway and headed north to the coastal village of Nuevitas, where it stopped. She opened her eyes wide and looked at what she pointed.

"Nuevitas," she said, thoughtfully. "Hmm. I wonder? It feels right, somehow. Perhaps they are just outside Nuevitas?"

"It's as good a guess as any," Earl said. "Rudy, you could check it out, couldn't you?"

"*Ja*. I will do so. Again, I can check the shape of the coastline against this map."

"Okay. So let's say that's where they are," Duncan said. "Now what? Where do we go from there?"

Earl looked up from the map and into his friends' faces. "I honestly feel we—or one or two of us at least—need to go there," he said quietly.

"Go there? You mean, physically?" Elizabeth asked.

"Right."

"I don't know." Duncan slowly shook his head. "I mean, we're the brains when it comes to the occult—or so we've been led to believe. But now we're getting into heavy stuff. Sneaking into Cuba? Come on, Earl! We're not the CIA, you know."

"But in a way we are," Rudolf said. "In a way we are the psychic CIA, if you will." He chuckled at his own idea, and the others joined in.

"You are right, my man," Guillemette enthused. "We are the psychic CIA. Let's face is, Dunk, we can do so much transcendentally, but that doesn't mean we might not have to do some physical stuff as well, to supplement it."

"Right!" Elizabeth spoke up. Duncan was surprised at the passion in her voice. "We took this on and we said, back at the hotel if you all remember, that we were all committed; that we were going to be into this all the way, no matter what it grew into. Well, are we or aren't we?"

Duncan had never seen Beth so resolute. Her cheeks had a touch of color and her green eyes seemed to flash as she looked around at her friends. She was right, of course, he thought. They were in this for the whole struggle. He hadn't known where events were going to lead when he first agreed to look into things for Bill Highland, but there had seemed to be a certain inevitability about the events as they unfolded. There had been no point, really, where he could have turned around and walked away, and this was no place to do that either. No, Beth was right. He—and he felt sure the others felt the same way—was in it to the end. Even if it meant that all of them would have to sneak into Cuba and meet the enemy face to face, they would do it.

"You bet we are, Beth," he said quietly. He turned to the others. "What about it, guys?"

"You betcha!" Earl said.

"Decidedly." Rudolf nodded.

"I'm only just warming up," Guillemette smiled.

"Good. Thanks guys." Duncan smiled at them. "Okay, so what's the plan? Rudy will project to make sure Nuevitas is where they are. Then what?"

"I will volunteer to go into Cuba and start to harass them," Earl said.

"And I will go with him, because I know the islands best and I wouldn't want to miss this anyway." Guillemette looked around defiantly, daring anyone to say she couldn't go.

"All right. Agreed! Rudy, I suggest you go and lie down as soon as possible and see if you can check on that. Meanwhile, we'll go over the logistics of getting you two over there." Duncan picked up the pencil and pad of paper Rudolf had been using the evening before and started making notes. "We'll need a boat to get you both there. Obviously you can't fly in. You're going to have to go in under cover of darkness, I guess. We'll have to check the fuel you'll need, tides and/or currents that could affect you, and the time it will take you to get across there. What about food? How long are you going to be there and exactly what will you do to harass their PKers?"

They settled down to work out the details.

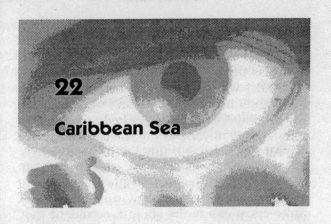

22
Caribbean Sea

The 1930 26-foot Chris-Craft Runabout leapt out into the sparkling blue ocean and tore its way across the calm blue water, its 225hp 6-cylinder Kermath engine screaming goodbye to the three figures on the dock. As the white wake behind the boat curved out of the bay and swung off into deeper water, Guillemette turned from looking back and waving to the figures on Prince George Wharf and settled down beside Earl, who held the wheel with the easy grace of a master mariner. She couldn't help but notice the slight smile that curled the corners of his mouth and she too smiled as she ensconced herself in the commodious horsehair-stuffed leather seat. Earl eased back the throttle a little and glanced at her.

"Nothing like leaving port at full bore, for effect. This bad boy can keep a steady 25 mph and get up to forty for short bursts like that. But I guess we can't keep up that pace all the way to Cuba."

"Not without going through our gas at a hellacious rate," she said. "No, we've got about a ten-hour journey ahead. Better settle to a more comfortable speed, Earl."

The sun glinted off the highly polished mahogany of the antique boat, the only vessel available for rent that was both large enough and powerful enough to make this journey. They had gassed up and stowed three extra gas tanks aboard, confident that they'd have sufficient to both get them to Cuba and get them back out again, at least to friendly territory.

Rudolf had gone out on the astral and returned to confirm that the Russians and Cubans were indeed nearby the village of Nuevitas. Guillemette and Earl had no real plans as to what they were going to do when they reached there, other than to harass the enemy so that they'd be unable to concentrate on their PK.

"Should we take weapons of any sort?" Earl had asked.

"No way!" Duncan was emphatic and Elizabeth and Rudolf agreed. "We're not trained for armed combat and we need to avoid anything that might lead in that direction. No! If it looks as though that sort of thing's going to be necessary then we withdraw and let Bill send in the Marines."

"Agreed." Guillemette nodded. "Besides, we've got a lot more going for us than nasty guns!"

"Oh?" Earl's eyebrows raised.

Guillemette smiled enigmatically. "Believe me," she said. "We can mess up these people a whole lot worse than by shooting them. You just stick with me, my man."

Staring out to sea, Earl smiled again as he thought of Guillemette's words. He glanced sideways at her. She was a remarkably attractive woman, he thought. Incredibly sexy, really. He surprised himself. He hadn't thought too much about women for a long time. He'd always kept himself so busy with his research; his lectures and workshops. He glanced at her again. Perhaps it was the knowledge that he was going to be alone with her for at least a couple of days, he thought. Whatever it was, yes, he thought she was damned sexy!

She suddenly looked up and caught his eye. He jerked his head away as though he'd been caught doing something he shouldn't have been. He felt his face burning and mentally kicked himself for behaving like a teenager. Guillemette's soft chuckle made him turn and look at her again.

"Earl Stratford!" she said in mock tones of admonition.

"What?!"

She shook her head and tut-tutted. "Beth's not the only one with ESP, you know."

"What?" He didn't know if she was serious or not. Surely she couldn't really have been reading his mind? Not exactly, surely? He didn't know what to think. He decided to change the subject and swept his arm across, pointing at the horizon. "Once we clear the end of Andros Island we'll have nothing but open water, I guess. Now don't forget you're the navigator, Guillemette. Have you checked our heading?"

She stayed looking at him for a long moment, a smile on her lips. Then, slowly, she looked down and pulled the charts out of the bag at her feet. She opened up the gridded paper and traced, with her finger, the route they had marked earlier with a red felt-tip pen. "Don't you worry, Earl. I'll see you don't wander off course."

It was nearly three hours later that they started to worry. No one had thought twice about the weather; it was always beautiful in the Bahamas, though Guillemette had made mention of the fact that they needed to check the forecast before they left. But somehow, in the rush of getting going, they had forgotten. Now, as the two in the fast-moving boat looked up at the sky, they saw that it was overcast and becoming darker by the minute.

"Better put up the top," Earl said. He throttled back the motor to idle and climbed back to where the tonneau cover was rolled back. He unsnapped the fasteners along the canvas and pulled the metal framework up to

Caribbean Sea

unfold forward over the seats. Once in place, with Guillemette's help, he brought up the canvas top over the framework and clamped it down along the windshield. "Sidecurtains too, I think," he said. They quickly pulled up the canvas-and-plastic sections and got them into place just as the first large drops of rain started to fall.

"Phew! Just in time." Earl settled back into his seat and brought the boat back up to speed. But he soon had to throttle back again. The surface of the ocean had gradually built up to giant swells that rose up two or three times as high as the top of the boat. The vessel had seemed a large cruiser when they left the island, but in no time, to Earl's mind, the big boat became a tiny floating piece of wood at the mercy of the enormous ocean. There could be no question of trying to stay on course. For now all Earl could do was keep the seven-foot-long bow pointed into the waves and hope for the best as giant raindrops pelted the windshield.

*

"Well at least they'll have good weather for the trip." Duncan turned off the radio after listening to the weather forecast. Apprehensively he had tuned it in, only remembering to do so long after his two friends had disappeared from sight across the blue vastness of the Caribbean Sea. He had been relieved to hear of nothing but sunshine and light breezes for the next two or three days.

The Committee

"Now let's see," he said. "They left at seven o'clock. We reckoned they should be there no later than six tomorrow morning, Right?"

Elizabeth and Rudolf nodded.

"That's the very latest," Beth said. "They should actually get there earlier than that and be able to get ashore before anybody's up and about."

"Oh, yes. They both know what they're doing. I'm not worried."

Before she left, Guillemette had made reservations for the three of them at the Drumbeat Club on West Bay Street, saying they would need a little relaxation and change of pace before the "war" proper began. No one had protested too loudly. Now the three friends were well pleased and got there early enough to secure a table near the front, where they could see the incredible drumming of Peanuts Taylor and other Bahamians, enjoy the singing and the marimba, and wonder at the agility of the limbo dancers. Ever mindful of their physical condition and how it needed to be at its peak for any and all psychic work, they passed up the tempting liquor concoctions and sipped lightly at plain soda-waters.

The show ended at ten o'clock and they were back at Guillemette's home within twenty minutes. They had a light supper and turned in.

"Up by five-thirty at the latest, tomorrow," Duncan said. "We need to be on hand for when Earl and Guillemette arrive in

Cuba. Then we can send them some psychic energy. They're going to need all the help they can get."

But a little after midnight once again they were all wide awake.

"It's like that icy cold back at the Hotel Jefferson," Elizabeth said. She had come through into the men's room and was now wrapped in a blanket and huddled close to a fire that Duncan had lit in the stone fireplace.

"*Ja*, it is definitely of psychic origin." Rudolf rubbed his hands together as he leaned toward the flames. "Duncan, pass me my notebook. It is beside my bed."

Duncan reached across and got a black, leather-bound volume and gave it to the German. The tall man opened the book and flicked quickly through the pages. Duncan saw that they were covered with the older man's fine, spindly handwriting, broken occasionally by neat little thumbnail sketches of objects, diagrams and symbols. Duncan came back in front of the fire and sat with his arm about the blanketed Elizabeth. "What are you looking for, Rudy?" he asked. "A spell of protection?"

"That is what it amounts to, *Ja*." He nodded and went on paging through the book. "Ah! Here we are. Now, bear with me one moment."

Throwing off the coat he had pulled about his thin shoulders, Rudolf stood up and extended his arms upward and outward, as though about to conduct some invisible orchestra. Suddenly, in a harsh, stentorian voice that belied his frail frame, he cried aloud three names which, to his listeners, sounded like ancient Greek or Latin or some primordial tongue.

For a moment nothing happened. Then there came a great gust of wind. Duncan half got to his feet, thinking the windows had blown open. But then he saw that they were fast closed. The wind lasted only a moment, then, as Rudolf repeated the words, the blast stopped abruptly and all was strangely still. Gradually the temperature returned to normal.

"Guillemette said that if we should come under psychic attack we were to go to her special room," Rudolf said, gathering up his jacket, book, and a small bag from the side of his bed. "I think now is an excellent time to do that. Come, she was insistent on this, and I feel she was right."

He led the way to a small room beyond the dining room. Duncan had not been in it before, and, as Rudolf lit an oil lamp, saw that one of its walls was made up of sliding glass doors that opened out onto a walled section of the rear garden. The other three walls were painted black. Filling the whole of one wall was what he recognized as an altar with a conglomeration of items crowding it. There was a carved, wooden figure of a man dressed in a top hat and frock coat. He wore spectacles made out of black wire. There was a beautiful female doll dressed in an elaborate white dress, wearing numerous necklaces and with her face painted with actual lipstick and makeup. There was a large, carved wooden snake, also wrapped in necklaces and coiled around a white egg. A large wooden cross was similarly hung with necklaces of beads and snake vertebrae. Several bottles of rum, some full and some part empty, were scattered about the altar together with herbs and flowers, fruit, nuts, and bowls of meal. An ornate gourd rattle, also decorated with beads and snake vertebrae and with a small silver bell attached to its handle, lay in front of everything else. Behind the altar, tacked up on the wall, were pictures of the Virgin Mary, Saint Patrick, and several other Catholic Saints. The room smelled of incense, as though a lot of it had been continually burned there over a very long period.

From the rough-hewn beams of the ceiling hung bunches of dried herbs, feathers, and dried flowers, together with silk banners, of various colors, bearing strange symbols. There was a large wooden cupboard with closed doors and, in the corner across from the doorway, a large wooden, iron-bound chest with a massive padlock on it, and what looked to Duncan like an old cavalry saber lying across its lid. The floor of the room was dirt, which surprised Duncan, since the rest of the house had wooden floors with rugs scattered over them. In the center of the dirt floor someone—presumably Guillemette—had trailed what looked like chalk dust or flour and drawn a large and incredibly intricate design. Duncan recognized it as a Voudoun *véve*, though which one he wasn't sure.

"Wow!" Elizabeth gazed in awe.

"You can just feel the power in this room," Duncan murmured as he gazed about him. "Yes, this is the place to be. No outside psychic force is going to penetrate this, I'm sure."

At Rudolf's bidding they sat on the floor within the confines of the *véve*. Huddled together, they sat there through the night, not daring to move and not able to sleep, until the pale glimmer of dawn began to lighten the windows.

"They're in trouble."

Duncan came out of his half-sleep as Elizabeth broke the long silence. "What d'you mean?" he asked. He could almost see Beth 'shifting gears', as he liked to call it; going backwards and forwards between the fully conscious mode and the clairvoyant mode.

"I—I don't know. I just know they're in trouble." She closed her eyes and knit her brows. "They seem to be lost . . . they're nowhere near where they should be and they—they're scared." Her body had fully relaxed and her eyes, closed, turned inward and upwards towards the position of the third eye. "I can pick up on Earl especially. He's very worried but doesn't want to show it." She

Caribbean Sea

smiled briefly. "That's just like him, isn't it? They've been through a really bad storm."

"A storm? But the weather report said . . ."

"I know. I know." Beth nodded. "But all I can tell you is, *they* had a bad storm."

"Are they anywhere near Cuba?" Rudolf asked.

"I don't know . . . *they* don't know. There's nothing but ocean all around them and they've no sense of direction."

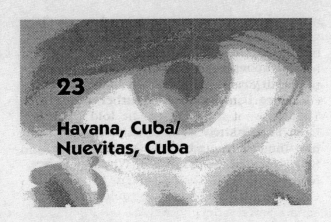

23

Havana, Cuba/ Nuevitas, Cuba

Nizar Hammadi wasn't happy to return to Cuba. He didn't really understand why Saddam couldn't negotiate without having to send him each time. He knew no telephone connection could ever be safe and secure but why was it he who had to come? He fingered his moustache; a copy of his leader's. But on the other hand, who was he to question Hussein's orders? On thinking back on it, the previous mission had gone well and Saddam had been well pleased. And it hadn't really taken that long. He sighed. Why did he find it so difficult to do such a small, simple job for the man he admired above all others?

He sat in the airport at Havana. This time there was no helicopter waiting to shuttle him to a meeting. There was nothing. He got up and paced the floor of the small office where he had been escorted and wondered what Castro was up to. The room had only a bare metal desk and a filing cabinet. Overhead a fan with a bad bearing made a continuous rattle as it turned slowly, doing little to cool the room. Nizar lit another cigarette. This was not a good sign, he told himself. Last time Castro had seemed pleased to see him and had treated him with every courtesy. So where was the man now? Why wasn't he, Nizar Hammadi, being taken to see the Cuban leader? A limousine could have been sent, or even a Jeep, surely?

It was over an hour after Nizar had landed that the door to the little office opened and Fidel Castro himself stood there. He was wearing sunglasses so Nizar could not see his eyes, but he had a scowl on his face.

"I cannot come running to meetings with Saddam Hussein's envoy every five minutes," he said. "What is it this time? I thought everything was decided."

Nizar sighed again. This wasn't going to be such a smooth visit.

"Saddam Hussein presents his compliments . . ."

"Cut the crap!" Fidel strode across to the window and stared out at the few aircraft sitting on the taxiway. There was not a lot of traffic. He pulled one of his eight-inch Cohiba *cigaros* out of his tunic pocket and stuck it in his mouth. He didn't light it. "Just get to the bottom line," he said.

Once again Nizar sighed. He extinguished his cigarette and dutifully addressed the back of the tall Cuban. "Saddam Hussein has merely asked me to remind you of the terms of the agreement between our two great countries. And he wishes me to respectfully draw your attention to the fact that he is to start moving SCUDs and Exocets four days from now. He would like your assurance that *all will be well* for their importation." He stressed the four words, as he had been instructed to do.

Castro remained looking out of the window, watching the progress of a twin-engine Piper PA23 Apache as it negotiated its way around an ancient Grumman G21 Goose amphibian which sat in the middle of the taxiway like an overweight albatross. He seemed not to have heard Nizar.

The Iraqi envoy waited patiently. Inwardly he fumed. Who the hell did this Cuban with his third-rate country think he was, treating a close personal friend of Saddam Hussein with such contempt? He'd have a strong word or two with Saddam about this when he got back!

Eventually Castro turned away from the window and walked to the door. As he opened it and passed through he spoke back over his shoulder.

"I have already given your leader my word on this. The timetable was laid out in the agreement. There was no need for him to send anyone here to harass us." He went out and closed the door.

Havana, Cuba/Nuevitas, Cuba

*

Ovideo Carlos de Céspedes Alderaguía sat at his desk looking at the telephone receiver he had just replaced in its cradle. Castro had sounded impatient. So, Hussein was applying pressure, was he? That certainly wouldn't please the Cuban *Comandante en Jefe*. If there was one thing Fidel hated it was pressure. He could be extremely stubborn when he wanted to be and dig in his heels harder than anyone else. But, it appeared that there was to be no negotiating; this was part of a previous agreement. Fidel was just annoyed that the Iraqi felt he could not rely on the word already given.

Seventy-two hours, Fidel had told Ovideo. "I want to see that satellite moving within seventy-two hours so that I can assure Hussein it will be out of the way by the time he wants it clear. I know you are on top of this, Ovideo. You don't like to be harangued any more than I do, so I'm just passing on word and I'll leave you to it."

"Thank you, Fidel. Yes, we are doing well. Rest assured the satellite will be moved with no trouble, easily within the time."

How he wished he could be sure that it would be so. The Russian colonel, Alexis Militsa, gave golden assurances but Humberto did nothing but bemoan the laziness of the whole group. Still, he did know how prone Humberto was to belittle everyone but himself. Ovideo sighed. All he could do was pass on Fidel's words and keep his fingers very carefully crossed. Time alone would tell.

*

"How is it *you're* so tired this morning?" There was no compassion in Humberto's question. He looked at the Russian almost accusingly. "You weren't screwing around all night with one of your Rusky women, were you?"

Alexis looked at the Cuban contemptuously. "Don't be too quick to judge others by yourself, Comrade," he said. "I do not, as you say, 'screw around with women', especially when I am in the middle of a mission."

Humberto's eyebrows went up and his face broke into a grin. "Oho! So it's the little boys you prefer, is it, Ivan?"

"And do not call me Ivan!"

The Cuban chuckled and turned away, shaking his head. "I had my suspicions about you," he said.

"Agh! You are not worth talking to!" Alexis also turned away, to the breakfast table, and busied himself poking through the pile of blackened toast, looking for a piece not too badly burned. He found one and scraped a thin layer of butter over it, then he poured himself a large mug of black coffee and drank it down quickly, without cream or sugar.

"You do seem a little under the weather," Nathan Wellesley observed, looking over the top of a book he had been reading while eating his breakfast.

"We are here on a mission." The Russian spoke quietly, enunciating carefully, his eyes fixed on a second mug of coffee he poured for himself. "And it seems I'm the only one serious about it. While you two were snoring your way through the night I was doing something."

Wellesley put down his book. "'Doing something'? What d'you mean by that, Colonel?"

The Russian drank half of the second mug of coffee and felt better. He dug a knife into a dark red jelly congealing in a jar, then thought better of it and crunched into the toast as it was. He chewed thoughtfully for a moment.

"You may have wondered why I am the leader of this group of talented people—I speak of the Moscovites, of course." He waited, half expecting a snide remark from Humberto, but the Cuban remained quiet. "As you may know, I was, for many years, instrumental in supporting the KGB with several of its endeavors. I have made myself useful to Dimitri Tupolev and, yes, to Yeltsin himself. It is not just my powers of administration that have endeared me to these important people. *Nyet!* It is my, how should I put it . . . ?"

"Your great opinion of yourself!" Humberto could contain himself no longer. "Shit, Alexis, I've never met anyone with such an overblown ego! And, as you admit, all you do is act the leader of this dumb bunch. Huh! It makes me sick! I take all the risks, going out on the astral . . . "

"Silence!" Dimitri roared the word and Wellesley almost dropped his book.

The Russian, slowly and deliberately, got to his feet and walked around the table to stand glowering down at the Cuban who, surprised at the other's outburst, sat with his mouth agape.

"You and your petty little journeys out of the body. What dangers do you face? I could do all that you have done without thinking twice about it."

"You can project?" Humberto sounded surprised.

"Projection is but a beginner's game. I am a Magus! A Master Magician. That is my talent that has been so useful to my country. Last night, while you two slept, I used but a little of my power to rid us of those incompetent amateur Yankees."

Humberto's mouth dropped open. A cigarette he had been about to light fell out of his mouth onto the table.

"You—you are a Magus?"

The Russian gave a short, curt nod.

Wellesley sat up and leaned forward. "Wait a minute, Militsa, what the hell are you talking about? Magician? Magic? What the hell's going on?"

The Russian ignored him, addressing himself to Humberto. "Yes. You ask why I look tired this morning. It is because I have been up all night unleashing a storm on those fools! Did you know they were on their way here?"

Havana, Cuba/Nuevitas, Cuba

"What? They were coming to Cuba?"

"Not just to Cuba. To Nuevitas. To this disgusting building . . . What an insult, to have to do our work out of this filthy ruin!"

"Well, we did have to move on pretty short notice," Wellesley said. "They'd found where we were . . ."

"*Da!* Again the incompetent Humberto! He let them follow him back there. Of all the fools!"

"And I suppose you could have done better?" The Cuban seemed to have recovered himself a little and stood, glowering at the stocky Russian face to face. Wellesley got quickly to his feet.

"Now then you two! Back off, both of you. Let's not lose sight of why we're here—never mind what sort of surroundings they've put us in. We've just been told we've got less than seventy-two hours to get that satellite moving. I don't think that leaves us too much time for bickering among ourselves, do you?"

Alexis was the first to move away. He spun on his heel and stalked back around the table. "You are right, as always, Comrade General. This worm is not worth my time."

"Why you . . . !"

"Enough!" Wellesley found himself shouting.

Alexis held up his hand. "I am sorry, General. That was my fault. Now, to work. We must get the group up and working right away. We will work them in the usual three shifts but will change every fifteen minutes. Agreed?"

Wellesley grunted agreement and, sullenly, Humberto nodded.

"Right. Comrade Gavilla, we will start with the local talent. Round up your people and they will take the first shift. I will organize my number one group to take over."

Obviously biting his tongue, the Cuban stalked from the room without saying a word.

"Alexis?" Wellesley could not contain his curiosity. "Just what did you mean by 'Magus', was it? And about unleashing a storm?"

The Russian ran a hand over his close-cropped hair and gave a wry smile. "I fear your expertise on matters regarding satellite placement has got you entangled in a web of occultism, Comrade General. I do not expect you to understand much of this. Yes, I am what is termed a Magus of the Fifth Degree O∴L∴L∴ That means that I have spent several decades—since my early teenage years, as it happens—studying the manipulation of forces you could not begin to comprehend. I was lucky in having good teachers; master occultists themselves. Perhaps when all this is over we can talk and I can help clear your mind. But, for now, we have work to do." He turned and went out of the room.

24

Caribbean Sea

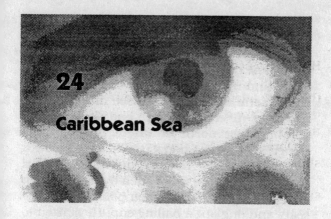

They were both soaked to the skin and huddled together, shivering. Eventually a cold, faint glimmer began to lighten the sky on the far horizon.

"I guess that must be east," Earl said. "Dawn is upon us."

"At last." Guillemette sat up and looked about her. Gradually she was able to make out her surroundings. The canvas top of the boat had been ripped to shreds and the side curtains were gone. There was water swishing about their ankles and the big Chris Craft had a decided list to port.

Earl tapped the compass. Someone had thoughtfully mounted it above the original small, central, instrument board, with its four dials. They had commented on the fact that it was a worthwhile addition. But shortly after the storm had struck, the previous evening, they had both been amazed to see the compass start to spin, and keep spinning at a tremendous rate as though driven by a motor. In no time they had become completely disoriented and now had no idea where they were. Guillemette was pleased to see that the compass had stilled itself again and showed them pointing just north of where the sun was struggling over the horizon.

"I don't know how we didn't sink," Earl said. "I've never heard of such a storm. It kept going all night." He reached back behind the seats and dug out a bailing cup. He started to scoop up the water and throw it over the side.

"What happened to the engine?" Guillemette asked. "I don't even remember it stopping."

"I do." He kept bailing. "It just sort of sputtered to a stop. Almost as though it had run out of gas, though there should've been plenty. I'd kept it throttled back quite a bit; just enough power to keep us heading into those damned waves. When it quit I really thought we were goners. We were tossed all over the ocean."

"Tell me about it." The Haitian woman tenderly rubbed the bruises on her arms. "Now how are we going to find out where we are? And which direction do we go?"

Earl looked at his watch. "Well, it's just after five. We know we're somewhere between the Bahamian islands and Cuba."

"We do?" Guillemette wasn't so sure. "How do you know we haven't been blown out into the Atlantic? Or up into the Gulf of Mexico, or God knows where?" She stood up and looked all around. There was no sign of land. "Ah, well! I guess there's a good chance we'll see something sometime soon. That's the advantage of being in the Caribbean—there always seem to be so many islands around." She didn't feel as hopeful as she tried to sound.

An hour later the floor of the front compartment was more or less empty of water, though the boat still listed to one side. Earl had the cover off the big, six-cylinder engine and was sitting up on the side of the compartment looking down at it with a frown on his face.

"I don't know diddly about engines," he said, scratching his beard with one hand while tracing a finger of his other hand around the letters of the name Kermath, emblazoned across the valve covers. "Least of all boat engines. If I can't run it in to my neighborhood mechanic I'm stuck."

"Just leave the top off for a while and let it dry out." Guillemette was even less mechanical than Earl but didn't want to admit it. She could see how depressed he was. "Crawl back to the after compartment, Earl, and see if our bags are still there," she said.

He adjusted his spectacles and did as she said. The classic boat had a rear seat for two, in the stern, behind the engine. They had previously referred to it as a rumble seat. Their bags and the spare cans of gas were stowed

The Committee

there. A tonneau cover was still tightly stretched over it.

"Eureka!" Earl cried, unsnapping the canvas. "We should have been back here with this stuff. There's no water here at all."

They settled down and ate some of the sandwiches they had brought with them in the bags. Guillemette would only let them have one each. She counted out the others, together with some apples and a jug of water. "We've got to ration ourselves till we see what our situation is," she said. "You never know. We could be out here for hours." She didn't say "days" but she thought it.

"We're bound to meet up with a fishing boat or something sooner or later," Earl said, munching on his sandwich. "I wish this boat had a radio. We never thought of that, did we?"

"Never thought we'd need one."

"Not to worry."

Three hours later the sun had climbed up into the sky and they started to feel its heat. Earl glanced up at it, anxiously.

"If we're stuck out here for any length of time we're soon going to get burned to a crisp." He climbed back to the rumble seat and returned with the tonneau cover. "Here! I think I might be able to fix this over the framework somehow so we can get some sort of shade."

They both worked at it and soon had a serviceable shelter. It was then they noticed that the bow of the boat had sunk a lot lower in the water.

"The seams may have got sprung, or something." Earl didn't know much about boats but he seemed to remember reading somewhere that clinker-built boats could let water in between the curving planks of wood that made up their hulls, especially after being battered in a storm for many hours.

"What can we do?" Guillemette asked.

"I have no idea."

Another hour and the water was up close to the top decking. Their compartment was once again awash and Earl gallantly bailed, but it seemed to be a losing battle.

"Try to start the engine again," Guillemette said. "If we could just get under way we might be able to keep the bow high enough up that it wouldn't let the water in."

"Worth a try."

Earl turned the key and pushed the button. The starter whirred half-heartedly. "Come on, baby!" he muttered. He let it up then tried again. And again.

"Sounds as though the battery's going."

"I know." His face was grim. He tried it in short bursts, but it was obvious the starter had no strength. "One more try then I'll let the battery rest," he said.

Once again it turned over then, suddenly and to their delight, the boat's big engine coughed. It didn't start but they threw their arms around each other.

"There's life in it yet!" Earl cried. "Come on, baby." He thumbed the button again. Again the motor coughed and almost started.

"Wait!" Guillemette cried. "Don't run the battery completely flat. It looks as though it'll start given half a chance. Let's let the battery sit for a minute or two and see if it can recover some pep. I know that's worked with my car before."

It was frustrating sitting there waiting. They watched the water lapping up over the nose of the boat and slowly advancing toward them. Finally Earl could wait no longer. He turned the key and thumbed the button.

The rest had helped the battery recover some of its energy. Though still far from its prime, it now gave the starter more of a push than the last time. Suddenly the engine roared; bursting into life. Earl threw his arms around Guillemette and gave her a kiss full on the mouth.

"Let's get the hell out of here!" he said. He advanced the throttle and the big Chris Craft started moving through the water once again. It still listed horribly to port and the bow didn't come up out of the water as much as they had hoped, but it was a little better and they both felt elated.

Guillemette pulled out the map from the side pocket, where it had remained safe from the storm. She spread it on the dash, to Earl's right, and studied it.

"Where d'you think we might be?" she asked. "Any guesses?"

"I'd say we have to be somewhere between the Bahamas and Cuba," he said. "Probably far more south and east than we'd planned. If we just head southwest by south I wouldn't mind betting we hit Cuba after all." He sounded almost cheery.

Guillemette hoped he was right and tried to feel as optimistic. But she had a bad feeling that she couldn't shake.

*

"We should have seen the coast by now, shouldn't we?" Earl was worried. It was past noon and they had been under way for over two hours. He looked at Guillemette. She stared out ahead of the boat and then back down at the map. She didn't say anything, but then it was the third time Earl had asked the question in the last half-hour.

He glanced at the bow of the Chris Craft. It was down on the waterline. He'd found that trying to gun the engine now drove the nose down into the water rather than up out of it, so they had to run at a quarter throttle. It was frustrating; the urge was to open it up wide and get somewhere . . . anywhere.

"There! Off to the right. Land, Earl! Land!"

Guillemette shouted excitedly and pointed. He screwed up his eyes and followed her extended arm. He couldn't see a thing but he trusted her. He turned the wheel slowly, so as not to swamp them, and gradually brought the

The Committee

boat around to a new heading. Then he saw it. Just the slightest smudge across the horizon but there was no mistaking it. Land. They were going to make it.

*

They were still more than 200 yards from the shore when the boat sank.

"Shit! I—I'm not very good in the water," Earl said. He splashed a lot but managed to stay afloat. Guillemette came alongside him and urged him toward the shore.

"It's not far," she said. "You can do it all right, Earl. If you like I'll try to pull you?"

"No. No, thanks. I'll manage." He gasped and kept getting a mouthful of water, but he floundered on. The shore didn't seem to be getting any closer and he was just about to give up when his feet touched bottom. "Oh, thank God!" Within minutes he was ashore, above the tide line, stretched out flat on the white sand and recovering his breath. The Haitian woman lay beside him.

"Well, that's a trip I wouldn't want to repeat," she said.

"Too bad about the boat." Earl sat up and looked back towards the water. "I would guess it was a classic. Shame."

"Do you think this is Cuba?" she asked.

"Has to be, doesn't it? Where else could it be?"

"I don't know, but wherever it is, we'd better get up in the trees there, away from the beach, before anyone spots us."

They got wearily to their feet and helped each other up the beach. Soon they were in the cool shade of the trees and pushing their way through the underbrush. Guillemette led the way.

The ground rose rapidly and soon they came out in a clearing and found they had been moving parallel with the beach. They were able to look down and see the waves breaking over a hundred feet below them.

"What's the area like around Nuevitas?" Earl asked. "High ground?"

Guillemette shook her head. "I don't think so. Besides, I can't believe we've been lucky enough to end up where we were aiming for. That would be too much to ask."

"I suppose you're right."

They moved on again. After a short distance they came to a narrow footpath winding through the trees.

"Might as well follow this," Earl said. "Has to lead somewhere. At least we may be able to find out where we are."

They moved along it cautiously. It twisted and turned so that they quickly lost all sense of direction. Earl was in the lead when they turned a corner and he came face to face with a scarecrow. At least, Earl took it to be a scarecrow. It was a life-size stick figure made out of tree branches; one stuck into the ground and another fastened across the first, like arms. On the "head" was an ancient black top hat. The figure had been clothed in a black frock coat and striped pants and, at its feet, there were three full bottles of rum together with a pair of black-rimmed spectacles and several bowls of meal.

"Baron Cimitère!" whispered Guillemette.

"What?"

"It is Gédé, otherwise known as Baron Cimitère, Baron Samedi, or Baron La-Croix."

"Quite a titled gent," Earl said, slowly walking around the figure and studying it. "Who is he?"

"He is a Voudoun *loa;* the god of the dead." She spoke in a hushed voice as she too walked around the figure. "In Haiti you will find such figures along the trails up in the hills. They are put there in case Gédé himself should happen to come along that way. Then he will find all that he needs and be pleased. Hmm." She stood and pondered for a moment.

"What is it?"

Guillemette looked about her, a puzzled expression on her face. "I didn't know they did this in Cuba. I thought they were more into Santeria than the pure Voudoun." She started pacing up and down and seemed to get more and more excited.

"What? What is it, Guillemette?"

"Earl! Do you think we could have possibly got to Haiti? Could we have missed Cuba altogether and come to my homeland?"

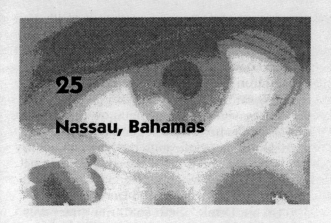

25

Nassau, Bahamas

"Explain to me a bit more about magic," asked Elizabeth. "All I know is rabbits out of hats and sawing the lady in half."

Duncan smiled. "Yes, there is that. Though if you want to get technical that's strictly prestidigitation."

"It's what?"

"Stage magic. Illusion; sleight of hand. But true magic is just that—magic. It's *making* something happen that you want to happen. A religious person might call it a miracle, though I've never believed in miracles myself. They're more like something happening even without you necessarily wishing for it. Very few and far between, I think."

"But magic isn't 'few and far between'?" Beth wrinkled her brow.

"Not at all. With some people it's almost an everyday occurrence. Certainly the old 'Wise

Ones' of the Middle Ages practiced it all the time. Most of their stuff could be explained away, today, as herbal workings or psychological reaction to suggestion. But there was still an awful lot that even today is inexplicable."

They sat together on a wicker loveseat suspended beneath, and swinging from, an old tree in Guillemette's back garden. Rudolf was in the house going through the herb cabinet in the Voudoun room and assembling what he termed "an emergency magic kit"; which had prompted Beth's question to Duncan.

"Go on, Dunk," Beth said. Her green eyes were big as they searched his face. Looking at her long, golden eyelashes, he thought how beautiful she was and found it hard to concentrate on his answers to her questions.

"The basis of most low magic is simply desire. If you desire something strongly enough you can bring it about."

"*Low* magic? As opposed to 'high' magic?"

"Uhuh." He was still looking at her lashes. "I'll tell you about high magic later. It can be very complicated—and dangerous. Low magic was simply the magic of the ordinary people; the common people, if you like. It had no connection with evil or devil-worship or anything like that. It was very positive and good. And, as I said, it was based on strong desire."

"You mean like the power of positive thinking?"

"Exactly! Yes. That's just what most so-called magic is. You want something so badly that it happens. I certainly believe that we all create our own realities and this is a part of that."

"But what about spells and charms, and bubbling cauldrons, Dunk?" She giggled; a delightful bubbly sound that made his heart skip a beat. He slid an arm along the back of the seat, as casually as he could.

"Most of that belongs to bad novels, late night movies on television, and good old Shakespeare," he said. "But, as with a lot of the stuff we connect with magic, there is a basis of fact behind the nonsense. For instance," he edged a little closer to her. "In order to get the concentration you need, to channel your energies into making things happen, it can help to chant something short and rhythmic."

"A chant? You mean like a spell?"

"If you like, yes. It's really just something to help you focus your attention. It doesn't have to be 'double, double, toil and trouble', it can just be one word repeated over and over again."

"Like 'love'?" Her face was close to him and he was captivated by her lips.

"Yes," he said. "Like 'love'. Just like love." He leaned forward slightly and their lips met. His arm came about her and drew her toward him. She came willingly. The kiss was long. When they finally drew apart neither of them was able to focus on where they were or what they were doing. They sat for a long moment, silent, catching their breath. Finally Beth again gave one of her soft giggles.

"Now, that was magic!" she said.

"*Bitte!* You two!" It was Rudolf calling from the house. "*Kommen sei.* We must plan what we are to do, *Nein?*"

With a sigh, Duncan got up and, taking Beth's hand, they went into the house.

The big map was spread out on the table and Rudolf was using a strip of cardboard to measure off lengths and then gauge them against the map's scale at the bottom of the sheet.

"Elizabeth, *meine liebeling,* you must try to make contact with the others. Let us try to pinpoint their position so that we will know how to proceed."

"We know they made land," Duncan said. "That was the last thing you got, Beth, wasn't it?"

"Yes." She nodded then sat down, closed her eyes, and tried to relax and make contact with either Earl or Guillemette. She found that she could connect with Guillemette only if Guillemette was also trying to contact her, but she could frequently pickup on Earl even when he was thinking of something else. For a long moment she sat and concentrated.

"For some reason I'm getting a man in a tall black hat and a black coat," she said, mystified. "It's very strange."

The two men remained silent, knowing that she worked better when she was not pressured for details.

"Ah!" She nodded her head and smiled. Her eyes remained closed. "It's Earl."

"What? Wearing a top hat and tails?" Duncan couldn't help himself.

"No, Dunk," Elizabeth said gently, and smiled again. Her eyes remained closed. "It's Earl I'm picking up on. He's been surprised, I think, by this figure, whatever it is."

"Would you describe it again, in as much detail as you are able?" Rudolf asked. She did so. "Aha! Yes, I think it is a representation of the Voudoun deity Gédé. *Ja*, that would surprise our young friend all right." He chuckled.

"What else, Beth?" Duncan asked.

She sat quietly for a long time before responding. "They've come out of a woods and are going downhill. There's a village ahead of them. Earl is walking behind Guillemette. She's breaking into a run. I feel happiness from her. Yes! Yes, she's very happy. She is running and Earl is puffing along after her. Now there's a group of people surrounding them. All black. They are all talking at once; I can't make anything out . . . Wait a minute . . . Yes! Guillemette is talking in French, I think. Something like it. Creole? My god! They're in Haiti!"

Beth's eyes popped open and she looked from one to the other of the two men.

*

"You need a submarine?" Bill Highland's voice remained calm but Duncan could easily detect the perplexity behind the question.

"To drop me off, yes, Bill. Just as soon as possible. And the Goodyear Inflataplane."

There was a long silence on the other end of the phone.

"Bill?"

"Yes, Dunk. Don't worry, I'm still here. You said the Goodyear Inflataplane?"

"Is there an echo on this line, Bill?" Duncan chuckled.

The Senator laughed. "You're right, Dunk. I said anything I could get for you I would. And I meant it. As a matter of fact there's a sub off the Florida Keys right now, I can use. But just tell me one thing—what the hell's an Inflataplane?"

"It was developed in the late 1940s and first flew in 1952. The first one was the GA-33, but I want the later development, the GA-447. I'm pretty sure the Smithsonian has it—possibly out at Silver Hill—but it may be that Goodyear themselves have it tucked away somewhere."

"The Smithsonian, you say? Or Goodyear?"

"There's that echo again."

"Seriously, Dunk, what is an Inflataplane?"

"Believe it or not it's an airplane that folds up into a small package about three feet by three feet by three. You inflate it with carbon dioxide into a full-size, single-seat airplane that flies just beautifully."

"You're kidding!"

Nassau, Bahamas

Duncan laughed. "No, Bill. I'm deadly serious. It was designed for the Army and the Navy, with the idea that it could be taken into enemy territory, or even dropped in by 'chute, and then pumped up to get someone out. Oh, by the way, it had a unicycle wheel with outriggers but was also done with a hydroskid landing gear. See if you can get the hydroskid, would you?"

"Sure. Sure. If I can get it I'll have a helicopter take it out to the sub pronto. Er, Dunk? Where are you going with this thing? Where do you want the sub to drop you off?"

"Cuba, Bill."

26

Haiti/Cuba

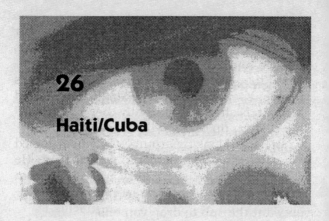

It was mid-morning when Earl awoke. For a moment he didn't know where he was. The rays of the sun poked through a small doorway to his left and slanted across the rough bed on which he was lying. A glint of sunlight through the walls and roof brought the realization that he was in a straw hut of some sort. He groped around, found his glasses and put them on. He turned his head and looked around.

"So you're awake." It was Guillemette's voice.

He turned his head the other way to find her sitting on the side of a similar cot to the one on which he was lying.

"Hi!" he said. "Yes, I'm awake. What time is it?"

"Time we were up and about," she said. "We must have slept all of twelve hours. Come on. Let's get something to eat."

He rolled off the low bed and followed her out the door, running his fingers through his tangled hair and beard as he went. He remembered they were in Haiti, among Guillemette's people, somewhere near a small town called Môle St. Nicholas. Apparently they had missed the eastern tip of Cuba by about fifty miles.

He stood looking around while he polished his glasses as best he could on his shirt. He felt grubby and wished there was a bathroom nearby, but he couldn't see anything resembling one and hesitated to ask Guillemette.

It wasn't exactly a village they were in; there were only a half dozen huts, scattered at wide intervals. Each had a small patch of land nearby that was being carefully nurtured. The looming edge of the forest threatened to engulf everything. There were few people about; an old, incredibly wrinkled, man sat outside the nearest hut, gazing off into space and muttering constantly to himself. A woman, almost as old as the man, stood in the middle of a patch of ground, scraping at it with a wooden hoe. She smoked a pipe and seemed unconcerned that the smoke from it blew back in her face all the time. On a nearby footpath a young, barefoot, girl of about twelve moved smoothly along with a large galvanized bucket balanced on her head and a live, flapping, chicken held by its legs dangling from each of her hands.

Guillemette explained that most of the people had long since left on the long trek to take their goods into market in nearby Port-de-Paix. No one had transportation here. Baskets, clay jugs, tin cans, piles of farm produce; all were piled up and balanced on the heads of the women, who would trudge for hours to get to a market where they might be able to make a dollar or two, if they were lucky.

Guillemette pulled a pot off an open fire and poured something from it into two wooden bowls. She brought one to Earl and took the other herself.

"What is it?" He sniffed, cautiously. It smelled a little like oatmeal but with another, tangy, aroma mixed in that he couldn't place.

"Don't ask," she replied and started eating, pushing the food straight from the bowl into her mouth with her fingers.

Earl did the same. He was pleasantly surprised; the alien concoction was delicious. He finished what he had, licked his fingers, and asked for more. With a smile, Guillemette gave him some.

"The others know we're safe," she said, when they finally sat back. "I guess Beth picked up on us. Anyway, they know we're here in Haiti and I assume they'll get on with things from their end."

"While we do what?" He didn't ask how she knew what she'd just related.

"Ah!" She smiled her all-knowing smile. It was one he was coming to know well and he wasn't sure if he liked it or not.

"You have ideas?"

"Oh, yes. You'll see."

"Can we get to Cuba from here?" he asked.

"We can — if we need to." She took the now empty food bowls and squatted down. Dipping them into the broken earth, she half filled them with the soil and swirled it around, rubbing with her fingers. She emptied it out then repeated the process. Finally she took a large leaf and wiped them out. They looked spotless.

"Since they know where we are I'd guess they're going to go ahead with alternate plans," she said as she worked. "So I suggest we attack from a different angle; from here, in fact."

"Attack from here?" Earl was puzzled. "I'm not sure I follow you."

She stood up. "You soon will. Come on. I'm going to introduce you to Voudoun."

They left the huts and walked along the path the girl with the two chickens had taken. Soon it divided and Guillemette took the right hand fork, which climbed up into the trees. In a short time they came out in a big clearing containing two large huts, three smaller ones, and a big, circular structure comprised of a wall-less, thatched roof held up by poles. There were two or three rows of crude benches set around the outer edge of this, something like an auditorium, Earl thought. A large pole held up the center of the roof and around this was grouped a pile of rocks on which stood a number of half-burned candles.

"What's that?" Earl asked, indicating the roofed area.

"That's a *peristyle*. You'll see. We're at a *hounfor* right now; that's this whole area, with all the buildings."

"Okay! And what's a *hounfor?*"

"It's a sort of Voudoun church. The big house on the left is where the Mambo and Houngan live — they're the priestess and priest. The other big building is where the *kanzo* stay."

"*Kanzo?*"

"People who're in training. Initiates, I guess you'd call them." She moved forward and Earl followed. She pointed to a small tree with an old tin bathtub sunk into the ground beside it. "This is for Damballah. He's the serpent *loá*. And over there, that's Erzulie's house." She indicated a small hut. Earl squinted through the door and saw a large brass bedstead inside, together with an elaborate dressing table, covered with bottles and boxes of make-up, and an open closet filled with dresses of every color imaginable.

"She must be quite a lady," he said.

"Oh, she is." Guillemette gave him a big grin.

"*Bonjour.* You must be Guillemette?"

They turned to see a tall, portly woman dressed all in white standing looking at them. Her eyes were deep and penetrating, but not unkind. Earl hadn't heard her come up behind them. He saw that she wore a white turbanlike headdress and a white dress. She had long strings of brightly colored beads strung across her body from each shoulder to the opposite hip, forming a cross. She carried a bottle of rum.

Guillemette bobbed a brief curtsey and then hugged the woman. They spoke together in what Earl took to be French. Guillemette finally indicated Earl and the woman came to him and put out her arms to briefly squeeze his shoulders.

"Welcome," she said.

"Thank you." He wasn't quite sure what to say and looked to Guillemette.

"This is my sister, Mambo Jannica," she said.

"Your sister?"

"Not literally, Earl. She is a mambo, as am I."

Earl didn't know what Guillemette meant but kept silent. Guillemette continued.

"We are going to be doing some work in the peristyle later on so you can take a break if you like and wash up." She pointed towards the largest hut. "There is some water inside and even some soap, I'm sure you'll be happy to hear. Give yourself a bath, Earl, and I'll bring you some clean clothes to put on. Okay?"

He nodded. The idea of a bath, albeit just a sponge bath, really appealed to him. He smiled at the tall mambo woman and hurried over to the hut.

The Committee

*

Nine people sat around a large wooden table in the center of the room, their eyes closed, their breathing shallow. Humberto Gavilla stood silently in the doorway watching them. His gaze moved slowly around, from one to another. He seemed satisfied. On the table in front of each person was a large, glossy, photograph of a United States Key Hole KH-14c surveillance satellite, the satellite that hung silently in space 22,500 miles above the Republic of Cuba. The photographs had been provided by General Nathan Wellesley.

Once in a while one or other of the people at the table would open their eyes to glance briefly at the photograph; to refocus their energies on the target.

After a while a muted chime sounded just outside the door to the room and, with sighs, the group around the table relaxed. Some rubbed their eyes, others stretched as though from a long sleep, many did quick neck- and shoulder-stretching exercises. Then, in orderly fashion, they got up from the table and filed out of the room, leaving the photographs on the table.

Almost immediately nine other people quietly filed in and sat down to take the vacated places. Among them was Alexis Militsa. The new group took a moment to take some deep breaths. They looked down at the photographs and studied them, then, closing their eyes, settled down to direct their energies.

Humberto remained standing for a minute or two then slipped soundlessly from the room.

"Think they're having any effect?" Nathan Wellesley asked Humberto as the Cuban came into the smaller adjoining room.

"Agh! I don't know. We must assume they are. They are the best in the world, I'll give our Russian friend that. My own Cuban people are supplementing them, yes, and they are good. Believe me they are good. But I have to concede that the Russians are better." He sat down and pulled out his pack of Popular cigarettes. He took out the last one in it and put it in his mouth, crushing the empty pack and tossing it into a corner of the room.

"Time marches on," Wellesley said. "Think we'll do it in time?"

Humberto smiled wryly. "That's the question we dare not ask," he said.

*

Guillemette stood proudly beside the altar. She could see Earl, who was dressed as she was, all in white, looking slightly uncomfortable as he perched on the edge of one of the front row benches and tried to take in all that was happening.

To her left, in an area between the benches, the three drummers and the *ogantier* were pounding out a powerful, hypnotic rhythm. They were dressed in colored shirts and blue jeans, two of them with kerchiefs about their necks. All were barefoot. The man with the big *maman* drum had it lying on its side and sat astride it, beating its goatskin head with both hands in rapid staccato fashion. Beside him was the man with the *seconde,* or *papa;* a slightly smaller drum which he kept upright and beat with two short sticks. Then came the *boula,* the smallest drum, beaten with bare hands. From the far side came the rhythmic "Chink! Chink!" of the *ogan,* a flattened piece of metal that was hit with an iron spike. Together the ensemble produced an exotic pattern of beats and counter-beats that could sway the emotions of the worshippers at a Voudoun rite and bring on the state of *ekstasis* that enabled the loá to come through and ride their followers like horses.

The villagers from miles around gathered regularly on a Friday evening, all dressed in their best, and filled the seats about the central area. But there was no general gathering of worshippers there that afternoon. This was a private rite. For now there was just Guillemette, Earl, the mambo Jannica and her houngan, the drummers, and half a dozen of the *hounsi.*

The *hounsi* were also dressed in white and followed the mambo in a processional dance around the inner circle of the *peristyle.* The houngan, or priest, stood in front of the central stone altar, the candles on it now all alight. He was a thin, wiry man, half the size of Jannica, his skin so dark it was almost black. He was dressed in a blue shirt and blue jeans. He had a straw hat on his head and a bright red kerchief tied around his neck. Like the others he was barefoot. In his right hand he carried a gourd rattle, decorated with colored beads and snake vertebrae. From its handle hung a small silver bell. He shook the rattle and chanted in a strange language as he moved around in a tight circle, with the steps of a complex dance. In his left hand he held a bottle of rum. At intervals he would take a mouthful of the liquid and spray it out onto the ground around the altar.

Guillemette smiled and nodded her head in approval. She had never met these people before but they were joined in the brother/sisterhood of Voudoun. They recognized her as a mambo in her own right and were happy to put their hounfor and its drummers at her disposal and to work with her.

Memories came flooding back and she wiped a tear from her eye. She had been too long away from Haiti and missed the moving rituals of her native chthonic religion. She watched as the mambo moved to the four corners and poured libations from a wooden bowl then came to the center post, the *poteaumitan*, and bowed low. Guillemette moved to stand beside Jannica and the two knelt facing the altar and started a lilting litany.

> *Papa Legba, Papa Legba,*
> *open wide the gate!*
> *Papa Legba, Papa Legba,*
> *open wide the gate!*

The Committee

Papa Legba we are here.
Open up the gate to let us pass.
Open up the gate for we are here.
Papa Legba, open wide the gate
  so that we can pass!

They repeated it over and over. The *hounsi* joined in as, led by the houngan, they continued dancing around the kneeling figures.

Finally they all quieted and the houngan picked up a bowl of meal from the altar and brought it to Guillemette. She took it and stood. Everyone moved back from the altar and was still. The drummers were silent.

Guillemette closed her eyes for a moment and felt all the old emotion and affection return. She remembered her training as a *hounsi-kanzo;* how her mother, the mambo, had seemed to be especially hard on her, just because she was the daughter of a mambo. She remembered the time of *couché;* the "putting to bed", as it was called. The twelve initiates—all in their early teens; all at puberty—living for thirty days in the close confines of the small grass hut. They had been stripped and all bodily hair had been removed from them. For nine days they had lain in the hut, on their left side, saying nothing and eating only food that was white. Each evening they had joined the mambo in prayers. As *hounsi-kanzo* they were later dressed in red. Only when they completed their training, and took the initiation, did they become true *hounsi,* or "spouses of the gods," and wear white. She remembered her lessons. She also remembered the time, many years later, when she too became a mambo and learned "the secret of the *asson*." How proud her mother had been.

Guillemette took the bowl and moved forward to draw the *vévé* before the altar. She moved swiftly, letting the meal fall from her fingers to trace an intricate pattern on the ground. At times her eyes closed but the *loá* guided her hand, completing a design that was several feet across. She was conscious of a soft murmur of approval from mambo Jannica, whose eagle eyes had followed her every move, and she felt good.

Then the drummers started up again. They began low and the beat was slow but, as Guillemette signaled to them, they gradually speeded up the pace getting louder and louder. As they played, the celebrants began once more to dance, all but the priests letting the music take hold of them and sway them around and around. Gradually the figures abandoned themselves to the power; faster and faster they moved, tracing enigmatic patterns with their feet across the *vévé*, treading the cornmeal into the ground.

Earl gave a start as one of the hounsi dancers suddenly let out a yell and fell to the ground. For a moment he didn't know what had happened. He watched as the woman, still screaming, rolled from side to side of the peristyle, then slowly stilled and lay there moaning. No one else seemed surprised. The houngan went to the woman and stood astride her, looking down at her. He shook his rattle and spoke to her in the language he had used at the start of the ritual. From the woman's lips came a reply in another voice; Earl could have sworn it was a man's voice. The two of them spoke back and forth for a few moments then the priest stepped away and the woman got unsteadily to her feet and stood stretching upwards, straight and tall.

Her eyes were closed but she turned her head as though looking back and forth at those all around her. Then she spoke in a loud voice, and it was that of a man. The mambo came forward and offered the woman an old military saber that had been leaning against the rocks of the altar. The woman took it and, stepping back, twirled it about her head. Her eyes opened and she smiled, a big grin which showed her teeth. "*C'est bon!*" she said, in the deep male voice. "It is good!"

Then Guillemette came forward and offered a bottle of rum to the woman. Earl could see that the bottle seemed to be nearly half full, but the woman stuck the end in her mouth, tipped it up and quickly drained it. Giving the empty bottle back to Guillemette, she wiped her mouth with the back of her hand and smiled even more.

"Father Ogoun," Guillemette said. "I have called you here for a very special purpose."

"I know that, child," the woman/loá replied. "It is about these plotters and workers on our neighbor island of Cuba, is it not?"

Earl was amazed. How could this simple peasant woman know about the Cuban group? He saw that even Guillemette seemed surprised.

"Why, yes! Yes, father. It is."

"What would you have me do, child?"

Guillemette recovered herself quickly. "They must be stopped," she said. "The magic they do is not good. I would delay them. I would interfere with what they are trying to do. They must not be allowed to succeed."

"Must not?"

"Must not!" Guillemette was firm as she repeated it.

Earl had heard of Voudoun worshippers being "ridden," as they called it, by their gods, the loá. Indeed they looked upon themselves as horses for their gods. To Earl it was still basically a form of channeling. Certainly looking at it as that made it easier for him to accept.

The woman/channel/loá threw back her head and laughed. The saber was once again raised and swirled in the air over Guillemette's head. Then came the words: "You will pay me, Guillemette!" and the woman dropped the saber and fell to the floor. Two of the other *hounsi* rushed across and dragged their colleague off to one side. She was left propped up against one of the benches, to recover at her leisure. The saber was replaced by the altar. Meanwhile the *hounsi*, Mambo, Houngan, and Guillemette threw themselves back into the dance as the drummers struck up again with a loud and stirring beat.

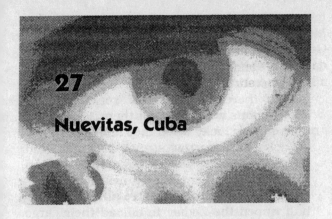

27

Nuevitas, Cuba

There were still almost two hours to go before dawn when the 18,700 ton Ohio class SSBN submarine USS *John C. Calhoun* stopped all engines and stood by in the Old Bahama Channel off the northeast coast of Cuba. In silence a small detail of men helped launch a 16-foot Zodiac rubber boat. It contained two men, together with a cargo of what looked like a large pile of folded sheets of rubberized canvas. One of the men gave a wave as the Zodiac cleared the hull.

The submarine's petty officer, Sloane Schreiber, kept the small boat's 60 hp engine throttled back, for quiet. Duncan hadn't wanted to use the motor at all but they were afraid they might not be able to row in with the load since the tide was on the turn. Duncan glanced up. He was glad of the overcast sky, making for near total darkness, but at the same time wished he could see where they were going.

It didn't take long for them to spot a thin line of phosphorescence ahead, where the waves were breaking on the shore. Duncan prayed there'd be no great rocks or other obstructions when they got there. He counted himself very lucky when they finally grounded on a smooth, narrow stretch of white sand. Quickly Schreiber jumped out of the craft and, with Duncan's help, they pulled it up as far out of the water as they were able. Then they half tipped the Zodiac to offload their cargo. Despite its weight, the mound of rubber moved fairly easily, sliding over the ground without too much trouble. Duncan and the Petty Officer managed to maneuver it up and under a line of mango trees and wild bushes. Since the rubberized fabric was black it was difficult, in the poor light, to tell how good a job they'd done of hiding it but they felt fairly confident it wouldn't be spotted unless that particular stretch of beach was well populated. And that Duncan doubted, since it was nowhere near a resort and, other than the abandoned villa that was his objective, there were no houses nearby.

Sloane Schreiber pushed the Zodiac back down into the water and, with a wave of his hand and a whispered "Good luck!" was quickly on his way back to the submarine. Within minutes the USS *John C. Calhoun* was once more under way.

Nuevitas, Cuba

Dressed in a black turtleneck and black pants, Duncan was feeling a little like James Bond, and consequently slightly ridiculous. He thought of Beth's parting comment: "Black is really not a good color for you, Dunk. You look so much better in pastels." He chuckled to himself. "Keep in touch," she had said. "Just focus your thoughts on me and I'll try to tune in to you." Well there was no problem there. His thoughts were forever focusing on her.

He moved along the shoreline, keeping close in to where the vegetation came down to the sand. Rudolf had tried to give him as many landmarks as possible, that he'd made note of on his astral journeys. Duncan felt confident he'd know when he came level with the old villa.

He came to a group of five tall royal palm trees that he could just make out silhouetted against the slowly lightening sky. He stopped and looked to his left. Yes, a little way back, about a hundred feet behind the first group, was a second clump of three slightly shorter palms. This was the spot. Taking a deep breath Duncan moved in off the beach, pushing as quietly as possible through the underbrush. The land rose sharply, about twenty feet, and then he came to an old picket fence. It probably marked the end of the villa's garden, Duncan thought. It was rotted and broken in places but he examined it carefully before clambering over it, in case there were any new wires attached, leading to warning devices at the house. He could see nothing.

He soon found himself in an overgrown grove of banana and plantain trees. He could smell jasmine and gardenias, which were everywhere, as were red, purple, and orange bougainvillaea, their vivid colors beginning to show as they caught the first rays of the rising sun.

Moving on, Duncan came onto a narrow, partly-cleared pathway and, following it, arrived at an old shed containing rusted garden tools. From there he could see the red roof of the villa itself. Duncan soon reached the dilapidated building. Then he came to a short flight of overgrown stone steps leading up to a terrace patio, with a broken stone balustrade around it. He didn't go up the steps but spent some time moving carefully along the front of the house, looking for lights in windows and listening for any sound of voices. There was neither.

He grew bolder and, moving up the steps, started peering through windows, but could make out nothing inside. By now the sun was starting to climb into the sky and he was becoming more concerned about being seen than about seeing. However he continued to look and listen and, drawing blanks, became bolder to the point of actually trying the doors that connected to the terrace.

Nuevitas, Cuba

The sliding glass door gave at Duncan's touch. He eased it open and slipped inside, scarcely daring to breath. As his eyes adjusted to the gloom he saw he was in one of the rooms he had visited when skrying. It was large but obviously long unused; dust was thick on everything. He moved through to an inner door and listened before easing it open. He was amazed to see the lightening sky.

The roof on this side of the house, and some of the other rooms along the passageway in which he found himself, was gone. Blackened fingers of wooden joists and rafters jutted out into the bare sky. Obviously there had been a fire and, judging from the smell, it had been a very recent one.

Half an hour later Duncan had determined that the villa was empty. He had found the cleaner rooms that had been used by the Russians and the Cubans, but they had all gone. The fire must have started in the kitchen, he decided, and spread to the adjoining two or three rooms before, somehow, it had been extinguished. Strangely it seemed not to have consumed the whole house. Frustrated, Duncan brushed off a chair and sat down in the blackened dining room and focused his thoughts on Elizabeth. Mentally he tried to let her know what the situation was. The enemy had gone and he had no idea where. But he wouldn't give up. He'd try his best to track them down.

The Committee

Duncan thought of astral projection. That would seem to be the easiest way to find them and it had certainly worked before. But he acknowledged to himself that he was not an expert at it and that, even if he were, it would be extremely dangerous to try it, especially right here in the enemy's camp, as he was sure Rudolf would have been quick to point out. So how else could he trace them?

He didn't know whether Beth sent the thought to him or whether he'd come upon it himself but suddenly, "out of the blue" it seemed, he thought of using a pendulum. The practice was known, in the field of parapsychology, as *radiesthesia* and had been found to be a very useful tool, not only to focus in on the subconscious but even to tap into the unknown. Duncan's own beliefs included the thought that there was indeed some sort of "collective unconscious," as espoused by people like Carl Jung, and that therefore the pendulum was tapping that, rather than any "unknown" as such.

He looked around for something he could use but could see nothing appropriate. Again he seemed to get inspiration from outside himself. He wore a fine gold chain around his neck, from which hung a nineteenth century British gold sovereign. It was his only concession to personal jewelry and he always wore it;

a gift from a very dear English friend. He pulled it out from under the turtleneck and slipped it off over his head. Holding the chain so that about six inches of it hung down with the weight of the sovereign on the end, he rested his elbow on the table and let it swing just off the surface. It finally settled down to become stationary.

Duncan cleared his mind and then concentrated on a question. He wanted to start with a question to which he knew the answer, to check the swing of the pendulum. He thought hard on the day of the week, thinking: "Is today Wednesday?" He had a momentary feeling of panic when he wasn't sure if it indeed *was* Wednesday, then remembered that it was. As he concentrated on the question, the sovereign started to swing gently to and fro, toward him and away from him. The swing increased until it was very definite. He stopped it and started from a stationary position again. Glancing up at the clear sky, now bright with sunlight, he concentrated on the question "Is it raining?" Immediately the sovereign swung across his body in wide sweeps, from left to right and back. "Good," he thought. Now he had established that a swing toward him and away again meant "Yes" and a swing across meant "No."

Duncan's next step was to draw a map. He looked around but could find no paper so, sitting once again at the table, he took a nail he had found jutting from one of the burned timbers and scratched on the surface of the charred tabletop. He scratched a rectangle to represent the house, crosses to represent the two groups of palm trees, and wavy lines to represent the oceanfront. Then, with the forefinger of his left hand pointing at the house symbol, he let the sovereign-pendulum hang down from his right hand, over the table top to the right of the crude map.

"Did they move out of here toward the ocean?" Duncan asked, out loud. He understood that it would work to just think his questions silently but somehow he felt it created a more positive effect to actually put them into words. He felt slightly silly, sitting there talking to himself, but soon lost all embarrassment as he became absorbed in the answers he received. He moved his left-hand finger down toward the wavy lines.

The pendulum started swinging from side to side.

"No," he muttered, and returned his left finger to the house rectangle. "Okay. Did they move off this way?" he moved his finger directly up on the map, away from the beach. The sovereign continued its swing from left to right and back.

"Hmm. Okay. How about this way? Did they go off this way?" He moved his finger back to the house and then traced a line off at a 45° angle to the left. The sovereign slowed and gradually turned to swing now towards him and away from him.

"Great! Okay." He stopped the swing so that it once more hung still. "Now, how far in that direction did they go? Less than a mile?" By continuing to ask he quickly established that the enemy had moved off and that they were now ensconced at a point approximately two and a half miles away, in the direction he had indicated. With a silent word of thanks to Reg Lee, the old English Gypsy who had given him the sovereign, Duncan put it back around his neck and set off after his prey.

*

It looked like an old church. Duncan knew that Cuba was officially atheistic, with Castro's regime expelling bishops and consistently downgrading the Christian tradition. What was called a Liberation theology had been established. This church, then, had probably long since been closed and abandoned. It must be just outside the town of Nuevitas, Duncan decided.

He crept up to the outside and listened. He heard no sounds from inside but, from the three or four Jeeps parked nearby, he knew he was at the right place. He moved a little closer to the doorway.

"Are you looking for me, Comrade?"

The Committee

Duncan spun around to find himself face to face with a fair-haired man with close-cropped hair, wearing an army-camouflage fatigue shirt and pants and pointing a Soviet Makarov PM 9mm pistol at his chest.

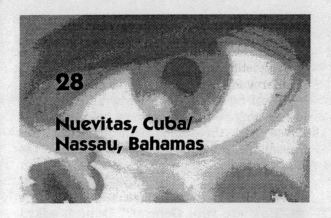

28

Nuevitas, Cuba/ Nassau, Bahamas

"You are an accomplished author, Mr. Webster."

"Thank you."

"*Da.* I have read some of your books. You write well."

Duncan gave up trying to loosen the ropes that tied him to the chair and looked around at the empty shell of a church in which he was held captive. Since the windows had been boarded up, the only light inside came from an oil lantern which stood on the floor not far from where he was sitting. They must have brought it with them from the villa, he thought. Three or four of the few pews still in the building had been pulled around to form a circle in the center of the floor space. About a dozen people were sitting on them, eyes closed, as though meditating. Over on the far side, on a slightly raised dais where the altar used to be, another group of people were sitting on the floor, leaning back against the wall, or lying on blankets spread on the floor.

The Cuban Duncan recognized as Humberto sat by the open doorway on one of the few unbroken chairs. He now held the pistol Alexis had threatened Duncan with. The Russian sat on an upturned box in front of his captive. Behind him stood General Nathan Wellesley, looking thin and a little haggard, and decidedly uncomfortable.

"How are you, General?" Duncan asked the older man, ignoring the Russian. "Enjoying the life of a traitor?"

Wellesley's eyes flashed momentarily, then dulled again, and his gaze dropped to the floor. Wordlessly he turned on his heel and walked over to Humberto, to stand beside him gazing out of the door.

"Nice touch." Alexis nodded and smiled.

"I don't know how the man lives with himself," Duncan said. "I could never betray my country."

"Perhaps you have never been in the position in which the General found himself." Alexis got up and stretched. "No matter. You have other things to worry about, I think."

"Yes!" Duncan snapped, hotly. "Like how to stop you and your band from moving the satellite. Why d'you want to do that anyway?"

"Let's just say it's as a favor to a friend." The Russian chuckled, then became suddenly serious. He moved close to Duncan and bent down to put his face close. Duncan could smell garlic on his breath. "Were you the one responsible for the fire?"

"What?"

"Don't play the innocent! Was it you who started the fire back down the road at the old villa?"

"No! Of course not. I wasn't even here then," Duncan protested. Then he bit his tongue. He shouldn't have admitted to being anywhere or doing anything. Nothing that might help these people.

"So!" The Russian stepped back a pace and stood looking down at Duncan, his arms crossed and his face thoughtful. "It would seem, then, that either our friends in the Bahamas were responsible or our other friends over the way in Haiti. Oh, yes!" He caught the look on Duncan's face. "Yes, we know they're there. They were not supposed to survive that storm I conjured up but, somehow, they did."

"What d'you mean?" Duncan asked. "That you conjured up?"

The Russian chuckled again. "Oh, you don't know what you have taken on, Mr. Webster. Something much more than you have ever written about, I fancy. I wish you were a more worthy opponent, I might have some fun. Now your Comrade Rudolf Küstermeyer, for example. How come he is not here rather than you? Oh! Don't tell me . . . he is more able to work from a distance. Am I right? Of course. *Da!* Your Comrade Küstermeyer would be a much more worthy opponent."

Duncan had a sudden idea. His arms were bound tightly behind his back, the ropes passing through the slats of the back of the chair. His feet were tied together but they were not fastened to the chair. He knew he had to do something to break the working of the group in the middle of the floor. If fire had done the trick before, why not again?

Praying that he had judged his distances correctly, Duncan suddenly pushed down with his feet and tipped the chair back onto its two rear legs, then rocked it up onto just one. He pivoted on that leg to swing the chair around, then tipped it all the way over. As he crashed to the floor he struck out with his feet. They connected with the oil lamp and sent it bouncing across the floor, scattering flaming oil in all directions.

Alexis gave a curse and jumped over Duncan to run toward the dais. The group in the center of the room came to their feet. Some of the women screamed and, with the people from the other group, who had similarly come to their feet, they all ran for the door. But the Russian had run to sweep up one of the blankets from the floor then, with shouts to the others, started beating at the flames. Humberto and one of the other men rushed across, picked up blankets, and joined him. Quickly the fire was put out.

Nuevitas, Cuba/Nassau, Bahamas

Alexis was breathing heavily as he dragged Duncan's chair upright. He swung his hand and slapped his captive hard across the face. Duncan's head snapped to the side and tears came to his eyes.

"You fool!" Alexis hissed. "Don't you realize that if that fire had caught hold and burned this place, you would have burned with it? How did you expect to get out?"

Duncan bit his lip. He realized that he hadn't really thought that through. The Russian was right. Still, he'd accomplished his immediate objective; the group of PKers was no longer at work. They were milling around together outside the church entrance, talking very excitedly in Russian and Spanish. It would take a while before they had calmed enough to be able to once again concentrate sufficiently to do any of their work.

The Russian turned to General Wellesley, as the American sauntered up to them. "I didn't see you helping put out the fire!" he snapped.

"Er, why no. No, I saw you men had it under control." Wellesley glanced at Duncan briefly, then away again. "Don't get so upset, Alexis. Everything's fine again."

"No thanks to you! You know we have a deadline. We've got to get this job done by Friday noon."

They both turned away from Duncan and walked out of the church, leaving him alone with his thoughts.

The Committee

*

"But we have to know what's happened," Elizabeth cried. "I mean, *really* know."

Rudolf sighed. "You think I need to astrally project to Cuba and see exactly what the set-up is?"

She looked up at him, her big eyes wide. He found it hard to ignore the appeal in those eyes. He sighed again.

"It could be very dangerous," he said.

"I know." She looked away. "I'm not really asking you to, Rudy. I—I'm happy to leave it to you. You know what's best." She turned back to him and he saw the glint of tears. "It's just that I'm so worried about Dunk. I know they've got him. I know he's their prisoner. It's just not knowing if he's really all right; what they might have done to him."

He moved to sit beside her on the couch, in the living room of Guillemette's house. He put his arm around her and suddenly felt very paternal. He no longer had any children of his own. He had once had a daughter; she would have been a little older than Elizabeth today if she had lived. But the Nazis had taken care of her. Rudolf had been a journalist for *Der Welt* at the outbreak of the Second World War. He had spoken out against the Hitler regime. He had lost his job as Hitler gained control, but continued to write articles in underground newspapers, urging that the people overthrow the tyrant. Consequently he had been targeted by the Nazis from the outset. He and his whole family—father and mother, wife and daughter—had been thrown into a concentration camp. Only he had survived to the end of the war.

"I will do it," he said quietly. "I will project there and see just exactly what the situation is." He kissed her tenderly on the forehead. Beth broke into tears and clung to him. They sat for a while gently rocking back and forth.

*

Alexis Militsa was angry. Things were not going smoothly. What should have been an enjoyable excursion to Cuba, to lead his group in a simple PK exercise, had turned into an all-out psychic war. He hadn't been prepared for that. He felt rusty. With the turmoil of the last few years, leading to the breakup of the Soviet Union, his expertise had been called upon less and less. In many ways he was delighted to be able to expand into other occult areas again. But he would have liked more notice of the need so that he might have consulted some of his rare books, still on the shelves of his not inconsiderable personal library in Moscow. When this was over, he promised himself, he would go back home and put himself through an intense refresher course of magic.

He sat on a straight-backed chair on the dais in the old church. A fresh group of PKers had finally got settled in the pews and were once again trying to focus on their objective.

The Committee

The others were now outside the building, resting in the shade of the nearby silk-cotton trees and plantains. The lantern once more stood alight on the floor, though now on the edge of the dais where Alexis sat. The Russian listened. He could hear the raucous cry of seagulls occasionally flying overhead.

He had taken the young American writer outside as well, and tied him securely to a tree. Alexis admired the man in a way; for both his occult knowledge and his bravery in what he had tried to do. Bravery or foolishness? Sometimes there was a very thin line between the two, he reflected.

The Russian rubbed his arms at the slight chill and turned to see where the draught was coming from. Then he became suddenly alert. The window, high up in the wall behind the altar area, where once there had been stained glass, was fully boarded up. No cracks or chinks. Yet even if there had been cracks, Alexis knew that the chill would not have come from them. No, he recognized the drop in temperature as signifying psychic activity. Someone, or something, was nearby.

He mentally drew a ball of protective light about himself then tried to relax and place himself in a trance. He found he couldn't do it very well on the hard chair and quickly moved across to lay down on a pile of two or three blankets, laid out on the floor by the wall. He closed his eyes, mentally taking himself through the steps to drop his conscious mind into the unconscious.

As Alexis stepped from his body he immediately saw the German, though the man now looked young and vibrant. He had obviously given his astral body the form his physical had known in his prime. But what startled Alexis more than this was the fact that the German was dressed in the purple robes of a Third Degree Magister of the Right Hand Path; one of the highest degrees of the positive magical orders and an indication that he was extremely accomplished in the Arts.

Their eyes locked and Alexis felt an immediate shock, as though he had been touched by a small electrical charge. Mentally he repeated to himself a mantra he used to give himself extra energy on the astral. It was one he had not had to draw upon in some years but the words came quickly back to him.

"Yes," came the thoughts from the older man. "Draw upon your reserves. You will need them."

Alexis's studies had leaned more toward the Left Hand Path—manipulation of the forces of evil, rather than the positive forces of good. His was a different order from the German's and, as though to flaunt his own knowledge, he wrapped himself in the vivid magenta robes of an Arch Mage Master.

"So!" breathed the German. "We are well matched."

"It would seem that way," Alexis acknowledged.

Outside the church the relaxing group began to get restive. Some of them got to their feet and stood muttering to one another. Nathan Wellesley noticed it and got to his feet also. His Spanish was poor but he had picked up a little Russian in his time in Moscow. He caught snatches of conversations.

"What's happening, General?"

It was the prisoner tied to the tree who had spoken. Wellesley moved over to Duncan.

"I'm not sure." It felt good to be able to talk to a fellow American, but he avoided the younger man's eyes. "They're saying something about psychic cold spots and charged ions. Any idea what that means?"

Duncan nodded and smiled. "I think it means John Wayne and the U.S. Cavalry," he said.

Wellesley looked at him in surprise.

From the door of the church the Russians and Cubans who had been sitting in the pews started emerging. They looked back over their shoulders then moved over to join their friends. Humberto pulled the Makarov pistol from his belt and went to look in at the door. After a moment he came back to the group.

"What gives, Humberto?" Wellesley asked.

The Cuban shrugged. "I don't know. They're saying something about electric charges but there is no electricity in this old place. Alexis is in there sleeping so I'm not going to disturb him. What d'you think we should do?"

Wellesley glanced again at Duncan then back to the Cuban. "Wait, I guess. You know how Colonel Militsa is. If he's asleep he'll wake up soon, he never naps for long. I'm not going to make any decisions without him."

The Cuban grinned. "Shit! You're afraid of him, General."

"And you, Gavilla? I don't see you standing up to him too much."

"Ach!" Humberto shrugged his shoulders. "I like to let him think he's the boss. But, perhaps you're right. We'll wait until he finishes his nap." The Cuban went back to the tree trunk he had been sitting and leaning against, and eased himself back down to it. Wellesley spoke out of the side of his mouth to Duncan.

"You know, I don't have to make excuses to you, Webster. But there was good reason for what I did."

"You regret it now?" Duncan asked.

"You're damn right I do!" The General spoke forcibly, though keeping his voice down so that no one else could hear. "Right from the start I regretted it. But there are some things which, once started, can't be easily stopped."

Duncan nodded. "I can understand that."

The flame in the lantern, standing on the floor inside the church, flared up high. The air was heavy and seemed to fuel the flame. Around the figure apparently sleeping on the floor there was an occasional crackle and the dim spark of static electricity. Suddenly the lantern flame flared even higher and the glass mantle shattered. The flame went out. The church was in darkness but for the slant of sunlight that angled in from the doorway and the now brighter crackle of static around the sleeping figure.

On the astral plane the Russian slipped to one side as a lightning bolt zapped down on the spot where he had been standing. He immediately had to dodge again as, with a mighty roar, a flaming chariot pulled by six blazing sun-fire horses crashed down upon him, bright knife blades spinning from the wheel hubs. Then came the crash of a huge, felled tree, slamming down within inches of where Alexis stood. One after another the images smashed into his astral existence, causing him to leap and jump from one side to another until, even in his astral form, he felt exhausted.

Suddenly he stopped and took a deep breath. The forms faded away and he saw the German standing looking at him.

"Damn you!" Alexis snarled. "They were mere forces of your imagination! They couldn't actually harm me."

"But of course not," acknowledged Rudolf, with an inclination of his head. "You *are* rusty, my friend, are you not? You should certainly have remembered something as basic as that. You cannot be hurt simply by my imagination."

A huge eagle screamed down on Alexis, a hideous scream coming from its open beak; its talons flashing in the light. It took all Alexis's will power to ignore it and not duck out of the way. Just as the eagle was about to hit him it disappeared.

"That's better," Rudolf said. "You learn quickly."

*

Alexis came out of his trance covered in sweat. He felt icy cold and shivered, wrapping the blanket around himself. It was dark and he wondered what had happened to the lantern. He cursed the German magician. How long had they been battling on the astral; faking out each other and trying to gain an advantage? It had taken him a long time to realize that the old fool was playing him for an idiot. He was just wasting Alexis's time and using up his energy. And he'd done a good job of it.

He cursed himself. Why hadn't he kept in practice? How had he allowed himself to slip into such a state of unpreparedness? He should have known, when it took so much out of him to conjure up the storm, that he needed to work seriously at his psychic exercises. Why hadn't he? Well, he thought, the answer was really obvious. He was involved in this stupid Cuban enterprise. He should never have got entangled in it. He should have insisted it was beneath him. But too late now.

He got up and stumbled across toward the doorway. He cursed as he banged his shin on

The Committee

the end of one of the pews. Finally he stepped out into the sunlight.

"Humberto!" he shouted. He needed to take out his anger on someone. The Cuban was always a good target. "Humberto! Where the hell are you?"

Humberto jumped up, scraping his back on the tree and cursing. "What?" he yelled, facing anger with anger. "What you want, Alexis?"

The Russian stood glowering for a moment then snatched the Makarov pistol from the Cuban's waistband and stuck it in his own belt. He glared at the various members of the group, all getting to their feet. Suddenly his head snapped around. "What the . . . ?"

Humberto turned to look where Alexis was looking. The tree to which Duncan had been tied was empty. The ropes that had held him lay on the ground.

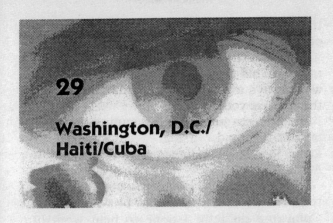

29

Washington, D.C./ Haiti/Cuba

"I understand the President is very concerned, Senator."

"And so am I." Bill Highland shifted the telephone to his other ear and noted some figures on a scratch pad. "Now, Koenig, with the shift you're seeing at the moment, how long before we lose track of Cuba altogether, supposing we can no longer correct the drift?"

"About twenty-four hours. There's just a tiny vent on the side of the KH-14c. When opened by remote it lets a small jet of hydrazine fuel escape, which nudges the satellite into position. It's just not powerful enough to compensate for what we've been seeing these last few hours, if this keeps up."

Charles Koenig sounded very concerned and the Senator could picture his face. Always something of a "worry-wort," as Highland had long ago dubbed him, Koenig was inclined to work himself into a state where his brow would be deeply furrowed, his hair thoroughly mussed, and his necktie pulled askew. But he was an excellent man to have working on any problem connected with computers or communications.

"I've got someone involved on another angle, which may stop the disturbance," Highland said. "I don't have immediate contact with him right now but I know he's working on this. I hope to hear from him soon."

"Well please let me know if and when you do hear from him, Senator," Koenig said. "And any suggestions he or you might have will be gratefully received."

Bill Highland hung up the phone and leaned back in his chair. Where the devil was Dunk, he wondered? The submarine had dropped him off with no problems, that he knew. But he was deep in what amounted to enemy territory, was unarmed, and his only means of escape was some weird rubber airplane! He shook his head. He doubted he would ever understand the boy.

*

Duncan lay on his back under a wild avocado tree, on a slope to the west of the church. He was watching the shadows lengthen as the sun sank down towards the far hills. He was not far from the old church. He didn't want to lose touch with the Russian group but definitely needed to stay out of their sight. He was still more than a little surprised at how Nathan Wellesley had loosened the knots of the ropes that had held him, so he was able to slip out of his bonds and escape. It seemed pretty certain, Duncan thought, that the General had been long regretting his act of defection and was now trying to make up for it in some small way.

As the sun started to disappear Duncan made up his mind what he had to do. The Committee was widely scattered and needed to get together for a conference. Very well, why not a "conference call," but on the astral rather than on the telephone? He chuckled to himself at the idea. It was risky he knew, but since Alexis didn't know exactly where he was, and was probably now busy reorganizing his own forces anyway, it seemed a safe bet to try for it.

Duncan sat up with his back as straight as he could. He closed his eyes and relaxed, taking deep breaths and then sending out thoughts to Guillemette saying "Astral conference, Bahamas; astral conference, Bahamas." In a very short time he felt a confirmation: his head started nodding of its own accord. It was as though he had suddenly decided to nod his head in agreement, yet he was not the one making it move. He gave a sigh of relief and then switched his aim to Rudolf. It took longer but eventually he got the same response; a gentle nodding of his head.

He lay flat on his back again and, once more taking deep breaths, filled his body with the protective light he envisioned coming up from the earth beneath him. It filled his whole body, then spread out around him until he was completely encased in an "egg" of psychic protection. Taking a few more deep breaths he went through a mental process of relaxing each and every part of his body, as Rudolf had taught him, and let his conscious mind drift down until he was in a medium trance.

Duncan's etheric double lifted up and out of his physical body to hover for a moment over the avocado bush. He gave a quick backward glance and then concentrated his thoughts on Guillemette's house in Nassau. He was immediately there.

Rudolf sat in a chair with Elizabeth in another chair opposite him. Guillemette and Earl were both already there, the Haitian woman looking solid and Earl appearing slightly transparent. Both were simulating sitting on the settee. Earl waved as Duncan arrived.

"Pull up a seat, Dunk—as if you need it! What a trip, eh?"

Duncan looked at Beth. She smiled. Her astral body was still sitting in her physical shell but, as Duncan arrived, she floated out and across to him and put her arms around him. Since they were both on the astral they could feel one another as well as if they had both been in the physical. He held her close and kissed her.

"I've been so worried about you, Dunk."

"Try not to, Beth. I'm all right. Honestly I am."

"Not to interrupt." It was Rudolf's voice. The two broke apart but kept hold of each other's hands. "Unfortunately we don't have much time. I think it will be well if we are as brief as needs be. We never know when our Russian or Cuban friends will come a'calling."

"Absolutely, Rudy," Duncan agreed.

Quickly they brought one another up to date with what had been happening. The others were intrigued by the happenings on Cuba.

"It was us who started the fire in the villa," Guillemette admitted. "I invoked Ogoun and he actually made it happen. I owe him a red chicken," she said aside to Earl. "Don't let me forget to give it to him."

"We seem to be doing well keeping them on their toes," Rudolf said. "Duncan, you took a chance with that lantern, but it certainly disrupted them. And then I was able to make some headway in distracting the Russian." He paused a moment before continuing. "He is a very dangerous young man, I must warn you all. That is one reason we must not be long here. He is very accomplished. I must admit that I had my hands full with him."

Duncan told them of General Wellesley's switch. They were all as surprised as he had been. "D'you think there's hope for him?" Earl asked.

Duncan nodded. "When I get back to reality I'll certainly let Bill know everything that happened. Meanwhile, I think he might turn out to be an ally. He could help a lot if we can cultivate him."

"So where do we go from here?" Guillemette asked. "Earl and I have got a handle on Haiti and can throw stuff at them from there, as we've shown. What's your next move, Dunk, my man?"

He shrugged. "I'm not certain yet. One thing I can tell you. They have a deadline. Whatever their reason for shifting the satellite, it seems they've got to get it done by about midday Friday, that's the day after tomorrow. A little over thirty-six hours from now. If we can just keep them disrupted till then, we'll have won."

"Sounds good," Earl said. "I think we can do it."

"I hope so."

Rudolf and Elizabeth nodded.

"Rudy," Duncan said. "Do me a favor and

give Bill Highland a call. Let him know what's happening, so far as you think he'll understand it. Thanks." He turned back to Guillemette and Earl. "Can you get a boat to get out of Haiti when the time comes?"

Guillemette nodded. "No problem."

"Good. Then when you do, meet me at Great Inagua—that island at the end of the Bahamian chain. I don't think the Inflataplane can get any further than that with the gas it carries."

Ten minutes later Duncan was back in his body and realizing just how hungry he was. He hadn't had anything to eat since that morning. He picked a couple of the wild avocados and ate them. It helped a little, but not a lot.

"Time to check on the enemy," he muttered to himself. He crept away and down the slope toward the derelict church.

When he got to the line of trees and bushes near the front of the building, Duncan saw that he was only just in time. The group was gathering together their few belongings and loading them in their Jeeps, preparing to leave.

"We'll go back to the villa," Alexis was saying. "At least there's food there. And those interfering busybodies may not guess what we've done. We don't have too much longer to work at the project. I think we can clean up enough space in one of the rooms the fire didn't touch so that we can get to it."

The Committee

That was enough for Duncan. He immediately made off himself, back toward the villa. If he got there far enough ahead of the Russians he could raid their supply cupboard and satisfy his own hunger. Then he could choose a good spot to hide.

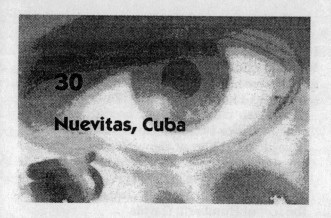

30

Nuevitas, Cuba

It was close to midnight when the Russians and Cubans came wearily into the half-burned house. Under Alexis's and Humberto's direction they cleaned off the dust on the table and some of the chairs in the large room that opened onto the terrace. Since there was no electricity in the house the food there was bread, biscuits, cheese, dried meats, fruit, nuts, and chocolate. There were also several bottles of water and cans of vegetable juice.

From his vantage point up in the crawl space over the ceiling, Duncan looked down on the PKers and, without knowing the language they spoke, knew they were not happy. He had brought some of their food and a bottle of water up into the roof with him and had enlarged a hole in the crumbling ceiling plaster so that he could keep a good eye on them and what they did. Right now, he thought, it looked as though they were all going to get some sleep. They were obviously tired.

The Russian, Alexis, did not sleep. The fair-haired young man prowled about the villa all night like an angry cat. Duncan did not dare sleep either, though he did manage to snatch one or two brief catnaps. He saw Alexis settle in a chair at the table, for an hour or so, scribbling in a notebook he kept in his jacket pocket, but then the Russian was up and about again. By dawn he was kicking at the feet of Humberto Gavilla.

"Come on, Gavilla! Time to get up. Get your people moving."

The Cuban irritably rolled over and pulled his blanket tighter about himself. Alexis kicked his buttocks.

"Up, I said!"

Humberto was on his feet in a flash, a black-handled knife in his hand, which he waved under Alexis's chin. The Russian looked startled and backed off.

"Don't you kick me, you Russian bastard!" the Cuban snarled. "I'm not one of your Red peasants! I'm here in the service of our beloved Fidel, and don't you forget it!"

Duncan held his breath as, for a long moment, the two of them stood there like statues glaring at one another. Then Alexis chuckled. The chuckle grew into a laugh. Humberto looked perplexed for a moment then he, too, started to laugh. He put away the knife. Alexis moved forward and, still laughing, put his arm around the other's shoulders.

"Humberto, my friend. Don't take me so seriously. I'm not working against you but with you."

Duncan breathed easier. But only for a moment. Suddenly the Russian's arm tightened to a rigid grip on the Cuban and his other hand came up out of his pocket with the 9mm Makarov pistol in it. He held it pressed to Humberto's head.

"Don't you ever draw a knife on me," he hissed. "And don't you *dare* call me a bastard! Now understand this. We are here to work together on this stupid exercise your idiotic leader has dreamed up. I am committed to it through my dedication to Comrades Tupolev and Yeltsin, and I do not back away from anything to which I have dedicated myself. Not even when I have to work with stinking Cuban dogs like you! Now, we will see this thing through to its triumphant conclusion . . . and then you and I will have a talk. You understand me?"

Humberto nodded his head. The Russian pushed him away and turned to look out of the window as though nothing had happened, sliding the pistol back into his pocket. Duncan saw the look the Cuban gave him.

By now the PKers were getting up from the floor and finding themselves something to eat before they started their day. They knew enough not to interfere with what was going

The Committee

on between their two leaders. Every one of them kept his or her eyes cast down and said not a word to anyone.

Duncan looked for General Wellesley and was disturbed not to see him anywhere. Thinking back, he didn't remember seeing the American arrive at the villa the previous night. What could have become of him, he wondered?

Soon the company was organized into two groups. Humberto sat with the first one. They tried to make themselves comfortable on the floor and on the few chairs that were available. It was obvious to Duncan that they were having a hard time relaxing sufficiently to project their thoughts out to the satellite they so desperately wished to move. He felt encouraged.

The second group sat around disconsolately awaiting their turn to try. Alexis watched them all for a few minutes then stalked off toward the kitchen.

"I wonder what he's up to?" Duncan thought, watching him go. Carefully, trying not to make any noise at all, he started crawling along the wooden joists. It was difficult moving. The roof had lost much of its support, both through age and from the fire. He could feel the rafters give slightly beneath his feet and quickly learned to spread his weight across two or more joists at the same time. The ceiling had crumbled in many places and left huge gaping holes. Gingerly Duncan eased himself around, hoping against hope that his weight would not be too much for the weakened ceiling, until he came to a smaller room. There was no sign of the Russian.

Duncan remembered that off from the entranceway, across from the kitchen, was another small room. It might have been a small bedroom or study, or even used as a cloakroom at one time. It had been slightly damaged by the fire. Duncan crept carefully along to look down into that room.

The hole he used was in one corner and did not give him a full view of the room, but he saw Alexis's legs and feet. The Russian had laid down on the floor and was apparently at last trying to get some rest.

"Good idea," Duncan murmured. "Perhaps I can do the same?"

He settled himself as best he could, stretched out along a wooden joist where it met and crossed another similar beam. He hoped and prayed he wouldn't roll off and fall crashing through the ceiling. It didn't take long for him to be asleep and for his astral body to be floating alongside his physical one, in the attic space. He was very conscious of the fact that the Russian, whom Rudolf had described as extremely dangerous, was also out of his body and only a few feet away.

Duncan remembered Rudolf's description of his journey when he first trailed Humberto from the Vandenberg Flight Center to the first villa in Cuba. Rudy had said that he changed his appearance a couple of times, so that he wouldn't be spotted. Duncan also thought of those pajama-clad figures he had seen passing through the control blockhouse in California; astral bodies of sleeping station personnel. With a smile, and concentration of thought, Duncan changed his shape into that of a small, dark-skinned, black-haired little boy, in Mickey Mouse-decorated pajamas, and clutching a teddybear. In that shape he descended to the ground floor of the villa and stood looking at the sleeping Russian. He had no idea where the man had gone or he would have considered following him.

It was more than an hour later that Alexis returned. He suddenly came through the wall of the room and stood for a moment beside his sleeping form. He glanced briefly at what Duncan hoped he would take for a small Cuban boy, then slipped into his body. In a flash Duncan was up beside his own body and slipping into it. He needed to keep up with the Russian at all times, if at all possible.

*

Sitting in the circle, Humberto was having a hard time concentrating. His thoughts kept going back to Alexis. He had grown to hate the cocky Russian. The man had embarrassed him in front of his own Cuban people. That could never be excused.

Humberto knew that things were not going well for the whole Russian-Cuban team. He could sense it; in fact he could see it. He glanced around. No one seemed able to relax and feel comfortable enough to do their job.

Sure, the Russian PKers had far more experience than his few Cubans, but they were also far more sensitive. They had lived their pampered psychic lives, watched over and provided for by powerful political patrons. They had obviously never before had to work under these sorts of conditions. Well, he'd show them! He, Umberto Manuel Alfredo Gavilla, would do what Fidel had asked. He and his Cuban psychics would move that *Yanqui* satellite with or without these Russians! And he would also teach that Alexis Militsa not to fool with a Cuban. He closed his eyes and focused his thoughts.

*

Duncan wished he had brought some sort of padding with him, up into the crawl space. The wooden beams were hard and he had to keep changing his position, being careful not to cause the weakened joists to make any sound. He had moved back from the little room where Alexis had slept, to look down once more on the whole group. He had hardly got settled again when the door opened and the Russian stalked in. The group in the center gave up all effort at concentration on the satellite and turned to look at their grim-faced leader.

"*Nyet! Nyet!* It will not do." He glared around, in turn looking each and every one of them in the face. "I am told that we have moved the target a number of times but that each time the Americans have managed to adjust and move it back. What we need now is

The Committee

one big, concerted effort. All of us, every single person, working at the same time; no split groups. That way, although we will only be able to send out our energies for a relatively short time, we'll be able to get the satellite moving to such an extent that they won't be able to stop it. Once we've started it moving like that, it will keep going by itself. Am I right General?"

He looked around for Nathan Wellesley, then seemed to remember something. Humberto chuckled.

"Yes, mighty leader," he smirked. "He's not here. You put a bullet in his back yesterday, if you remember? Because you thought he helped the young *Yanqui* get away."

So that was what had happened to him, thought Duncan. Well, the General had certainly paid his dues in full. But it did seem a shame.

"Never mind that," Alexis snapped. "You've heard what the decision is. But none of you is in any shape to do this last work right now. We still have time on our side. Tomorrow morning is our deadline. All right! You will all take a break. Relax! Lie on the beach; go play in the surf, if you wish." He smiled like a benevolent father handing out candies to his children. "Whatever you like. It is just important that you relax."

"Relax?" Humberto asked. "In a half-burned ruin of a house like this? That's not going to be easy."

Nuevitas, Cuba

"You *will* relax," Alexis spoke through clenched teeth. "Because you will be ready to work by the time it is dark tonight. Everyone!" His eyes bored into Humberto's. "No excuses." He turned on his heel and stalked out of the room.

Duncan sat back. So that was it. He knew that if the group did manage to move the satellite with any force then there was no way it's shift could be stopped with the remote control of its maneuvering jets. This was it! They had to stop this concerted effort no matter what. He took a deep breath. At least they had a little time to prepare.

Duncan eased himself up and once again cautiously crawled across the rafters to check on the Russian. Alexis was back in the small room, writing in his journal. Good, thought Duncan, then it should be safe to do a quick astral trip.

He was surprised, on arriving in Haiti, to find Guillemette waiting for him. She was in the peristyle of the Voudoun hounfor, hovering over the central altar area. He saw Earl, still in his body, sitting on a bench on which Guillemette's body-shell was stretched out.

"How did you know I was coming?" Duncan asked.

The Haitian woman smiled. "I've been keeping my eye on you through my crystal ball. I couldn't hear what was being said but as soon as I saw you settle down I knew you were going to project."

Duncan quickly filled her in on what was happening in Cuba with the PK group. "I've got a rough plan sort of half-formed in my head," he said. "Perhaps between us we can fine-tune it. Why don't we both pop over to old Rudy and have another conference?"

"No need." They both turned at the sound of Rudolf's voice but couldn't see him anywhere. There came a low chuckle. Then a small hummingbird, that had been hovering by the post over the altar, instantly changed shape into that of the old German. "You see? Don't forget that on the astral you can change your form to anything you desire, human or non-human."

"I've discovered that," Duncan said. "In fact I did it just a short while ago to check on where the Russian had gone."

"He didn't see you, did he?" Rudolf asked anxiously.

"No." Duncan shook his head. "I wanted to follow him but he'd already left his body when I got to it so I had to just wait there. He noticed me when he returned but I was looking like a little Cuban kid so he didn't really see me as such."

"Hmm." Rudolf didn't sound too comforted. "I cannot emphasize enough how careful you must be with that man."

"I know, Rudy. I appreciate your concern. Thanks. I'll be careful."

They discussed the situation and the upcoming psychokinesis session that was to be done by the combined Russians and Cubans. All three agreed that it could be very serious. If the PKers got the satellite moving with any great momentum it would be impossible to stop it.

"We will stand by," Rudolf said, "and you must send us word as soon as they prepare to start, Dunk. Then we must strike, and strike hard. Our Russian friend is very sensitive to psychic activity, so if I travel to him he will not be able to keep from coming out onto the astral to meet me."

"But you won't do battle with him all by yourself?" Duncan said.

"I must do," said the German. "Despite all your intentions, both of you, you would not know how to handle the situations that might arise. *Nein, mein lieb Freunds,* you must promise me you will not get caught out of your bodies by him."

Duncan and Guillemette looked at one another but said nothing.

"You, Duncan," Rudolf continued, "can act on the First Level, interrupting the group's concentration in some way. And our lovely Guillemette Flaubert can weave her magic from the relatively safe distance of Haiti."

"Trust us, Rudy," Duncan said. "We'll do all in our power to break up this plot. But, what exactly are you planning on doing on the astral? If he does come out to you, what then?"

"It will not be easy," the German said. "He, obviously, will be trying to disconnect me from the silver cord, so that I can no longer return to my body. Meanwhile I will be trying to bind him."

"Bind him?" Guillemette asked.

"*Ja*. He is a follower of the Left Hand Path. He can call upon the Black Powers to aid him and I can call upon the White. It is the old, ever recurring story of Good against Evil. But if I can bind him in golden chains of light, he will be my prisoner and I can turn him over to those Light Workers who will be able to refocus him, so that he may come back and finish out this life in a positive and worthwhile manner, as a servant of the Right Hand Path."

"Sort of a psychic soul-saving," Duncan murmured.

"In effect, yes." The German nodded.

"Great!" Duncan said. "Okay. If anyone can do it, you can, Rudy. We're all behind you, you know that. The Committee is going to be the victor in this battle."

Rudolf beamed and they all took hands for a brief moment.

"So," Duncan continued, "you two go back now, bring Beth and Earl up to date and instruct them on how to send us their power, to supplement ours, then we'll all be in it together. Okay?"

"Okay!"

"*Ja!*"

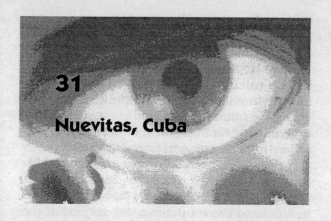

31
Nuevitas, Cuba

The sun had already sunk below the horizon when Alexis called his people together. To Duncan, back in his observation position above the ceiling, it was obvious the day's rest had done them all a world of good. There was even some good-natured banter between one or two of the PKers. Although he couldn't understand what was said there was no mistaking the chuckles and smiles.

Humberto was the only one who didn't seem to have benefited from the day's relaxation. Duncan noticed that he hardly took his eyes off Alexis. He did all that the Russian asked of him but it was obvious he was nursing some dark inner feelings.

"Time to call in the cavalry," Duncan thought. He settled down and closed his eyes, bringing his focus onto Guillemette first and then onto Rudolf. He quickly got responses from both of them. "Now for it," he muttered to himself, as he brought his attention back to his immediate surroundings.

Below, Alexis arranged the seating of his people, placing the Cubans in a tight inner circle surrounded by an outer circle of the Russians. He himself was to sit in the very center of them all with Humberto, in with the circle of other Cubans, immediately behind him.

They were about to begin when Duncan noticed a marked drop in temperature. It became obvious that Alexis had also noticed it. His head came up like a dog sniffing at the opening of a can of dog food. His gaze swept around the room. He raised his hand and everyone stopped talking.

"*Da* . . . it is as I thought. All of you, take a few moments to do some preliminary stretches and psychic warm-up exercises. I will then lead you in a moment."

With that he sat down in a yoga posture, closed his eyes and, after two or three deep breaths, became completely still. Duncan knew that he had left his body.

Duncan had not actually given Rudolf his word that he wouldn't also astrally project; no more had Guillemette. They had both carefully avoided any such promise and Duncan knew that the Haitian woman had every intention of aiding the German, whether he would welcome it or not. He lay down and closed his eyes.

Duncan found himself in a surrealistic landscape of stark, multicolored mountains with scattered bare trees and bushes. Dark, monstrous purple clouds above raced across a somber, deep blue sky, accompanied by occasional flashes of lightning and rumbles of thunder. Standing on the pinnacle of a huge black rock, not far in front of him, he saw Alexis, impressively dressed in robes of Magenta and gold. With both hands the Russian held above his head a mighty sword that had a wavy blade, from which came occasional flashes and blue sparks like static electricity.

Beyond the Russian Duncan could see Rudolf, though it took him a moment to recognize his old friend. Looking forty years younger, the German stood atop another tall peak, resplendent in robes of purple and green. His right hand held a staff as tall as himself. It was of dark, rough wood, carved and inscribed in places with ancient runes. At its tip there was a massive quartz crystal which seemed to glow with its own inner light.

Duncan blinked a couple of times and muttered to himself. "This looks like the cover of a fantasy magazine! Don't tell me we're going to have the battle of the opposing magicians!"

But even as he looked Alexis disappeared. In his place was a screaming, three-headed hawk which flew straight at Rudolf and swooped down on him, the trio of razor-sharp beaks seeking to bite through the silver cord which Duncan could make out trailing away from his friend.

"Of course!" Duncan thought. "Alexis wants to break Rudy's cord, so that he can't return to his body." He knew that the break had to be made where the cord joined the astral double, which was why the demon-hawk tried so desperately to get in close. But the German blocked its attack by swinging the great staff across his body. Flashes came from the crystal at its tip and, when one of them caught a wing of the hawk, caused it to scream and feathers to fly.

In an instant the hawk became a savage lion and pounced on Rudolf. But, a split second before it landed, the purple-clad figure had become a knight in silver armor whose shield held back the raging animal. Instantly Alexis was himself again, his wavy-bladed sword arcing through the air, to cut Rudolf's silver cord. Only just in time did the German deflect it with a heavy mace he held in his armor-gloved right hand.

Duncan watched in total fascination as the two dueled across the astral landscape. It became obvious that, rather than trying to cut the Russian's astral cord, Rudolf was simply trying to subdue the man and bind him with golden rope that, from time to time, would materialize in his hands; but both were lightning fast and seemed able to anticipate the other's every move.

It seemed that the battle raged for hours, though Duncan knew that there was no such thing as time beyond the First Level of earthly existence. Suddenly the Russian seemed to have Rudolf in his power. He had given himself the body of a heavyweight wrestler and pinned the German on his back, on the edge of a rocky ledge halfway up a ragged mountain. Duncan moved in close, though keeping out of the Russian's line of sight. With a cry of triumph, Alexis materialized a knife in his hand and prepared to swing it down to cut the cord. Duncan concentrated and sent his thoughts into action. The clouds above opened up and torrents of water cascaded down on top of the two men. It was as though a waterfall had suddenly started over the top of them. The Russian was swept from Rudolf and disappeared over the side of the ledge. Rudolf came to his feet as the waterfall ceased and immediately his eyes locked with Duncan's.

"What are you doing here? Get away!"

The thought hit Duncan forcibly. No words of thanks, not that he expected any, just the order to go. But there was no time for further communication between them. The Russian appeared beside Rudolf, again wielding his wavy-bladed sword. Duncan quickly assumed his guise of a young Cuban boy and walked away.

"One point to you, old man," Alexis said to Rudolf, ignoring the tiny figure. "I would not have been affected by that thought form if I hadn't allowed myself to be."

Rudolf bowed his head briefly in acknowledgement, without letting on that it was not he who had brought down the torrent. Even though he had not been expecting Duncan's deluge, Rudolf had reacted swiftly enough to know that the water could not have any effect on him if he did not allow it to. Only an actual astral being, in whatever form he or she took, could affect him.

Again the battle raged, with each having close calls. Then, once again, it seemed that Rudolf was in the Russian's power. But, as the wavy-bladed sword swung downward, a tiny hornet flashed in to viciously sting Alexis on the back of the neck. With a cry, he actually dropped his sword and leapt up and away. Duncan knew that it was no thought form this time, to have such an effect on the magician. He was right. The hornet settled some distance away and became Guillemette. She smiled grimly at her victim.

Alexis cursed the black woman and flung what looked like a bolt of lightning at her. She did not move or flinch and it dissipated with a hiss as it encountered an invisible ball of protection about her.

"I will deal with you when I have finished with this old man!" Alexis cried, and turned his attention back to Rudolf.

This time the German went on the offensive. He suddenly appeared behind the Russian, dressed as an ancient Roman gladiator. He carried a net of golden rope, which he threw over the figure before him. Only just in time Alexis ducked out of the way, changing existence. Suddenly the Russian seemed to have Rudolf in his power. He had given himself the body of a heavyweight wrestler and pinned the German on his back, on the edge of a rocky ledge halfway up a ragged mountain. Duncan moved in close, though keeping out of the Russian's line of sight. With a cry of triumph, Alexis materialized a knife in his hand and prepared to swing it down to cut the cord. Duncan concentrated and sent his thoughts into action. The clouds above opened up and torrents of water cascaded down on top of the two men. It was as though a waterfall had suddenly started over the top of them. The Russian was swept from Rudolf and disappeared over the side of the ledge. Rudolf came to his feet as the waterfall ceased and immediately his eyes locked with Duncan's.

"What are you doing here? Get away!"

The thought hit Duncan forcibly. No words of thanks, not that he expected any, just the order to go. But there was no time for further communication between them. The Russian appeared beside Rudolf, again wielding his wavy-bladed sword. Duncan quickly assumed his guise of a young Cuban boy and walked away.

"One point to you, old man," Alexis said to Rudolf, ignoring the tiny figure. "I would not have been affected by that thought form if I hadn't allowed myself to be."

Rudolf bowed his head briefly in acknowledgement, without letting on that it was not he who had brought down the torrent. Even though he had not been expecting Duncan's deluge, Rudolf had reacted swiftly enough to know that the water could not have any effect on him if he did not allow it to. Only an actual astral being, in whatever form he or she took, could affect him.

Again the battle raged, with each having close calls. Then, once again, it seemed that Rudolf was in the Russian's power. But, as the wavy-bladed sword swung downward, a tiny hornet flashed in to viciously sting Alexis on the back of the neck. With a cry, he actually dropped his sword and leapt up and away. Duncan knew that it was no thought form this time, to have such an effect on the magician. He was right. The hornet settled some distance away and became Guillemette. She smiled grimly at her victim.

Alexis cursed the black woman and flung what looked like a bolt of lightning at her. She did not move or flinch and it dissipated with a hiss as it encountered an invisible ball of protection about her.

"I will deal with you when I have finished with this old man!" Alexis cried, and turned his attention back to Rudolf.

This time the German went on the offensive. He suddenly appeared behind the Russian, dressed as an ancient Roman gladiator. He carried a net of golden rope, which he threw over the figure before him. Only just in time Alexis ducked out of the way, changing his shape to that of a small bird and winging out between the meshes of the net. Instantly Rudolf was a hawk and flashed in on the small bird. Again just in time, Alexis became himself and fended off the attack with a swing of his sword that took feathers from the hawk's back.

The scenery changed to that of a strip of beach, and as Rudolf turned to look for his opponent the Russian became a huge crab whose pincer claw reached up to snip the German's silver cord. Instantly Duncan, in his guise of a small Cuban boy, kicked sand all over the crab. It was just enough to give Rudolf a chance to slip out of the way.

The Russian stood, as himself, and looked at the little boy clutching his teddy bear, now ankle-deep in surf.

"You fool!" His lip curled. "You are the American, I see. You amateur! You have forgotten to change your eyes; they are blue!" In less than a second he was on Duncan. But Duncan had learned quickly from watching the bout between the two masters. As Alexis grabbed him he turned into a fish and slipped right out of the Russian's hands, flopping down and into the water, to disappear along the tideline.

The scene changed again and again; one moment the two magicians were battling in a desert and the next in the heart of a dense jungle. Then they were in a bare room, then in an ancient stone castle. Wherever they went, along went Duncan and Guillemette, watching eagle-eyed for a chance to leap in and help their old friend.

A chance seemed to come when the Russian trapped Rudolf in a musty building, not unlike the old villa the PKers were working from. As Alexis once more prepared to swing his sword, Guillemette appeared alongside Rudolf and taunted the Russian. Alexis allowed his attention to be distracted from Rudolf but, in an instant, had the black woman in his grasp. Duncan didn't wait. He rushed in and was about to grasp the Russian from behind when a strange thing happened. The figure in the Magenta robes suddenly seemed to check, and let go of Guillemette. He straightened up and dropped the sword, staggering back a pace. Duncan saw a black-handled dagger materialize between the man's shoulderblades. Even as the three friends watched, Alexis's silver cord snapped away from him like a taught line that had been cut.

"He's been killed!" Rudolf cried. "He's been killed on the earth plane."

Duncan knew at once what must have happened. While the Russian was out of his body, fighting for his life on the astral, Humberto had wreaked his vengeance and stabbed Alexis from behind.

"You two, get back to your bodies and do whatever else you can to stop the group work," Rudolf said briskly, taking charge. "We still have our other battle to win. I will take this astral body and lead him to Helpers who may be able to guide him back to the side of goodness and light. Oh!" He paused and smiled. "You disobeyed me but—thank you. Both of you. Now get going."

As Duncan came back to consciousness in his physical body he became aware of the sounds of anger, fear, and distress in the room below him. He rolled over and looked down. As he'd suspected, Humberto had stabbed Alexis and was even now retrieving his knife and wiping off the blood on the Russian's clothing. The inner and outer circles of PKers were broken up, many of the Russians huddled silently against a far wall while the Cubans gathered around Humberto, all talking at once. As Duncan watched, the Russians in the group seemed to reach a decision and started to move quickly out of the door of the room. Humberto made no attempt to stop them. Duncan soon heard the sound of the automobile engines starting and knew the Russians were leaving.

It seemed to Duncan unlikely that the remaining Cuban psychics would get reorganized sufficiently to work comfortably together on their project, but there was still a chance they might be brought under control and given direction. Whether or not they alone would have the power to accomplish the movement of the satellite, Duncan doubted but couldn't be sure. He knew he had to do something to completely disrupt them, once and for all.

The Committee

His clue came from Guillemette. At least he assumed it was her at work. The house started to shake, ever so slightly, as though in a minor earthquake. It wasn't too severe but certainly enough to disrupt concentration and to cause the PKers to draw close to one another and mutter in concern. Even Humberto didn't seem to know what to do.

Duncan seized on the suggestion of earthquake that Guillemette had given and, standing up, grasped the roof beams and started to bounce up and down on them. Old as they were, and badly weakened by the fire, tiebars began to snap where they joined with roof trusses. Plaster started to cascade down on the group below and then one or two beams actually broke free and crashed through the ceiling. The Cubans wasted no time in rushing out of the house. Before Duncan could stop the effect, the whole roof gave way and, him with it, came crashing down in a shower of dirt and dust.

As Duncan lay there, momentarily dazed, he was aware of the sound of the remaining Jeep starting up and driving away. Happily he smiled. The Committee had won.

*

Duncan still had to get out of Cuba. Bruised and dirty, he made his way back to the beach and walked as quickly as he was able along to where he had left his escape vehicle. He breathed a huge sigh of relief; it was still there. He dragged the pile of folded rubber out from under the bushes and positioned it on the sand.

The Goodyear rubber Inflataplane model GA-33 had first flown in 1952. It was made of a substance know as *airmat*, a technology which bonded two outer rubber surfaces with an inner weave of nylon fabric. The nylon prestressed the load-bearing surfaces and reduced the material's flexibility, making it solid, yet inflatable. The airmat could become incredibly rigid, yet, when the cells were deflated, it folded up like any other rubber material.

The original airplane made of airmat had a simple, open cockpit and basic controls, but flew extremely well. A later, improved model—the one which Duncan now started to unfold—was designated the GA-447 and had an enclosed cockpit with a flexible canopy.

From the pile sitting on the sand, Duncan unfolded one wing then walked around and unfolded the other. The fuselage and empennage were next, then the nose and "front office." The small, 40hp Nelson four-stroke engine, with its two-blade propeller, sat on top, just behind where the pilot would be.

Duncan didn't worry about creases in the material, knowing that as it inflated they would all come out. He checked the layout, then moved to the right side, just behind the wing, and attached the bottle of carbon dioxide. He also had a handpump, for emergency use, but was pleased to find the bottle worked fine. As he turned the knob there was a hiss of gas and the plane started to inflate. Within eight minutes it was fully inflated, and he disconnected the bottle. Once the engine started a pump would take over, constantly topping off the air pressure and keeping it steady throughout flight.

He did a walk-around, checking out control surfaces and making sure all the control wires were free and clear. Then he took a nylon cord that extended from the rear of the plane and tied it securely to the tree under which he had originally hidden the plane.

The original Inflataplanes had utilized a single landing wheel under the fuselage, with an outrigger for balance on the end of each wing. A later variation—the one Duncan had got—utilized a simple hydroskid in place of the wheel, which made it an ideal water landing and take-off aircraft.

Duncan pulled out the plane to float on the gently undulating water. He turned over the propeller a half dozen times, to prime the carburetor, then switched on and swung it. It only took a couple of tries before the little engine burst into life. Duncan scrambled into the cockpit.

His feet fitted snugly into the "toe gloves" attached to the control cables. He moved the short, central, stubby stick and saw that the control surfaces responded all right. He revved the engine and watched the temperature come up. The little plane had only three basic instruments—engine temperature, altimeter, and indicated air speed—but Duncan had asked to have a compass added. "Just like so many ultralights I've flown," he thought as his gaze swept over the instruments.

He gave it full throttle then pulled the release on the cord tying the plane to the tree. At it came free the little craft surged ahead, skimming across the water, and in less than one hundred feet, as he eased back on the stick, it broke free and was airborne. Duncan set a course for Great Inagua Island, the Bahamas.

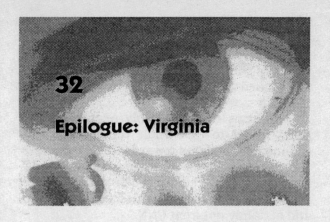

32
Epilogue: Virginia

"In an Iraqi television broadcast from Baghdad, Saddam Hussein made an unprecedented attack on Cuba and on Fidel Castro, aligning him with the United States and criticizing him for 'actions contrary to the advancement of peace'. No response was forthcoming from the Cuban leader. In other unrelated news from Cuba, the Minister for Foreign Affairs, Ovideo Aldereguía, has apparently been replaced after thirty-five years as Castro's right-hand man . . ."

Senator Bill Highland pushed the mute button on the television remote and looked around at his guests. Duncan and Beth sat side by side on the settee, with Earl and Guillemette in armchairs on Beth's left and Rudolf to the right of Duncan. They were once again in Bill Highland's Virginia residence, with the Websters waiting on them. Mr. Webster kept looking hard at each and every one of them and then shaking his head and quietly "tut-tutting" to himself. Mrs. Webster kept a very straight face and would look at no one as she passed around cups of coffee and a plate of cookies.

"It seems that's the only reference we're going to get to this whole thing," Highland commented, nodding towards the television.

"Not that any of us should be surprised," Duncan said. "We certainly didn't expect to get news and coverage of battles on the astral, and certainly not from CNN."

Everyone chuckled.

"Do you think they will try it again?" Rudolf asked, his face serious.

"I don't," Earl said.

"Nor do I," Highland agreed. "Though believe me, if there's anything that looks the least little bit like this metaphysical type of thing, you guys are going to be the first I'll contact. Incidentally," he looked around at each of them. "Did I tell you? The President sends his thanks. He has even less idea of what you did than I have, but he said we are in your debt anyway."

"*He* said that?" Duncan asked.

"Well," Highland selected a cookie from the plate Mrs. Webster had refilled. "I told him to say it, I have to admit. But he took my word for it and was totally sincere," he added quickly.

"Does he know what sort of a Committee it was you'd organized?" Elizabeth asked.

Epilogue: Virginia

The Senator shook his head. "He was quite content to leave it to me, after I assured him you could handle anything that came along."

Elizabeth looked around. "Well, I don't know about anyone else," she said, "but I shall be very sorry to see this end, in spite of all the dangers."

"What are your plans, Dunk?" Highland asked. "Back to California and your books?"

Duncan nodded. "Yes. I've got a fast approaching deadline now. Must get back to the keyboard." He smiled at Beth and put his arm around her. "Though I may not be alone out there for too long."

Beth blushed slightly. "I've got some things to tidy up in Ohio, then I'm going to be going out to spend some time with Dunk. Who knows? It may be a long time!"

"Good for you," Guillemette said. "I've got to go back to my island paradise." Everyone made mock sympathetic noises and she laughed. "I know! I know! Someone's got to live there! But you know you're all invited to come down anytime you like."

"I, for one, may well take you up on that," Earl said, tugging at his beard and smiling broadly at her. "You can tell me more of your fascinating tales of Voudoun."

"I'd love to."

"And you, Professor Küstermeyer?" Highland asked.

"Ah! I have students awaiting my return. And, like our young friend Duncan here, I must get on with a book I am writing. *Ja*. I have plenty to occupy myself."

"May I make a suggestion?" the Senator asked. They looked at him. "I'm sure you're all good enough friends that you're going to stay in touch with one another anyway, right?"

"Right." They nodded their heads and continued to look at him questioningly.

"Well, I was wondering if it might not be such a bad idea if you perhaps got together on a regular basis. Just a couple of times a year, perhaps. You know, to just check that everything was going all right?"

There was a brief silence.

"'Just to check that everything was going all right'?" Duncan grinned at his friend. "Come on, Bill! You mean you'd like us to make this a permanent committee, is that it?"

"Well," the Senator grinned sheepishly. "I did discuss it with the President and he did say he'd have no objections. In other words, I could continue picking up the tab for you five to get together every six months and trade stories. How's it sound?"

"And you, of course, would be sure to let us know if there was any particular agenda for these meetings, right?"

"Something like that."

They all laughed and raised their coffee cups in a toast.

"To 'The Committee'," said Duncan.

"The Committee!"

STAY IN TOUCH

On the following pages you will find some of the books now available on related subjects. Your book dealer stocks most of these and will stock new titles in the Llewellyn series as they become available. We urge your patronage.

You may also request our bimonthly news magazine/catalog, *Llewellyn's New Worlds of Mind and Spirit*. A sample copy is free, and it will continue coming to you at no cost as long as you are an active mail customer. Or you may subscribe for just $10.00 in the U.S.A. and Canada ($20.00 overseas, first class mail). Many bookstores also have *New Worlds* available to their customers. Ask for it.

Llewellyn's New Worlds of Mind and Spirit
P.O. Box 64383-134, St. Paul, MN 55164-0383, U.S.A.

* * *

TO ORDER BOOKS AND TAPES

You may order books directly from the publisher by sending full price in U.S. funds, plus $3.00 for postage and handling for orders under $10.00; $4.00 for orders over $10.00. There are no postage and handling charges for orders over $50.00. Postage and handling rates are subject to change. We ship UPS whenever possible. Delivery guaranteed. Provide your street address as UPS does not deliver to P.O. Boxes. UPS to Canada requires a $50.00 minimum order. Allow 4-6 weeks for delivery. Orders outside the U.S.A. and Canada: Airmail—add retail price of book; add $5.00 for each non-book item (tapes, etc.); add $1.00 per item for surface mail.

FOR GROUP STUDY AND PURCHASE

Our Special Quantity Price for a minimum order of five copies of *The Committee* is $14.97 cash-with-order. This price includes postage and handling within the United States. Minnesota residents must add 6.5% sales tax. For additional quantities, please order in multiples of five. For Canadian and foreign orders, add postage and handling charges as above. Mail orders to:

LLEWELLYN PUBLICATIONS
P.O. Box 64383-134, St. Paul, MN 55164-0383, U.S.A.

Prices subject to change without notice.

THE MESSENGER
by Donald Tyson

"She went to the doorway and took Eliza by her shoulders. 'But you mind what I tell you. Something in this house is watching us, and its thoughts are not kindly. It's all twisted up and bitter inside. It means to make us suffer. Then it means to kill us, one by one.'"

Sealed inside a secret room of an old mansion in Nova Scotia is a cruel and uncontrollable entity, created years earlier by an evil magician. When the new owner of the mansion unknowingly releases the entity, it renews its malicious and murderous rampage. Called on to investigate the strange phenomena are three women and four men—each with their own occult talents. As their investigation proceeds, the group members enter into a world of mystery and horror as they encounter astral battles, spirit possession—even death. In their efforts to battle the evil spirit, they use seance, hypnotic trance and magical rituals, the details of which are presented in fascinating and accurate detail.

Llewellyn Psi-Fi Fiction Series
0-87542-836-3, 240 pgs., mass market   **$4.99**

THE SANTERIA EXPERIENCE
A Journey into the Miraculous
by Migene González-Wippler

In this raw, emotional account, Migene González-Wippler reports her own encounters with Santería as researcher and initiate. You will meet extraordinary people and witness unbelievable occurrences. All are Migene's lifelong experiences with Santeria.

Explore *the truths* about this magico-religious system from the inside, as Migene reveals her childhood initiation and later encounters with the real and extraordinary powers of the babalawo (high priest of Santería). Learn of the magical practices of the santeros (priests of Santería). Learn actual ebbós (offerings and rituals) that *you* can do to enlist the aid of the African deities!

0-87542-257-8, 400 pgs., mass market, illus.   **$4.95**

Prices subject to change without notice.

POLTERGEIST
A Study in Destructive Haunting
by Colin Wilson

Objects flying through the air, furniture waltzing around the room, dishes crashing to the floor. These are the hallmarks of poltergeist phenomena. Now Colin Wilson, the renowned authority on the paranormal, investigates these mysterious forces in a fascinating and provocative work.

Countless cases of poltergeist mischief have been recorded from the days of ancient Greece and Rome to the present. But what are poltergeists? Where do they come from? Why do they appear and how do they interact in our world? In this comprehensive study, Colin Wilson examines the evidence regarding poltergeists and develops a masterful and definitive theory of the forces that surround us and are contained within each one of us.

0-87542-883-5, 448 pgs., mass market   **$5.95**

THE LLEWELLYN PRACTICAL GUIDE TO THE DEVELOPMENT OF PSYCHIC POWERS
by Denning & Phillips

You may not realize it, but you already have the ability to use ESP, Astral Vision and Clairvoyance, Divination, Dowsing, Prophecy, and Communication with Spirits.

Written by two of the most knowledgeable experts in the world of psychic development, this book is a complete course—teaching you, step-by-step, how to develop these powers that actually have been yours since birth.

Psychic powers are as much a natural ability as any other talent. You'll learn to play with these new skills, working with groups of friends to accomplish things you never would have believed possible before reading this book. The text shows you how to make the equipment you can use, the exercises you can do—many of them at any time, anywhere—and how to use your abilities to change your life and the lives of those close to you. Many of the exercises are presented in forms that can be adapted as games for pleasure and fun, as well as development.

0-87542-191-1, 272 pgs., 5 1/4 x 8, illus., softcover   **$8.95**

Prices subject to change without notice.

SECRETS OF GYPSY DREAM READING
by Raymond Buckland, Ph.D.

The Gypsies have carried their arcane wisdom and time-tested methods of dream interpretation around the world. Now, in *Secrets of Gypsy Dream Reading*, Raymond Buckland, a descendant of the Romani Gypsies, reveals these fascinating methods.

Learn how to accurately interpret dreams, dream the future, dream for profit, remember your dreams more clearly, and willfully direct your dreams. The Gypsies' observations on dreaming are extremely perceptive and enlightening. They say that dreams are messages, giving advice on what is most beneficial for you. Many times these messages could mean the difference between happiness and misery—if not life and death.

In today's fast-paced, often superficial world, we need to listen to the Gypsies' words of wisdom more than ever. Listen to your dreams and achieve success, riches, better health—and more—in your waking hours!

0-87542-086-9, 224 pgs., mass market, illus. $3.95

SECRETS OF GYPSY LOVE MAGICK
by Raymond Buckland, Ph.D.

One of the most compelling forms of magick—perhaps the most sought after—is love magick. It is a positive form of working, a way to true delight and pleasure. The Gypsies have long been known for the successful working of love magick.

In this book you will find magicks for those who are courting, who are newlyweds, and love magick for the family unit. There is also a section on Gypsy love potions, talismans and amulets.

Included are spells and charms to discover your future spouse, to make your lover your best friend and to bring love into a loveless marriage. You will learn traditional secrets gathered from English Gypsies that are presented here for the first time ever by a Gypsy of Romani blood.

0-87542-053-2, 176 pgs., mass market, illus. $3.95

Prices subject to change without notice.

HOW TO DREAM YOUR LUCKY LOTTO NUMBERS
by Raoul Maltagliati

Until now, there has been no scientific way to predict lotto numbers ... they come up by chance. But overnight, you may find them through a trip into the dimension of the collective unconscious, where "time" and "chance," as we know them, do not exist. *In How to Dream Your Lucky Lotto Numbers,* you will be introduced to an actual dream interpreter, who will guide you in picking your lucky lotto numbers! Author Raoul Maltagliati explains such things as: Why we dream ... How to isolate the key points in a dream that point out your lotto numbers ... How to find the numeric equivalents of dream... The importance of the day and the month during which you have your lotto dreams. An extensive dream dictionary helps you discover what numbers you should pick based on your most recent dreams.

0-87542-483-X, 128 pgs., mass market, illus. $3.95

HOW TO SEE AND READ THE AURA
by Ted Andrews

Everyone has an aura—the three-dimensional, shape-and-color-changing energy field that surrounds all matter. And anyone can learn to see and experience the aura more effectively. There is nothing magical about the process. It simply involves a little understanding, time, practice and perseverance.

Do some people make you feel drained? Have you ever been able to sense the presence of other people before you actually heard or saw them? If so, you have experienced another person's aura. In this practical, easy-to-read manual, you receive a variety of exercises to practice alone and with partners to build your skills in aura reading and interpretation. Also, you will learn to balance your aura each day to keep it vibrant and strong.

As we develop the ability to see and feel the more subtle aspects of life, our intuition unfolds and increases, and the childlike joy and wonder of life returns.

0-87542-013-3, 160 pgs., mass market, illus. $3.95

Prices subject to change without notice.

SECRETS OF GYPSY FORTUNETELLING
by Ray Buckland

This book unveils the Romani secrets of fortunetelling, explaining in detail the many different methods used by these nomads. For generations they have survived on their skills as seers. Their accuracy is legendary. They are a people who seem to be born with "the sight" ... the ability to look into the past, present, and future using only the simplest of tools to aid them. Here you will learn to read palms, to interpret the symbols in a teacup, to read cards ... both the Tarot and regular playing cards. Here are revealed the secrets of interpreting the actions of animals, of reading the weather, of recognizing birthmarks and the shape of hands.

The methods of divination presented in this book are all practical methods—no expensive or hard-to-get items are necessary. The Gypsies are accomplished at using natural objects and everyday items to serve them in their endeavors: Sticks and stones, knives and needles, cards and dice. Using these non-complex objects, and following the traditional Gypsy ways shown, you can become a seer and improve the quality of your own life.

0-87542-051-6, 240 pgs., mass market, illus. $3.95

THE BUCKLAND GYPSY FORTUNETELLING DECK
by Ray Buckland

Over the past 200 years, gypsy families have designed their own versions of the Major Arcana to be used with a poker deck for divination. One such Romani deck is that of the Buckland family of Gypsies, presented here for the first time ever! The Buckland Gypsy Fortunetelling Deck consists of 22 Major Arcana and 52 Minor Arcana. They are very different from the Tarot and are a fascinating and effective tool for divination. Included with the deck is a 36-page instruction book that includes all necessary information needed to use the cards.

**0-87542-052-4, Boxed set: 74 cards,
36-pg. instruction booklet** $12.95

Prices subject to change without notice.

GHOSTS, HAUNTINGS & POSSESSIONS
The Best of Hans Holzer, Book I
Edited by Raymond Buckland

Now, a collection of the best stories from best-selling author and psychic investigator Hans Holzer—in mass market format! Accounts in *Ghosts, Hauntings & Possessions* include:

- A 37-year-old housewife from Nebraska was tormented by a ghost that drove phantom cars and grabbed her foot while she lay in bed at night. Even after moving to a different state, she could still hear heavy breathing.
- A psychic visited with the spirit of Thomas Jefferson at Monticello. What scandals surrounded his life that the history books don't tell us?
- Here is the exact transcript of what transpired in a seance confrontation with Elvis Presley—almost a year after his death!
- Ordinary people from all over the country had premonitions about the murders of John and Robert Kennedy. Here are their stories.
- What happened to the middle-aged woman who played with the Ouija board and ended up tormented and possessed by the spirit of a former boyfriend?
- Here is the report of Abraham Lincoln's prophetic dream of his own funeral. Does his ghost still roam the White House because of unfinished business?

These stories and many more will intrigue, spook and entertain readers of all ages.

0-87542-367-1, 288 pgs., mass market   **$4.95**

Prices subject to change without notice.

ESP, WITCHES & UFOS:
The Best of Hans Holzer, Book II
Edited by Raymond Buckland

In this exciting anthology, best-selling author and psychic investigator Hans Holzer explores true accounts of the strange and unknown: telepathy, psychic and reincarnation dreams, survival after death, psycho-ecstasy, unorthodox healings, Pagans and Witches, and Ufonauts. Reports included in this volume:

- Mrs. F. dreamed of a group of killers and was particularly frightened by the eyes of their leader. Ten days later, the Sharon Tate murders broke into the headlines. When Mrs. F. saw the photo of Charles Manson, she immediately recognized him as the man from her dream
- How you can use four simple "wish-fulfillment" steps to achieve psycho-ecstasy—turning a negative situation into something positive
- Several true accounts of miraculous healings achieved by unorthodox medical practitioners
- How the author, when late to meet with a friend and unable to find a telephone nearby, sent a telepathic message to his friend via his friend's answering service
- The reasons why more and more people are turning to Witchcraft and Paganism as a way of life
- When UFOs land: physical evidence vs. cultists

These reports and many more will entertain and enlighten all readers intrigued by the mysteries of life ... and beyond!

0-87542-368-X, 304 pgs., mass market $4.95

Prices subject to change without notice.

THE LLEWELLYN PRACTICAL GUIDE TO ASTRAL PROJECTION
The Out-of-Body Experience
by Denning & Phillips

Yes, your consciousness can be sent forth, out of the body, with full awareness and return with full memory. You can travel through time and space, converse with nonphysical entities, obtain knowledge by nonmaterial means, and experience higher dimensions.

Is there life after death? Are we forever shackled by time and space? The ability to go forth by means of the Astral Body, or Body of Light, gives the personal assurance of consciousness (and life) beyond the limitations of the physical body. No other answer to these ageless questions is as meaningful as experienced reality.

The reader is led through the essential stages for the inner growth and development that will culminate in fully conscious projection and return. Not only are the requisite practices set forth in step-by-step procedures, augmented with photographs and visualization aids, but the vital reasons for undertaking them are clearly explained. Beyond this, the great benefits from the various practices themselves are demonstrated in renewed physical and emotional health, mental discipline, spiritual attainment, and the development of extra faculties.

Guidance is also given to the Astral World itself: what to expect, what can be done—including the ecstatic experience of Astral Sex between two people who project together into this higher world where true union is consummated free of the barriers of physical bodies.

0-87542-181-4, 266 pgs., 5 1/4 x 8, illus., softcover $8.95

Prices subject to change without notice.